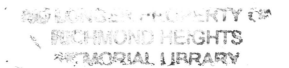
THE MARAUDERS' ISLAND

Hen & Chick Book One

TRISTAN J. TARWATER

Cover Artist: Mildred Louis
Editor: Annetta Ribkin. You can find her at
www.wordwebbing.com
Design: Chrisanthropic Studios

Paperback ISBN: 978-0-984008-99-5
HardcoverISBN: 978-1-942062-99-8
ePub ISBN: 978-1-942062-98-1

To my mom.

Chapter 1
A Misplaced Mage

Azria rested her arms on the windowsill, staring out onto the sparkling Merchant's Bay of Hitha. The shouts of mariners and cries of seagulls drifted over the warm, salty breeze which rippled the sapphire-colored water. Boats from all shores were docked, their colorful flags and gleaming sails the first hint at what diverse wares lay below their deck.

But Azria's eyes were on the horizon, looking for ships sailing into the bustling bay. The bright light of the midday sun shimmered off the water's surface, the warmth soaking into her arms. Her dark brown eyes strayed from boat to boat, their bows all pointed towards the busiest port of Miz, but none of the ships were her mother's. Azria frowned.

"Your last day under my tutelage and you spend it staring out the window," Hiezh sighed, the armful of scrolls he carried rustling as he placed them back into their wicker box.

"She's supposed to be here today," Azria said. She pulled herself away from the window, her wood and metal bracelets jingling lightly with the movement. "I told her this was my last day as a student. I have it in writing, in her own hand: *I'll be there that day, to take you aboard my ship. Then you'll really learn what wonder is.*" Azria remembered getting the letter a month ago, on her birthday. By far, the best gift she had received.

"You can't go with her until I take you before the guild and have you tested before a council of mages, among other things," Hiezh scolded. He lifted the lid of a trunk and placed the scroll box inside, locking it with the key he wore around his wrist. "Even if your mother does come to get you, she might not come today, Azria. Pirate Queen Apzana is not known for being prompt."

"I wish you wouldn't call her that," Azria said, looking down at the desk she used for her studies. She wrinkled her nose and sat down, looking at the spell she had just written. A water purification spell. The words, swirls of black, blue, green, and red written in her careful, flowing handwriting still glistened on the bone-white paper. "Bad publicity is still bad, you know?"

"Like anyone listens to me anyway," Hiezh said. Azria watched him as he walked to the small kitchen and began picking through a bowl of fruit. Hiezh had been a good teacher. She had been studying under him for ten years now and his stern and humorless demeanor had grown on Azria. He dressed better than he had in her earliest memories of him. Her mother's money made sure of it. Today he was what would be considered dressed up for him, his hair freshly braided and oiled, the creases in his stark white linen kilt and vest sharp and clean. "I'm just a mid-level spellweaver with no ambitions in the inter-island spats which are always popping up." Hiezh picked up a mango and brought it to his nose, sniffing it.

"It's what makes you more bearable than the other Innates," Azria said. She watched him pick up another piece of fruit before he frowned, crossing to the other table where the basket of cassava bread was kept. "What are we waiting for?" she groaned. "Can we go check in with the council already? I'm bored!"

"Ah, to be young and unaware of bureaucracy," Hiezh said dryly, frowning at the empty bread basket. "I already told you we would have lunch first. In addition, you have a thing called an appointment. We will get there early for your appointment, and we will naturally have to wait to be seen an hour after the time they gave us. This is the natural order of things," he said. "The chiefs can't seem to get their law and order sorted out, but of course the magic makers streamline everyone into infinite frustration." Hiezh put his hands on his hips and looked to Azria. "I don't have food for lunch."

"Didn't Nana bring you food from the market?" Azria asked. Her grandmother usually brought groceries to Hiezh on the first day of the week and often brought him meals. Hiezh shook his head and walked into his bedroom.

"No, I was stupid and told her not to worry about it this week," she heard him call from the room. "I knew she would be busy preparing for your big dinner tonight." Hiezh emerged, tying his money belt around his waist. "I'll make up for my folly by taking some of the leftovers."

"If we're going out to eat, can we please go to Puffer-fish Lane for food?" Azria asked, trying to keep any anxiety out of her voice. "I think the fritters there are better."

"Also, Poesh doesn't eat there, right?" Hiezh laughed, seeing Azria's face darken with embarrassment. "Sure, I don't feel like seeing that sand crab or his teacher either."

"Thanks," Azria muttered. Out of the other magic trainees she had to deal with, Poesh was the worst. As Innates of Hitha, they had been part of the same crèche, the tutors all taking turns teaching Hitha's future guild members. For the first five years of her training, Azria benefited not only from the training Hiezh offered but the social aspects of studying with other Innates and the guidance of other mages of Hitha's guild.

All that had changed when the rumors about her mother began. First, that her mother was a pirate, which resulted in teasing and the questioning of the many gifts her mother sent. Then one day Poesh said Azria's father wasn't of Miz. Once the second rumor began spreading, Azria took her lessons alone. A pirate for a mother was one thing but a woman who shared her bed with foreigners, who loved another land and its people more than her own? That was too much for proud Miz. When Azria did encounter Poesh and his friends, it usually ended in words she would later regret, not because she hadn't meant them but because of the things he said to her, and the laughs of anyone who heard them. Azria hoped she wouldn't see Poesh today, not before her testing. She asked the Goddess to do her this one favor before she followed her teacher out the door.

The afternoon sun shone high in the bright blue sky, the humidity eased by the fresh sea breeze. Azria walked down the tree-lined street behind her teacher, shyly waving hello to everyone they passed on the dusty road.

"What do you feel like eating today?" Hiezh asked, still walking ahead of her. "You mentioned fritters but maybe some rice balls?"

"If you want," Azria said, looking back towards the sea once more. Food was not at the forefront of her thoughts. Just past the swaying palms and brightly flowering bushes, she could make out the port and the boats, the horizon empty of other vessels. A frown pulled at the corners of her mouth as Azria wondered if her mother would show up.

"When was the last time you got a letter from her?" Hiezh asked quietly.

"My birthday," Azria replied. "So not that long. She said she would come get me when I was finished with my studies."

"You said that, Azria," Hiezh sighed. "But you know as well as anyone, the sea can be a treacherous mistress. The winds and waters may not have been in her favor. Plus," Hiezh said, more quietly, "there's the complicated matter as to whether she is even allowed in this port or not."

"I just don't think she would say she would come get me if she wasn't going to," Azria said. "What would she stand to gain by lying to me?"

"When it comes to writing letters, many people write what they most desire, not necessarily what they're capable of," Hiezh said, slowing his pace so Azria could join his side. "It's easy to say what you want with ink and paper. It's another thing altogether to carry it out."

"I guess," Azria said, her gaze straying again towards

the port. "Though one would think, by writing it down it'd make it more real. Like writing a spell."

"There is something similar between the two acts," Hiezh said with a nod and a bit of a smile. "You saying that makes me feel like I haven't totally failed you as a teacher."

Azria laughed. "You've been a good teacher, Hiezh, you must know that."

"I've had a lot of time to fix my mistakes," he said, smiling at her. "I still remember the first day I met you."

"My mother was there," Azria said with a nod.

"Yes," Hiezh said. "You had been manifesting ability for six months already. She interviewed many mages before she picked me."

"I remember clinging to her leg and staring up at you," Azria laughed. "You seemed so tall and scary!"

"In your defense, I was a mess back then," Hiezh half said, half muttered. "She didn't tell me she was coming with you and my home was...unacceptable."

"Didn't Nana clean it before I started my lessons?" Azria asked. The memories she had of those days were vivid but fractured. Her mother coming in and out of the city to check on her, always with strange and wonderful gifts. Nana singing and cooking in the background, no matter where Azria seemed to be. Hiezh instructing her, telling her to focus, please, focus, stop. Playing on the beach with the other children, before her mother became news and then notorious.

"If you mean to ask if Nana felt compelled to, yes, you remember correctly."

"I don't know who's gotten more out of my studies, you or me." Azria smirked. She waved at the woman at the fritter stand as they approached, climbing up onto one of the stools set at the counter for customers. "I'll take two yucca fritters."

"Three of the same and a crab salad to split," Hiezh said, sitting beside her. Azria watched as the woman took the grated vegetables and formed them into flat patties, sliding them gently into the oil. The oil boiled and popped as the fritters danced, the steam wafting over the air and making Azria's stomach grumble. The woman chopped chilies and ground spices for the salad, the sound of the knife against the cutting board a happy note to Azria's swirling thoughts.

"What if my mother doesn't show up?" Azria murmured. Saying the words made a lump form in her throat, and Azria swallowed hard, wishing she hadn't said them.

"What?" asked Hiezh.

Azria kept her eyes on the cook as she poured them each a cup of coconut water. She tried to decide if she should repeat her question or try to brush it off. "What if," Azria said, staring at the counter, "what if she doesn't come back?"

"Well, it would put a dent in your plans," Hiezh said. "Seeing as how you don't have any."

Azria rolled her eyes at Hiezh. She had wanted some reassurance, not a reminder of her lack of ambition on Miz. As an Innate she had been required to study under another wizard. But she was sixteen now and should have a plan on what to do with her skills. Many of the chiefs and traders looked for wizards to help them with their building projects and farms. Azria had politely refused the few people who had offered her work and resented those who never would have dreamed of asking her. Her ability to create and weave magic was good enough for the mages to initiate her, acknowledging the power born in her through Mizian blood. But the rumors of her father being a foreigner made Azria incomplete in the eyes of some. Sometimes she felt it, under the gaze of those who knew the gossip. But for Azria, the truth was a mystery she pondered while sitting with Nana in the living room, pretending to study her scrolls while her grandmother embroidered beautiful patterns on the edge of garments.

"At least I know I won't be homeless," Azria said. "Nana would never throw me out. She loves me too much."

"Even Nana wouldn't hire you. Your embroidery is terrible," Hiezh said.

The woman placed their fritters before them served on big green leaves, the colorful and fragrant crab salad heaped in a mound in a small wooden bowl. Azria blew on her fritters, waiting for them to cool down. She watched as her teacher picked one up, hot as it was and took a bite, his mouth falling open, moaning quietly as steam billowed from his mouth.

"Hot?" Azria asked with a laugh.

"So good though," Hiezh said with his mouth full, trying to chew and breathe out to cool his mouth. Azria laughed and picked up a spoon, starting in on the cool crab salad. They quietly ate their lunch, not speaking to each other. Azria listened to the sounds of the street, other food stands and people selling their wares. The familiar and comforting aromas of roasted coconut and grilled fish, spices from all five islands being ground, charred, and chopped for meals hung in the air. Her thoughts strayed towards the little house with its black chickens in the yard, Nana at home, mending clothes or embellishing something of Azria's. Was she so eager to leave Miz, the sights and sounds she knew, for something different? To leave Nana and Hiezh for a woman she hadn't seen for five years?

Nana said, it had been so long since Azria had seen her mother, the girl still saw Apzana with the eyes of a babe and mixed her mother up with those teenage thoughts of being on her own. Did her mother ever wish she slept in a bed on land? On the other side of the horizon is the best treasure, was the saying.

Azria thought of the city she grew up in, the streets she knew well and faces she recognized. Hitha knew her and didn't seem too interested in keeping her. But Miz was more than Hitha. Gethe, city of the Northern Bay was far but just as big, and the people there received more foreigners. Perhaps rumors of her mother hadn't spread to ports with more diverse populations; perhaps they wouldn't even care. In a new city, Azria could get a fresh start, still surrounded by a culture she was raised in. Once she had her credentials as a caster, she could probably move to one of the other ports if she desired.

"Is it time to go in for my testing?" Azria groaned, pulling herself away from thoughts of the future.

"About that time," Hiezh said, draining his cup. "You ready?"

"Ready to get out of here," Azria said, hopping down from the stool. Hiezh just nodded and together they pushed through the crowd towards the High Seat of Hithan Mages.

"What do you mean, I didn't file the paperwork correctly?"

Azria stood next to Hiezh and looked up. She knew her teacher's tones and his moods and this was the kind of mood that generally ended in something breaking. If the woman behind the counter was aware of this, her response was only a slight smirk. She wore the same bleached white linen garments most Mizians wore, her dark hair braided and plaited atop her head, two writing styluses decoratively placed within her locks to keep them in place. The blue-and-yellow stole she wore around her neck told Azria she was also a mage, as well as a secretary for the Hithan Mage Guild.

"What I mean is, yes, you made your appointment. But there was more to do to get Azria seen and acknowledged today than make the appointment." The secretary pulled out several sheets of blue reed paper, the paper used by mages for such official things, black and deep blue ink laying out various rules and asking for certain information. "If you fill these out and pay the fees—"

"Fees?" Hiezh interrupted. Azria looked at his hands, gripping the edge of the table, his knuckles yellow. "What fees?"

"The processing fee," the woman said, matter-of-factly. She pointed at a section of one of the documents with a thin, carved bamboo pointer. "As well as a renewal fee if you wish to vote in matters of Hithan mages. Your vote expired two months ago."

Azria bit her lip. She couldn't tell if she should laugh or cry. Hiezh's face was comically infuriated but if what the woman said was true, Azria would not be received among the society of wizards today. Awkwardly she straightened her clothes, not sure what to do with herself as the two other mages spoke in very different tones.

"I filed that," Hiezh said insistently. "I filed it. And I paid."

"There's no record of it, Mage Gowde. Do you have the receipt?" the secretary said. Azria watched as the woman cocked her head to the side slightly, as if challenging him. She was obviously not put off by Hiezh's irate behavior, her demeanor cool and business-like. "If you have it, we can get this settled."

"Why would I have it on me if I thought it was—" Hiezh started. He threw his hands in the air and turned away. "You know what, this is so typical of the mages, to change the rules at the last minute."

"The last change to the law was made two months ago, and voted upon unanimously by all attending mages. The change in the registration fee was made six months ago." The secretary placed the paperwork on the table and looked up at him from her seat, placing the fingertips of her hands together and smiling at him. "Now, would you like to fill this out, as well as the other pertinent paperwork? And pay your fees?" She turned her attention to Azria. "You haven't been teaching her with an expired license, have you?"

"No, no, of course not," Hiezh said. Azria frowned as her teacher grabbed the paperwork and turned, walking away from the table. "We'll be back shortly!" he called out. His shoulders hunched over slightly as they walked away from the licensing office. He did that whenever he was annoyed.

"If I don't get seen today, I'll be extremely upset," Azria said, not bothering if her words irritated Hiezh further. "I know I gave you the mail for the licensing a few weeks ago, Hiezh. You filled it out and sent it."

"I may have gotten into an argument with someone who works in the records office," Hiezh muttered, pinching the bridge of his nose. "If you don't get registered today, it'll be because of my big mouth, not negligence."

Azria stopped in her tracks, narrowing her eyes at her teacher and crossing her arms over her chest. Hiezh usually kept to himself and since he didn't drink, rarely went to the taverns the other mages frequented. Still, from time to time he did go, to talk to mages who could still stand to converse with her sarcastic teacher. "You can't keep from arguing with a drunk person, can you?"

"Not when they are so incredibly wrong, Azria." Hiezh sighed. "Next time I see Gizh in the street, I'm going to twist his stole around his neck."

"Alcohol doesn't completely wipe people's memories," Azria said, shaking her head.

"Are you sure? I have personal experience to the contrary." Hiezh brought his hands to his head and groaned, pulling at his braids. "Azria, I will get you registered. I swear it by the Holy Depths."

"Glad to know there's more than just my uncertainty that's ruining my future here in Miz," Azria said. She looked down at the dirt road, ignoring the sights and sounds of the marketplace. "Now I have my teacher's enemies to blame." Azria felt as if her body was heavier, as if not knowing what tomorrow held was a weight on her shoulders. "What other terrible thing is going to happen today?"

"Never say that," Hiezh half whispered, half hissed.

Azria opened her mouth, wanting to say something rude but she stopped, a familiar face in the distance catching her eye. A smile spread on her lips as she waved, never more relieved to see her grandmother till now. "Nana!"

The old woman hobbled across the street, walking with an uneven gait. An accident in the old woman's youth had resulted in a broken knee; her walk and the hard wooden cane, its handle a heavy, metal crab claw, were among the things Azria associated with her grandmother. Nana waved back, easily making her way through the marketplace crowd despite her infirmity.

Her long off-white skirt showed brown at the hem from the dirt road.

"I thought I was late but it looks like I've caught you before your testing, Azria," Nana said. She smiled from under her broad-brimmed hat. "I wanted to be there to hug you after the mages received you as one of their own!"

"About that," Azria said, her eyes darting from Hiezh to her grandmother. "I hope you didn't plan anything elaborate to celebrate."

"Nothing much," Nana said, rocking back and forth on her heels. Azria knew this gesture. She was lying. "I was just going to make some food. Five spice stew. With rice. And plantain. And maybe something sweet at the end." All of Azria's favorite foods. "It's not every day you finish your studies and become a mage in your own right."

"Well, I am done teaching her," Hiezh muttered, looking to the side, as if trying to avoid eye contact with the old woman. "She'll have to form her own discipline now."

"Except I didn't get to test today," Azria said, not able to keep from glaring at Hiezh. She thought about the boats in the harbor and if her mother would return that day. If her mother came, expecting a full-fledged mage of her daughter, and found her denied due to a clerical error, what would she say?

Nana's face screwed up with confusion, her grip tightening on the head of her cane. "Why didn't you get to test, Azria? You've completed your training and turned sixteen! Hiezh said you were ready for the testing. What's the matter?"

"There was an issue with some paperwork," Hiezh said sheepishly, still avoiding the old woman's gaze.

"And there may be an issue with my own charter," he added in one breath, wincing slightly as he said it.

Nana scowled and picked up her cane, holding it ready to strike Hiezh. "You chicken brain, you can't even keep your paperwork straight with Azria filing your mail?" Hiezh flinched and with a flick of her wrist, Nana whacked Hiezh once on the arm, making the older mage jump in pain. "And where were you headed just now?" she asked, still holding her cane, ready to strike again.

"Back home to go through the paperwork I have," Hiezh said. He rubbed his arm, frowning at the old woman. "I have my charter there. I need to find it."

"It doesn't matter if you find it," Azria said. She started walking down the street, intending to head back to her grandmother's house, her home. "It's so late in the day, even if we could sort it out, there wouldn't be time to get it all processed in time for me to be seen today." Paper, having no legs, moved slowly. That was the saying among the five islands of Miz. "We can start in on it tomorrow and hopefully I can test within the next few weeks." If they applied tomorrow, she could probably get another appointment in four weeks, three if she was lucky. The mages weren't known for making exceptions or being speedy. In a month's time she could be an official member of the Hithan Mage Guild. Azria swallowed hard, thinking of the next few weeks ahead of her and how they would stretch and seem endless.

"I hope you don't blame me," Hiezh said, falling in besides her.

"Why shouldn't she?" Nana asked, coming up on the other side. Azria slowed her pace to accommodate her grandmother, the old woman's presence her only comfort at the moment. "You're the one who can't keep some paperwork straight."

"I'm not the one who requires the paperwork!" Hiezh said. "If this was the old days, I would test her myself and say she was a mage, part of our Order. But things are different now." Hiezh lowered his voice, and Azria watched him look around, obviously looking to be sure no one was listening before he spoke. "After all the infighting, the mages thought they'd make up for the lawlessness by having more rules. They just made magic boring and cumbersome."

"You don't remember the old days, Hiezh, before the Triumvirate came and went," Nana said, matching Hiezh's volume but with more nostalgia in her quiet words. "They were wilder, almost worse than the ma-rauders that ravaged our shores. They fought in the streets and in the forests. They formed covens and ri-valries. They brought the tide in and out and carved caverns into mountains."

"They proved to themselves they needed laws," Azria said, leading the way through the busy streets, past food vendors and sandal menders. "They caused so much chaos, they shattered the peace. And when the chiefs rose up, the mages started the Guilds, im-posed their own rules, rather than have those without understanding force their decisions upon them." Azria knew the history of the mages well. Every Mizian did. "Better the mages rule themselves than those who don't understand how magic works."

"Don't or won't?" Hiezh said with a wry laugh. "The leaders of each of the five islands want the power of the mages. They use the mages, they go through the pre-cious paperwork to pick and choose who to use, like a tool in the toolbox. One to build a faster ship, one to make the purple rice grow faster and in less space. If mages didn't have to appeal to five chiefs, maybe there would be fewer rules."

"As annoying as the rules are, a mage of Miz is respected in every port," Nana snorted.

"Meanwhile, I can't get the respect of my peers because of who my parents are, or might be," Azria interjected, no longer concerned with the politics of Miz and its history. She was the one rejected at the guild office today, for reasons clerical or otherwise. "Even if I were to pass the test, which I could, easily, Poesh and them would whisper behind my back and cost me work, if not my reputation."

Of all the things which had remained after the Triumvirate had risen and fallen, Mizian pride remained. Azria's ability to weave magic had been the proof the Guild needed as to her parentage but the rumors still lingered. Azria remembered the way Goezh's parents had pulled him back over the threshold away from her. The disappointed look on Nana's face when Azria told her about it, sobbing at the kitchen table. Not understanding what 'rumors' were and why it mattered who her father was. She didn't care who he was and why would he be a foreigner? Why did it mean other apprentices wouldn't play with her? Why was Hiezh her only confidant and friend?

Azria sighed heavily, rubbing her eyes with the palm of her hand. She was tired. Tired of training for a world that wasn't sure she belonged there. Tired of Hiezh's cold way of expressing care. Tired of waiting for letters from her mother and trying to remember what she looked like.

"If you both don't mind, I think I need to be alone for a while," Azria muttered. Nana's face fell with disappointment, the corners of her mouth drooping with a slight frown. Azria sighed and wrapped her arms around the old woman, embracing her as warmly as she could at the moment, given her mood. "I'll be home for dinner, I promise. I just need some time to think."

"Don't be too long, granddaughter," Nana said. The old woman craned her neck forward and laid a dry kiss on Azria's cheek. She smelled of the cooking spices and the warm woods they burned at the altar for incense. "You know I hate serving cold food."

"And I hate eating it," Azria laughed, pulling away. She smiled one more time at Nana and Hiezh, noticing the concern in their eyes. "I'll bring something for dessert."

"I'll get everything sorted with the Guild, I swear," Hiezh said.

"You better," Azria said, not wanting to spare her tutor's feelings at the moment. "See you both later," she said, turning and leaving, sure they were waving farewell. Azria didn't bother turning around to make sure. She'd see them sooner than she'd like.

The market stretched before her, rows of sun-bleached white awnings fluttering in the breeze around her. Azria looked over the wares absently, seeing the same sandals, shawls and snacks being sold at every turn. The words of her countryfolk were usually comforting and familiar, but at the moment they seemed bland and monotonous. Azria walked down one row of booths and instead of turning down the next, walked away from the market district, pointing her sandals towards the beach, walking into the wind.

The shore stretched white as the insides of seashells in front of her, the ocean a brilliant sapphire sparkling with hints of emerald and turquoise under the golden sun. Miz was called the 'Crown Jewel' of the Floating Chain and never did Azria believe it more than when she was on the beach. She walked off of the cobblestone street, her feet sinking into the sand. Without thinking she bent down and untied her sandals, carrying them in her hand as she walked further down the beach, the fine, white sand smooth against her feet.

Seagulls swooped and shrieked in the sky above and in the distance several pelicans were gliding in a lazy line over the surf. Other beach goers walked and sat, eating lunches or poking at the shells and half-dead creatures which always washed up on shore. Azria walked until she thought she was in the middle of the beach and sat down, staring out at the ocean.

The sea crashed and lapped at the shore, the noise rushing in her ears like a familiar, raucous tune. Out on the azure waves she saw ships. Fast, long fishing boats from white-beached Hitha, sailing vessels of all shapes and sizes from the Redlands, Kamer, and the other wide, flat lands to the north. Boats from the other islands of Miz bobbed on the waves. Past them the shores of the other islands of Miz shimmered. All of the islands, even the Black Island, were encircled by the warm, clear waters of the Sapphire Sea.

Azria sighed, picking up a handful of sand. She felt the small, fine grains slip past her skin, slip out of her fist and watched as they blew away in the wind. She flexed her fingers before she picked up another handful, feeling the heat in her chest, head, and belly which always rose up when she began to form her magic. She felt it swirl and glow inside of her as the heat coalesced and then trickled through her nerves, running down her arm as she felt out the properties of the white, clean sand. Slowly the sand stopped falling and came together, forming a hard, tight ball. Azria opened her hand and as she did, the sand flattened, her eyes leading the way as it settled into a hard, thin sheet. She could still see the grains of sand within it, dancing within the plane. As she drew in her breath, the granules loosened their hold on themselves and melded together, her hand warm under the newly formed plane of clear, brown glass.

"Azria?"

Azria jumped, startled to hear her name. She felt the heat in her body swirl and surge as it tried to dissipate, her vision blurring for a moment as she turned to see who it was.

A short man, by Mizian standards, and he wasn't from Miz. His build, stockier and muscled, filled out his clothes, but they were all wrong. Instead of the typical linen kilt most Mizian men wore, he wore brown pants that stopped right above the knee and seemed to be tucked in at the waist. His hair was very straight and greased back, the sides of his head shaved. Golden earrings adorned his big ears. The sleeved jacket was dyed a very deep blue, with black and silver embroidery flashing when he moved. His sharp brown eyes sparkled with excitement. At his waist, two curved knives hung from a thick leather belt, their hilts made of bone and carved with writing.

"Azria, is that you?" he asked again. From his accent, Azria thought he was probably from the Golden Islands, far to the south. She didn't know anyone from the Golden Islands. Her eyes darted from side to side, looking for anyone who might see her speaking to him. "By Her Lap, you look just like them," he said, shaking his head side to side.

"Do I know you?" she asked, standing up quickly and taking a step back. The man put his hands up in surrender, a smile revealing straight white teeth and one black tooth, made of some kind of stone. While his round face looked young, the lines at his eyes and around his mouth told her he was older.

"The last time I saw you, you were a baby," the man said.

"That's not what I asked," Azria said, looking around again. The beach seemed suddenly empty.

"No need to worry," the man said. He brought a hand to his belly and he bowed to her at the waist, standing up straight before he smiled at her again. "My name is Bolo of the good ship *Hen & Chick*.

"I'm here to take you to your mother."

Chapter 2
Reconciled

Azria's mouth went dry as sand, her heart thumping in her chest. Had he just said what she thought he said? All this last year, Azria had anticipated her mother coming, daydreamed about it. This wasn't exactly the way she had pictured it: standing on the beach with a stranger. Azria narrowed her eyes at the man called Bolo, not sure what her next step should be.

"And who is my mother, exactly?" she said, crossing her arms over her chest. She still held the piece of glass in her hand, and she gripped it with her fingers in an attempt to keep her hands from shaking.

"Well, with that attitude, it's obvious," he said, rolling his dark eyes. "Captain Apzana Chiwde is your mother. And you're her daughter, Azria Chiwde." He chuckled, his eyes sparkling as he looked her over. "You've grown so much these last few years! You don't remember me, do you?"

"I don't," Azria said, not sure if she should feel embarrassed for not remembering him. "Why would she send you to come get me?" Azria asked, glancing to either side of him. "Here? At the beach?" She frowned as the realization hit her. "Were you following me?"

"Yes, I was," Bolo admitted, holding his hands up again. "On your mother's orders," he added quickly. "I'm the first mate. Your mother told me to find you at Hiezh's home and follow you from there. Once you were alone, I was to approach you and ask you to come with me to our home. It's docked at the Far Bay."

"Our home?" Azria asked. She thought of Nana and the wooden table where Azria had eaten almost all her meals. The way the floor cushions felt when she knelt on them, and her bed with its cool, embroidered sheets.

"Meaning my home, your mother's home and the rest of the crew's, of course," he said.

"Why did she tell you to wait until I was alone?" Azria asked, still frowning.

"Because the *Hen & Chick* is for you alone, Azria, not Hiezh or Nana," Bolo said with a smile. "You're the one she wants to see. You're the reason she's back in Hitha."

"Right now?" Azria asked, flustered with the timing of it all.

"I know you were really busy staring out into the ocean but yes, right now would be ideal," Bolo said, a hint of exasperation in his voice.

"Well," Azria mumbled. She dug her toes into the sand, wondering what she should do. Part of her wanted to run towards the Far Bay, up onto the ship. But she knew Nana waited for her at home. Azria could imagine Nana stooping over the fire, singing over it and stoking the embers to flames with her wet hands. How long would it take to go see her mother? If it made Azria late for supper, surely Nana would understand. After what had happened today, the thought of sailing on a boat away from Miz was even more tempting than before. Perhaps her mother would sympathize with her, after Azria told her about the trials of the day. Azria pressed her lips together and then nodded, tossing the piece of glass to the sandy shore. "Alright, let's go."

"Great!" Bolo said, clapping his hands together. "Come with me." He held out his arm, offering it to her. Azria tilted her head to the side as she slipped on her sandals, confused by the gesture. "Sorry," he said with a chuckle, dropping his arm to the side. "Old habit. I forget Mizians don't like touching each other."

"What? That's not it," Azria said, feeling slightly offended. "It's just so hot here. We enjoy the feel of the breeze as we walk."

"It's hot in the Golden Isles, as you call them," Bolo replied, already starting to walk across the beach, back towards the street. "But if two people are walking together, they're arm in arm."

"I thought you were from there," Azria said. She didn't mean for it to sound smug but as soon as she said it, she realized it did. She examined Bolo's face to see if he was offended. Instead he just shrugged. "You're far from home," she said, quickening her pace to catch up with him.

"The *Hen & Chick* is my home, Azria," Bolo said, smiling happily before he stepped onto the street ahead of her, the tall palm trees throwing their cool blue shadows over them. He put his hands on his waist, tucking a thumb behind the hilt of each of his blades, a strange gesture to accompany a smile. "It has been for some time now."

"How long have you known my mother?" Azria asked. She saw Bolo's eyes dart towards her and then away, as if he was going to say something but then thought better of it.

"A long time is all I'll say for now," he said. They walked quietly down the palm tree-lined street, Azria ignoring the stares they received from other Mizians. Bolo knew more than her but wasn't saying anything. She wondered if he had been ordered to do that as well.

"Everybody knows my mother better than I do," Azria said with a shrug.

"The sooner children realize this, the better," Bolo replied, turning his head back slightly to look at her.

"Do you know my father?" Azria asked. He wasn't much taller than her but his strides were long and quick.

"Would it surprise you if I said I did?" Bolo answered.

"Is he part of the crew?" Azria asked.

"Your father?" Bolo asked, raising his eyebrows. Something about this was funny to Bolo. Azria frowned as she watched his face grow more serious, as he forced his smirk into a frown. "No, he isn't."

"But he is from the Golden Isles, right?" Azria asked, not sure if she wanted the answer or not. "Did they meet there? Does my mother still love him?"

"That story's not mine to tell, Azria," Bolo said with a sigh, obviously holding back. Azria wrinkled her nose at him in annoyance.

"You're no fun," Azria muttered, rolling her eyes.

"I've been told otherwise, but never by young wizards with a head full of questions."

"How many wizards have you met before?" Azria asked, not caring she was asking yet another question.

"Four, not including you. You're by far the shortest mage I've ever met," Bolo said.

"Height has nothing to do with magic ability," Azria said, her cheeks growing hot.

"Not very imposing though, don't you think?" Bolo asked, the corners of his eyes wrinkling with mirth.

"I think I'm as good a mage as all the ones you've met. Maybe better!" The last two words fell from her lips before Azria could stop herself.

"We'll see who's best very soon, I'm sure," Bolo said with a laugh. Azria wasn't sure if she should try to clarify or justify her statement. As far as mages of Miz went, Azria had little difficulty with the various disciplines Hiezh had taught her over the years. She excelled in manipulating objects and had trouble with illusions but they weren't unattainable. But Azria knew magic users of different shores spun different spells. To say she was better than any of them was presumptive. She hoped Bolo wouldn't take her words seriously. He hadn't seemed to take any of them too seriously so far.

As they turned down the road leading to the Far Bay, Azria's stomach fluttered with excitement. Footsteps quickened with anticipation till she hurried past Bolo, scanning the harbor for a boat she recognized. She thought she remembered the *Hen & Chick*. It had two green sails and a black-and-white chicken carved into the masthead. Her mother had acquired the ship five years ago, about the time she stopped visiting. Boat after boat bobbed in the water but Azria didn't see the ship. "Are the sails still green?" she asked, squinting against the setting sun.

"You have a good memory," Bolo said. "They haven't been green for a long time. They're white and black now, and the flag is always changing." He winked at Azria, catching up with her as they came closer to the docks. Other sailors waved as they walked by, the sounds of loading and unloading interspersed with the songs sailors sang to make the work go faster.

Finally Azria spotted the ship, its striking black-and-white sails crisp against the clear blue sky. Even from afar, she could tell the chicken at the mast had been painted recently, the feathers carefully carved by a skilled hand so they looked real. It looked like one of Nana's many chickens.

"Here she is," Bolo said, pushing past her and starting up the gangplank. Azria slowed to a stop, chest tightening as she looked up at the ship. Bolo stopped halfway, turning and looking at the girl curiously. "Come on now," he said, holding his hand out towards her. "Don't tell me you're nervous!"

"I haven't seen her in five years, how am I supposed to feel?" Azria asked, hoping she didn't sound afraid or accusatory. Azria stood at the foot of the gangplank, playing with her bracelets nervously as she thought about the woman she would see on board the ship. What would her mother think when she saw her? What if her mother didn't recognize her? "She never told me why she didn't come back. All I had were rumors and a promise that one day, when I was done with my studies, she'd come get me." Azria felt her eyes sting, the threat of tears starting to simmer in her throat. "I know five years isn't long for you, but for me, it felt like forever. What if she doesn't recognize me? And why did she come back now?"

"Five years is almost a third of your life, Azria!" Bolo said. "It was a long time. She knows that, and she knows it was hard for you. If you come with me," Bolo said, still holding his hand out towards her, "in time, all your questions will be answered. If you're too angry to see her, I'll tell her that and she'll understand. But I think you're more curious than angry."

"All my questions?" Azria asked, still looking at Bolo's hand. She couldn't help but narrow her eyes in disbelief.

"As many as she can answer," Bolo admitted. "Please. She's waiting for you."

Azria took a deep breath. Taking Bolo's hand in hers, she stepped onto the gangplank, the wood creaking under her feet. The young mage had been on boats before but those had been fishing boats, local pleasure taxis which went to the other islands of Miz. She had been on her mother's vessels before but mostly she remembered waving at them from the dock as they pulled away. Azria quickly ascended the ramp and stepped onto the ship, feeling it bob in the water beneath them.

The deck gleamed with cleanliness, freshly washed and smelling of wood and tar. Overhead the sails flapped quietly in the sea breeze, gulls spinning overhead. "Where is everybody?" Azria asked, looking around.

"Out for shore leave," Bolo said. "Enjoying the sights and sounds of your fair city."

Azria walked slowly across the deck, looking at the masts and long, thick ropes that ran up the sails and across, holding things down and keeping things up. Towards the rear of the ship the cabin was painted in bright colors with patterns of red and purple passion flowers. The door to the cabin stood open. Azria walked slowly towards the open door, thinking she heard humming. If Bolo followed her, she didn't hear him. Azria approached, her heart thumping harder and harder in her chest the closer she drew.

The humming stopped as soon as she reached the threshold. Azria put her hand on the side of the doorway and peered inside.

Her mother, Captain Apzana Chiwde, sat at a table, her sandaled feet propped up . Azria's gaze went to her face first. It was the same face she remembered: smooth, dark skin, a cheek Azria used to press her cheek against. A full mouth which would break into an even wider smile or sing a song. Eyes the color of the earth, lined with short lashes. Her clothes were similar to Bolo's: short, black trousers that fit loosely and a red jacket embroidered with gold floss. Earrings carved from some sort of green stone hung heavy on her earlobes and an ornate gold collar hung around her neck. On the table was a wide-brimmed hat, woven from bamboo. Her mother looked up from the map she was reading and stared back at Azria with warm brown eyes.

"Azria," Apzana said. Long-fingered hands folded the map before she stood from her chair. She was somewhat smaller than Azria remembered, but still two hands taller than Azria. Azria started to take a step back but stopped herself, too overwhelmed to speak. She tried to recall the last time she had seen her mother. What had she been wearing? What was the last food they shared together? Azria drew in her breath, forcing herself to breathe steadily. She wouldn't be overwhelmed by this situation. She wouldn't show it, at least.

"Mama?" Azria said, her voice much quieter than she intended. Her mother blinked. She walked around the table and stood in front of Azria, grabbing her hat from the table before bowing low at the waist.

"I'm honored to have a mage of Miz before me," Apzana said, standing up straight. Azria frowned slightly, trying not to let her confusion show on her face.

"Mage?" she asked. Azria pulled herself away from the doorway and stood up as straight as she could, trying to match her mother's more business-like demeanor. This wasn't what she was expecting.

"Yes," her mother said. The older woman nodded and walked past her, ducking slightly in the low doorway. "In our letters, you told me you'd be done with your training today. It just so happens I'm without a wizard for my crew." Her mother walked out onto the deck and Azria turned in the doorway, facing her.

"Do you normally have a wizard in your crew?" Azria asked. Had her mother always had an accent? Her mother's words were Mizian but similar in tone and cadence to Bolo. She must have spent a lot of time in the Golden Isles at some point.

"We do," her mother said, tentatively. "But well, our last one...let's just say he isn't with us anymore."

Azria didn't like the way that sounded. She didn't like anything about this situation. She hadn't been sure what to expect when she came aboard her mother's ship but it was definitely not this. A job offer? "What happened to him?" Azria asked, not sure if she wanted to know the answer.

"Blood mages of Kamer are hard to keep around," Apzana said with a shrug. "It's just the way it goes. Kamerians of all paths are unpredictable and their magic tends to result in...messy endings. But a mage of Miz, bestowed with a charter by the Guild?" Apzana looked to Bolo and nodded. "That's got an anchor on it."

"Let me get this straight," Azria said, feeling her anger starting to simmer in her belly. "I'm going to be late for dinner with Nana because you wanted me to become part of the crew?"

"Well, not quite," Apzana said. "I need to see you in action of course. Many a mage has misrepresented themselves on paper." She raised an eyebrow at Azria, the brim of her hat casting a shadow on her face.

Azria felt her face burn. Her mother wanted a demonstration, did she? Azria realized she had been clenching her fists this whole time and she stretched her fingers, keeping her breath as steady as she could. She tried to think back to all the letters they had sent over the years, and if this was the person who had represented themselves in those written words and gifts. Was this the reason her mother had left her behind? Too busy seeing to her purse to take care of her own daughter? Azria looked around the boat and considered setting it on fire.

"Take your commission to the crabs," Azria said. If she rushed she could still get to Nana's without her grandmother being the wiser. She started to walk back towards the gangplank, finding Bolo standing in her way.

"This is endlessly hilarious to me," Bolo said over her shoulder, obviously addressing Apzana. "Finally, some-one is talking back to you."

"People not talking back keeps them alive, Bolo," Azria heard Apzana say. "So," her mother called. "You're just going to leave without doing a single trick? Not even to humor your own mother?"

Azria stopped, her hands balling into fists again. She turned to face the captain. Azria could see her own face staring back at her. The same eyes, the same mouth. The same smirk. Azria frowned, too angry to cry. "No," she spat. "I didn't come here for a job. I came here to see my mother." Azria pointed two fingers at Bolo, trying to dampen her anger by misdirecting it. "And you, you said if I came with you, I would get answers. Instead I get demands from a stranger. You're both liars." Azria turned this way and that, trying to figure out how she was going to get off of the ship, Bolo standing firm in front of the gangplank. "Get out of my way," she ordered Bolo.

"Nope," Bolo said with a shrug. "I don't take orders from anyone but Apzana."

"It's true," her mother said. "It's one of the reasons he's such a good first mate. Feel free to make him move, though," she said.

"Wait, let's not be too hasty," Bolo said, his voice pitched with panic. "Apzana—"

"Stay put, Bolo."

"But—"

"Hold your ground, Bolo."

Azria wrinkled her nose, thinking about her mother's words. "You think I'll use magic to get off this boat," she said. The smile on her mother's face told her she was right.

"I think you'll stay on the boat, actually," Apzana said with a shrug. "Why go back to Nana and Hiezh and Mizian life when you can sail the Floating Chain? See the Skyward City from the Emerald Pass? The sea wolves on the silver waves of Kamer? The forested beaches of the Red Lands?" Apzana shrugged. "You've seen Miz and all it has to offer. Why not go see what else the world has to show you?"

"Just because Miz has offered, doesn't mean I've taken it all up," Azria scoffed. Her mother's words were more tempting to Azria than anything she had ever heard before. Still, Captain Apzana's presumption, her dismissal of all Azria knew and loved tilted Azria's chin up. She wouldn't be swayed so easily, as much as she wished to bend. "You know, I'm only sixteen, and just coming into my commission. There's more to Miz than its sights and foods. There's a lot to stay for."

"At sixteen, I wanted to leave home," the captain said, the look in her eyes telling Azria her words were true. "I stared out at the sea every day and thought of the lands which lay beyond the horizon. The music of foreign tongues. The color of strange silks."

"We're not the same person," Azria murmured.

"You don't know that for sure," Apzana said. Azria's gaze darted towards her mother. "I know," she began. "I haven't been here these last five years. There are reasons for that, good reasons. I tried my best to have a relationship with you while my relationship with Miz was constantly changing. I hope you can understand that. I know you're smarter than me, and more sensitive, so I think you can."

Azria stood there, not sure what to do or what to say. The boat rocked under her feet, caught in the gentle lull of the waves, the sounds of other boats and other sailors seeming far away. If Azria left the boat, she'd never learn anything about her mother, would she? If she stayed aboard, it may be hard but it'd be something. Somehow she'd reconcile her ideas of her mother with the truth.

"What do you generally ask of your magic users and what's the pay?" she asked.

"Ha, this is getting even better," Bolo said.

"Get below, Bolo," Apzana said, annoyance in her voice.

"As first mate, I am requesting to see her skills, Captain," he said, a hint of mock professionalism in his voice. "She'll be reporting to me, after all. I would also like to ask her some questions, perhaps—"

Apzana shot him a look that stopped him from talking. He laughed nervously as Apzana walked towards Azria. She looked taller, bigger. Azria swallowed hard and told herself she had nothing to worry about. She thought of memories of when she was younger, of her hand being much smaller, cradled in the warm, calloused hand of her mother, walking down the lane with her. Letters that ended, 'my heart floats on my love for you,' that smelled of spices and salt. Her mother came closer till she was standing right in front of Azria, peering down at her. Azria clenched her fists and blinked, the opening words for a barrier spell floating into her mind and flowing towards her fingers.

"Smart and clever," her mother said, a smile breaking the seriousness of her face. "Not that I'm surprised. You were smart as a child." Azria watched as her mother's face softened, her gaze drifting away for a moment before she snapped back to her more business-like demeanor. "The ship's magic user is asked to provide cover for the ship when needed, even odds in fights and tend to wounds too serious for our surgeon. Any material cost for all spells we ask you to weave will be covered by the ship. In addition, you will receive a portion of any income the ship gains while you are aboard equal to your fellow sailors and you will be expected to report and share fifty percent of any wealth gained off-ship while you are under our employ.

"You are also allowed to borrow against the ship's funds, at interest and if you are ever imprisoned and convicted of a crime, the bail will be paid for your release. However, you will have to remain on the ship till your debt is paid and you will then be left at the next port town, no matter how far away from home or hostile." Apzana smiled. "Not that it should be a problem."

"Right," Azria said, nodding. Those terms seemed fair, for the most part. The most troubling part was the imprisonment bit but Azria didn't plan on breaking any laws any time soon. "What's the average yearly income of each sailor?" she asked, her mind conjuring images of coins from every shore and stamp, gemstones raw and faceted, aromatic woods and spices able to make someone swoon with their richness.

"Reported, each sailor made a hand and four fingers of gold," Apzana said. "At least that's what the appraiser and accountant agreed upon."

"What about the death clause?" Bolo chimed in. The captain gave Bolo a sideways glance.

"No need to bring it up," Apzana said. "If something happens to her, her pay will go to me. I'm her only kin."

"What about Nana?" Azria said.

"What about Nana?" Apzana asked, amusement in her quip. "She's being cared for, don't you worry about that. Worry about getting aboard this ship, Azria. The sea will always be here for us."

Azria almost answered back, a smart answer already on her tongue. But she stopped herself. What her mother said seemed wrong at first but Azria knew it to be true. All her short life, the sea was always present. Its tides came in and out, its waves shifted and crashed but always there was the salty, vibrant water which hugged Miz in its strong, deep arms. The sea brought food, the sea brought news, and it brought souls to and from this world.

Azria wasn't sure what her future on Miz held. Without a commission from the Guild, she couldn't practice the arts she had studied these last ten years.

Would Hiezh get the correct forms in order this time? Would the Guild find some reason to remove his mantle and turn out Azria?

"Answer me one question first," Azria asked.

"Alright," Apzana said with a nod. "What?"

"Is my father of Miz?" Azria asked, looking up into her mother's eyes. If she lied to her, Azria would be able to tell. She was sure of it. Azria saw a flash of sadness cross her mother's gaze but if Azria hadn't looked for it, she never would have seen it.

"No," Apzana said, shaking her head. "He's not."

"Is he alive?" Azria asked.

"That's a second question," Apzana pointed out, sounding more amused than annoyed.

"You're right," Azria said with a shrug. "Well, you wanted to see magic. Here it goes." Taking a step back, she followed her breath through her body, the way it filled her lungs and belly, spreading its life through her. She planted one foot behind her firmly, knowing the boat moved on the water but she was grounded on the deck of the ship.

Azria felt the water in the air, moving erratically, invisible but there. Closing her eyes, it moved on every breeze, caressing her skin. She exhaled slowly, her breath meeting the water. As she pushed her energy out, the moisture began to move together in one motion. She felt its power in her hands, rippling through her fingers as she willed it, spinning the water into a clear, shining ball.

It spun above her head, over her outstretched hand. Azria couldn't help but smile as she felt the sphere of water cool as it moved, heat dissipating around her. With her other hand she gathered the heat and concentrated it, drawing it into a single, fiery point at the tip of her finger. Her left hand began to shake but she steadied herself, remembering her breathing, remembering she could stop whenever she wanted to. With a flick of her wrist, the point of heat shot through the air, through the middle of the glimmering sphere of water. The water absorbed the heat and like a balloon, expanded and then popped audibly, a blanket of steam expanding through the air and drifting down on them.

"Well, I'm glad to see the money I paid Hiezh was put to good use," Apzana managed. Azria swore the smile on her mother's face was an expression of pride. She couldn't tell for sure. Apzana raised her eyebrows and looked to Bolo. "I'd say you're hired," Apzana said.

"When do we leave?" Azria said, barely able to believe the words spilling from her lips. A grin spread across her face, her cheeks already aching, but she didn't care. Excitement boiled like a tide pool in her belly.

"First light tomorrow," Apzana said. "You've got till mid-evening to get your affairs in order. All who plan on departing with us will be on deck or left behind."

"Mid-evening?" Disbelief washed across Azria's face. "So soon?"

"I only had one piece of business in Miz," Apzana said, starting to walk back to the small room. "It's been tended to. I expect you on board by mid-evening and you will have everything you'll need with you. Actually, Bolo?" she said, turning back around to face them.

"Yes, Captain?" he said.

"Go with her, help her pack and take this to Nana and Hiezh." Apzana entered the room and emerged a moment later with two packages. One was wrapped in red and blue silk, tied with a piece of thin, sisal rope. The other was a dark wooden box, intricately carved with depictions of strange flowers Azria didn't recognize. "The bundle's for the old woman, the box is for the teacher." She walked up to Bolo and handed them over. "Do not under any circumstances allow Nana to refuse the gift."

"I'll do my best but I'm not putting my life on the line to give that woman a present," Bolo said. He looked to Azria and winked. "Come on, you. We've got a lot to do."

"Wait," Apzana said, her voice soft but strong. Azria turned and before she could react, her mother was hugging her, holding her close. "Thank you," she heard her mother say, quietly, in a voice she hadn't used since she had said Azria's name. "Thank you, my sweet girl."

"Thank you for what, Mama?" Azria said. It felt strange, to be embraced by her mother, something she hadn't done in so long.

"For coming aboard the ship. For being patient."

Azria pulled back slightly, looking up into her mother's face. "Mama, what was I supposed to do?"

Azria closed her eyes as her mother bent to kiss her on the forehead. "What we're supposed to do isn't always easily done. I'm proud of you." Apzana smiled and wiped the wet kiss away. "We have a lot to talk about. But remember, I am Captain Apzana first."

"I know, I know," Azria said, looking away. "I'm glad I can see you as the captain, instead of reading about it!" Azria smiled up at her mother, excitement fluttering in her chest. "We have time now."

"Speaking of which," Bolo said. "If you want to eat dinner with Nana and get back by mid-evening, we should get going."

"Of course!" Apzana said, smiling broadly. "I wouldn't deny you one last meal cooked by Nana's hand." She gave Azria's arms a slight squeeze before she pulled away.

"Are you coming with us?" Azria asked, the idea of everyone she loved sitting at the same dinner table again filling her with joy.

"Oh, I don't think that'd be a good idea," Apzana said, smiling, something like sheepishness in her expression. "I've much to do before the rest of the crew starts coming in. Give Nana my regards. And tell Hiezh I said hello. I'll see you this evening." Her mother gave her one more hug before she turned and walked back towards the cabin, disappearing into the small, colorful room.

Azria was part of the crew. The realization made her heart thump, a grin returning to her already beaming face.

"Alright, I don't want your dinner to get cold," Bolo said, moving aside so Azria could pass to the gangplank. "After you," he said, trying to gesture towards the ramp as he held the two presents in his hands.

Azria felt as if she was floating down towards the dock, the ramp barely registering under her feet. She briefly considered turning around and going back onto the ship, never stepping foot on Miz again. But she had to say goodbye to Nana and Hiezh.

She stood on the dock, the wood creaking under her feet, looking to Bolo. "I'll lead the way," she said.

"About that," Bolo said, scratching his eyebrow with his thumb. "I know I said I would escort you home, but I just remembered I had to do something personal. If I go with you now, there's a chance I won't get to it. So I was going to suggest we part ways for now." Azria must have frowned because Bolo put his hands up. "I won't be long, I promise! I'll pick you up at Nana's after evening meal. It'd mean a lot to me, and getting on the good side of the first mate isn't bad for a new sailor." He grinned. This was a cocky man, if Azria had ever met one.

"As long as you promise," Azria said finally, noticing the relief on his face. "Do you know where Nana lives?"

"If she hasn't moved, I know," Bolo said, already backing away. "Remember, evening meal. I'll come get you and you better be ready! Oh, and I guess you should take the presents." He walked back, pushing them into her arms before she could protest. "Make sure they get them!" he ordered her before he turned and started off again.

"Bolo!" Azria called after him, watching him hurry towards whatever personal errand he had to run. "What's the real reason my mother didn't come with me to dinner?"

"Because she's sworn to never step foot on Mizian soil again!" he called. The smile on his face didn't match the gravity of his statement. He waved goodbye to her before he turned and started jogging down the flower-lined street.

Azria watched him run, shocked by what he had just said. Was this true? Part of her wanted to go back to the ship and ask her mother about it. But she had a bag to pack if she wanted to be on the *Hen & Chick* when it left the bay. "I'll ask her about it when I get back," she said to herself, reveling in how wonderful she felt. Shifting the two gifts in her arms, Azria turned and started down the street, quickening her pace till she was running down the road, her excitement making her feel as if she could fly.

Chapter 3
Gifts and Goodbyes

"Nana?" Azria called up the garden path. "Nana? Hiezh?" She fumbled with the two packages as she tried to shift them under one arm, placing her hand on the small wooden gate. Without looking, she undid the latch as she had so many times before, the wooden gate swinging open smoothly. Nana's gate never squeaked; the old woman was fastidious in the maintenance of her property. Azria hurried up the narrow, stone-lined path, the mango trees throwing cool shadows across the ground, the air scented with the flowers of Nana's many spice and herb plants. A black chicken darted across the path in front of her, clucking as it disappeared into the bushes. Azria hopped up the wooden stairs and stepped across the freshly swept veranda, the spicy aroma of her dinner making her stomach grumble.

"Azria!" She heard the old voice call from the back of the house. Nana appeared in the doorway. Even from the front of the house, Azria could see the frown on her face. "Where have you been, girl?! I've been watching your plantain get cold!"

"Where's Hiezh?" Azria asked excitedly, ignoring the old woman's admonishment. "I have something for each of you."

"Is it an explanation as to where you were?" Nana said, annoyance in her voice. Azria put the bundles down on the couch and started walking towards her bedroom, Nana limping to catch up behind her. "Hiezh will be by later. He's talking to the record keeper of the Guild, to see if he can't get you another appointment before the end of the week."

"It's nice of him to try, but it's pointless," Azria said. She breezed into her room, walking over to the wicker chest in which she kept her clothes.

"Azria, what about supper?" Nana huffed. Azria heard her thump her cane on the wooden floor. Azria turned to her grandmother, putting a hand on her shoulder.

"I'm too excited to eat, Nana," she said, the same excited grin returning to her face. "I need a traveler's bag. The bundle wrapped in silk is for you. It's from my mother." Azria rushed back to her chest, lifting the lid to look over her clean clothes.

"Your mother?" Nana murmured.

Azria picked up a linen dress and shook it out, dried leaves spinning down into the chest, taking their scent with them. It wasn't her best dress but a boat probably wasn't a place for best dresses. "Yes," she said, draping the dress over her arm. "She's back, just like she promised me." Saying the words made Azria's cheeks hurt. Just a few hours ago, she had doubted her mother would come and now she was picking through her belongings, getting ready for a new life.

"So she told you to just pack your things and join her, did she?" Nana said. Azria heard hurt in Nana's voice, though she knew the old woman was too proud to admit it. "I have to say, I'm not surprised."

Azria laid the dress she had picked out on her bed. Nana gripped the crab claw of her cane, looking towards the door, as if she wanted to leave. "My mother's leaving at first light tomorrow and says I have to be on the boat by this evening," Azria explained, hoping her words wouldn't further upset her grandmother. "A man named Bolo is coming to fetch me."

"Bolo? Feh!" Nana said, thumping her cane on the wooden floor again. "That troublemaker is probably turning a table over on Green Way right now."

"Is he a troublemaker?" Azria asked, not able to keep from smirking. It didn't seem too unlikely, just after their brief meeting. But if Nana had something to say about Bolo, Azria definitely wanted to hear it.

"That he is. He's also one of your mother's oldest friends," Nana said with a nod, her previous confident demeanor returning. "I'm sure you'll hear all about it once you have wood and water under your feet. Well, don't let an old lady keep you from your work," Nana sighed, dismissing herself with a wave of her cane.

"No, Nana," Azria said, calling after her. The old woman stopped in her tracks, looking over her shoulder as she waited for Azria to speak. Azria held her hand out towards her grandmother, motioning for her to join her. "You've been to more lands than I have. Could you please help me pick out clothes for the journey?"

"Hmph," Nana said, shrugging her shoulders. But she walked over and stood beside Azria, the warm aroma of coconut cream and cinnamon wafting off of her clothes. Azria watched as her old, gnarled hands felt the fabrics of the garments, rubbing the cloth between her fingers. "I'll say this, and hopefully you're not too young to heed an old woman's words," Nana said. "Pack light. You often find the things you need on other shores. All you really need to take with you is the love of those you leave behind." Nana looked down into the chest, looking over Azria's clothes with a chuckle. "That being said, I'd bring your rainy season skirts and tunics, and the heaviest shawl you have. A belt is good on a ship, especially if you can keep things in it. Hold on, girl. I've got just the thing." Nana gave Azria's shoulder a squeeze before she limped out, leaving the girl in the room alone.

Azria's hands went to her favorite summer skirts. She wondered what the salt air and high winds would do to the white, sheer fabric. Her mother wore trousers. Maybe she could buy something less susceptible to breezes in the first port they reached. Maybe a rice picker's skirt, which she could fashion into pants? Azria folded the thin garments carefully and opened her jewelry box, a carved wooden box inlaid with shells to form the image of a seabird. Maybe she should bring her jewelry, to sell. That was a thing sailors and pirates did, she had heard, to make money to pay debts or ransoms during trying times.

Azria looked at her jewelry and grimaced. All her Mizian jewelry was fairly plain compared to even the simple pieces her mother wore. Shell jewelry and hair accessories, typical of current trends in fashion. A wooden cuff inlaid with mother of pearl was probably the most ornate piece made in Miz she owned, a gift from Nana when she had turned ten. Nana had one similar to it herself and Azria picked it up, holding it in her hands. Why hadn't she worn it to her test today? Azria slipped on the bracelet, smiling at the familiar weight on her arm.

Her hand slid over the more ornate pieces, cold bracelets and earrings made with coral, jade and small beads of bright yellow gold. There was even a pair of bracelets set with a stone of deepest blue, speckled with silver, a night sky laden with stars. Gifts from her mother. Some of her fellow magic students had scoffed at them. Goezh had asked what ship her mother had stolen them from.

Azria huffed and upturned the jewelry box, spilling it all onto the dress she intended to take with her. She wouldn't be seeing Goezh or the rest of those crabs ever again. At least she hoped she wouldn't. Azria rolled her dress up around the jewelry so it formed a tight bundle, smiling to herself as she wondered what other treasures she might find on other shores.

"I found it," Nana said, entering Azria's room. Two rainy season skirts were draped over her arm but in one hand she held a large belt with pouches, mother of pearl buttons glinting on the worn brown leather. In Nana's other hand was a knife. "These served me well on my travels abroad. The belt's made of fine Kamerian leather, crafted by Mudnebis." She held all the items out towards Azria, waiting for her to take them. "You can keep your money in there, dried food. Chewing leaf if you decide to take up bad habits once I'm gone from your life."

Azria took the belt and skirts but only looked at the knife, noting the empty sheath in the belt. "Take this too," Nana said quietly, holding the knife out towards Azria. The dark blade shimmered with ripples of glimmering black threaded through the metal. The hilt was bone white and smooth like a tooth or tusk of some large animal.

"But Nana," Azria said, trying not to sound too embarrassed. "I don't know how to use it."

"Then learn," Nana said, lifting her chin slightly. She pushed the hilt into Azria's hands, placing her hands atop hers. "It's an old knife, but good. Never used it on the person I got it for. Maybe you'll find a good reason to use it. I hope not, but I'd rather you have it and not need it than need it and not have it."

Azria blinked, taking the blade from Nana. She rubbed her thumb over the hilt, feeling a spot which had been carved and then rubbed smooth. A name had been carved into it and erased, an old Mizian vengeance tradition. She felt it in the blade, magic scraped away by an untrained hand but scraped away nonetheless. "Who did you get the knife for?" Azria asked, not sure if that was the real question she wanted to ask.

"Some woman I used to know," Nana said. She chuckled, but Azria heard the sadness there, and Nana's eyes shone with tears the woman was too proud to let fall. "There was a time I was full of vengeance, my little Azria. It gave me something to do but nothing to speak of." Azria slid the knife into the sheath, feeling the weight of the weapon in the belt. "Then your mother left you with me and I had lots to do. Because I traded a life with a knife for a life with you, I have many happy memories." Nana smiled, handing her the skirts before she put her hands on her shoulders, looking Azria over with pride in her sharp, dark gaze. "So I'm sad to see you go but happy to see you join your mother's side. It is truly where you belong, my little heart." Nana placed a dry kiss on her forehead. "Now, please tell me you have time to eat something before you pack?"

"I should. I don't have to be back till evening," Azria said, nodding. She placed the items on her bed, not sure if the feeling in her stomach was hunger or excitement. Noise in the front room drew both their attention, Azria frowning in the direction of the front door. "Bolo?" she called, walking out of her room. "Is that you?"

"Bolo?" Azria heard the voice of her teacher in the front room, disappointment in his voice. "Why would you think I was Bolo? By the maelstrom, is Bolo in Hitha?"

"He is, Hiezh. He's taking our Azria to her mother," Nana said, following Azria out of her room. "Please, keep your opinions of others to yourself, mage."

"Somebody needs to warn her," Hiezh said, sitting down at the kitchen table. He poured himself tea from the pitcher, frowning as he took a sip. "Nana, you should put less hibiscus in your tea."

"Hiezh, you should put more manners in your bearing!" Nana scolded "This will probably be the last time we have Azria here for a meal and she likes hibiscus in her tea."

"There's no accounting for taste," Hiezh said, putting his hands in his lap. "Anyway, I'm here with a reason to celebrate. I managed to get another time set up for you to test before the Guild, Azria."

"When is it for?" Azria, already knowing what the answer would be.

"Three days from now," Hiezh said, smiling. "All I had to do was—"

"I can't," Azria interrupted, watching his smile drop. "I'm leaving tonight. And I might never come back."

"Azria, there's no need to be so dramatic," Hiezh said, rolling his eyes.

"No, it's true," Azria insisted. "My mother sent

for me. When Bolo comes, I'm going with him. My mother's docked in the West Bay and she's taking me with her. As of tonight, I'll be another member of the crew of the *Hen & Chick*."

"She speaks the truth," Nana said, her voice full of gravity. "Apzana is back for Azria, like she said she would be."

For a moment her teacher just sat there, staring at Azria with his mouth open, as if he didn't understand what she had just said. He finally took another sip of his drink and shook his head. "If you don't have your commission—"

"It's just paper," Azria said. "Having it or not having it doesn't make me more or less of an Innate. It won't make me more or less likely to keep on in my studies."

"But it will give you validity in Miz and other cities," Hiezh said. Nana went out the back door, shooing chickens away from the entrance. "Even in Kamer, having the backing of the Guild, being part of an Order is taken seriously. Why did I train you for this if you weren't going to see it through to the end?"

"The end of a mage's training is not the certification," Azria argued, plopping into the chair across from him. "Also, I'm pretty sure you trained me because my mother paid you to."

"Azria, do you really think our relationship as teacher and student is based solely on money?" Hiezh asked, hurt in his voice. "Your mother didn't pay me to get you out of fights with Goezh or give you advice when Erizana started spreading rumors about you."

"With all that said, why should I stay in Miz when my peers hate me?" Azria said.

"They don't hate you," Hiezh said. "They're just stupid kids."

"Who grow up to be stupid adults I'll have to deal with," Azria said, pointing a finger at him.

Hiezh's mouth popped open to talk but he stopped. "I can't really argue with that," he admitted, shrugging. "But don't think stupid people are only on our shores. Miz doesn't have the monopoly on idiots."

"Spoken like a true scholar," Nana snorted, setting down a bowl of mashed plantain fried in garlic oil in front of them.

"My mother is leaving tomorrow morning with her crew," Azria said. "I haven't seen her in five years and you think I should forego joining her to get—"

"What we've been working towards these last ten years," Hiezh said. He scooped a mound of plantain into Azria's bowl, shaking his head. "A commissioned mage is worth more than one without one. A mage in a Guild can do magic in Miz!"

"The mages who made the Black Island didn't have commissions," Azria said, narrowing her eyes at her teacher.

"You're not nearly as skilled as them," Hiezh laughed. "That was a different time, Miz was very different then! Magic was wild, the Triumvirate had just fallen apart—"

"Shush," Azria hissed, looking over her shoulder. "Don't mention them in front of Nana. Not again."

"Don't mention what?" Nana said, carrying a tray through the open doorway.

"Nothing. Hiezh is saying I should stay in Miz and forget about my mother," Azria said, sticking her tongue out at her teacher.

"I know we both love Azria," Nana said, placing a bowl of purple rice on the table. "But we knew this day would come. Apzana is a lot of things, but she's not a liar. She said when you turned sixteen, you'd be leaving with her. Maybe it isn't so much we didn't believe her as we don't want you to be gone from our lives, Azria."

"I'll have to find another student," Hiezh grumbled, crossing his arms over his chest. "Do you know what it looks like, that my sole student didn't receive a recognition from the Guild? Who will hire me to tutor their children?"

"I'm salting my food with my tears," Azria said, putting a scoop of plantain into Hiezh's bowl.

"What about the work I put in?" Hiezh said, his voice pitching higher. "All the times I helped you?"

"Hiezh, please!" Nana snapped. She set a tureen down with a bang on the table, making both of them jump. "It's hard enough to have her go without hearing you choke about it. You sound like a seagull! If Apzana hadn't dragged you out of the gutter, you'd be drunker than a sailor without a ship, or dead. Be grateful she cleaned you up! If your future in Miz is destroyed by the disappearance of one little girl, your future was built on the sand to begin with."

"I'm just saying," Hiezh said quietly, not looking at Nana. "It feels like Apzana is taking our future away from us."

"I'll be sure to tell her that when I see her," came the voice in the doorway. Azria looked up to see Bolo standing there, leaning against the wall. Hiezh slowly put his face in his hands as Bolo entered the home, while Nana nodded her head to him in greeting and Bolo bowed to the old woman. "It's an honor to see you, Enza."

"For now," Nana laughed, smacking him on the shoulder. "You'll be sassing me soon enough, Bolo. Should I get you a bowl?"

"I'll get one myself," Bolo said, smiling warmly at

Azria. She watched him move through the kitchen, surprised at how familiar he was in the cozy space. "I went to the market to see to some business and thought, why eat at a stall when I could have some of the worst food in Miz?"

"See what I mean?" Nana said, thumping her cane. She looked to Azria, her words serious but her face full of merriment. "These sailors, their humor is as dry as their mistress is wet."

"I have a lot of possible responses to that, but there are children present," Bolo said, returning to the table.

"Hey," Azria said, frowning.

"I was referring to Hiezh," Bolo said, sitting down next to him.

"So, when are you leaving? " Hiezh asked, already frowning.

"Oh, Hiezh, you act like I was the worst thing to happen to you," Bolo said with a grin, putting his elbows on the table and his chin on his hands. He batted his eyelashes at Hiezh, drawing a groan from the mage.

"You were the one who had an issue," Hiezh grumbled, obviously trying to keep his voice down in an effort to keep Azria and Nana out of their conversation.

"Did you two...uh...?" Azria asked, her voice trailing off. She wasn't sure what to ask but apparently Bolo was more familiar with Miz than she had thought. Hiezh kept his personal life to himself mostly, not that there was much to speak of. As Azria had witnessed, he lived a quiet life which consisted of teaching and being annoyed by virtually everyone else he came into contact with.

"Save yourself the headache," Nana said. "These two were like fire and water. Everything they touched just wound up destroyed or wet." Hiezh blushed and Bolo laughed nervously as Nana sat down at her place at the table, scooting her seat up. Bolo served the older woman first, Nana nodding in thanks as he spooned hot, spicy stew into her bowl.

"There's not much to talk about that's suitable for supper talk," Bolo began, apparently finding his words. "But yes, once upon a time I looked for Hiezh when our ship made port here. It was a mess from start to finish," he said, the smile on his face telling Azria it hadn't been all bad.

"You still don't like plantain, eh," Hiezh asked, looking into the sailor's bowl. He waited for Bolo to put the ladle back in the tureen and served the sailor.

"No," Bolo said. "Never will, I don't think."

"You're so abnormal," Hiezh said, wrinkling his nose at Bolo, though a smile played on his face as well.

"Says the man who can start a fire with a few words and a hand gesture," Bolo quipped, a hint of annoyance in his voice Azria was surprised to hear.

Azria took the ladle and waited for her teacher to offer his bowl to her. She put two scoops of stew into his bowl, knowing he'd get a third later. "I don't remember any of this," she said. "When was the last time you were in Miz, Bolo?"

"I'll serve you," Bolo offered, taking the ladle before anyone else could. Azria smiled and picked up her bowl. "How many scoops do you take, Azria?"

"One for now, please," she said.

"Moderate, like your mother," Bolo said, winking at her. He spooned the stew into her bowl and placed the ladle back in the tureen. Azria inhaled the yummy, spicy aroma of the stew. The five spices were perfectly blended into one fragrant mélange and thin slices of peppers and smashed cloves of garlic accented the chunks of shrimp, crab and white fish. Oil gleamed red at the surface of the rich broth and shredded herbs added freshness to the heat of Azria's favorite stew. Nana held her hand towards Azria, who took the old woman's hand in her own, taking Bolo's in her left. She watched and stifled a giggle as Bolo offered his hand towards Hiezh, Hiezh frowning and hesitating before he accepted Bolo's hand in his. They bowed their heads as Nana spoke the blessing.

"Great Goddess, thank you for this food we are about to eat. Let it bring strength to our bodies that we may put our hands to ordering this world you have placed us in. Wash us in your wisdom."

"Wash us in your Wisdom." Azria said the close to the prayer and heard Hiezh say it, Bolo's voice absent from the closing words. She looked to him, raising an eyebrow when he caught her eye.

"To answer your question," Bolo said, "the last time I was in Miz, you were nine." He looked to Nana, the old woman nodding slightly to the sailor before he continued. "Your mother and I were visiting, both to see you and for business. I only stopped by to say hello and see how you had grown. Your mother generally wanted you all to herself when we were docked."

"Why won't she step foot on Mizian soil?" Azria asked. Hiezh stiffened, holding his spoon in mid-air. Nana slowly brought her hands to the table, as if bracing herself. Bolo looked to the old woman, who again gave the slightest nod before he answered.

"Well, to be honest, to avoid arrest."

"So it's true," Azria said quietly. "She is a pirate."

"A pirate is just a word sailors use to describe someone who is doing better than them," Bolo said with a shrug. "Oh, the *Hen & Chick* has pulled in more hands this year, they must be dealing in stolen merchandise or clandestine affairs. It's just jealousy." Bolo stirred his stew, looking off to the side. "Miz hasn't always been a friend to Apzana, Azria. Even if the charges were dropped, it'd have to be a good job to bring her boat to these shores."

"Wait, what are the charges exactly?" Azria said. She knew her food was getting cold but Bolo was giving her answers to questions Azria had held onto for years. Hiezh hunched over his bowl, eating quietly and Nana fixed her brown, hard gaze on Bolo.

"You know, there are just so many, I am going to leave it to Apzana to answer them!" Bolo said with a grin.

"What country is the *Hen & Chick* registered under, if the police can't just board and take her in?" Azria asked. Any Mizian ship was subject to Mizian search but maritime law said boats were extensions of the nations they were registered under, regardless of where their captains were from. Officials could board foreign ships and charge individuals or whole crews but it took evidence to be able to do so. If someone had found evidence which would allow her mother to be arrested... "You haven't been studying your flags, have you?" Bolo asked, wagging a finger at her.

"Golden Isles, Azria," Nana said. The old woman smiled but something in her expression looked like sadness.

"Not anymore," Bolo said. "The *Hen & Chick* is Golden Isle made but she got our sovereignty switched over to Buriq earlier this year. For no reason at all." Bolo winked at Azria, dipping his spoon into his food.

"I'll believe Apzana does something for no reason

the day Miz falls into the sea," Hiezh muttered, taking another bite of food.

"Azria, please, eat," Nana chided. "This will probably be our last meal together for a while. You'll never get to your rice if you don't start now."

"I'm sorry, Nana," Azria said. "I'm just so...excited! I'm finally getting answers and I'm more curious than hungry."

"It won't keep so I can't send it with you," the old woman sighed. "You've got days of water that tastes like wood and hard bread before you, girl; eat up."

Azria dipped her spoon into her cooling stew, thinking of all the times she had sat at Nana's table and eaten her cooking. A day hadn't gone by in her memory where she hadn't eaten something Nana prepared. "Is there a galley on the *Hen & Chick*?" she asked quietly between bites.

"Actually, there is!" Bolo said, slurping the last of the stew. "The captain does enjoy food so we always have a cook on board. Our newest cook isn't much older than you. She's from the south."

"Where will we be going first?" Azria asked again, ignoring the look Nana gave her.

"I'll let your mother tell you, Azria. Finish your food before Nana strangles me," Bolo said. He grinned at Nana as he stood from the table, taking his empty bowl. "I'll take yours too, Hiezh, if you like."

"No, I'll help Nana finish this stew," Hiezh said, serving himself a mound of rice.

"Did you two open the gifts Apzana sent you?" Bolo asked, walking into the kitchen.

"Gifts?" Hiezh asked, looking up from his bowl. "I wasn't told there were presents."

"I forgot my mother sent them," Azria admitted with a shrug. "Nana and I got busy with packing."

"I thought I would open mine after you had gone, Azria, to brighten my day after you leave it," Nana said. She put her hand on Azria's and gave it a squeeze. "Apzana sends me gifts when every day, I thank the Goddess I was able to take care of you."

"She is thankful for you, Nana," Bolo said, returning to the table. He stood behind his chair and put his hands on the back of it, looking to Azria. "A ship is no place for a babe, especially not a babe like her. Apzana will never be able to show you how grateful she is for taking such good care of Azria all these years."

"Well, I want to open my present," Hiezh said, standing up. He walked into the sitting room and found the two items, looking to Azria. "Which is mine?"

"The box," Azria said.

"Might as well bring mine here, Hiezh," Nana said with a sigh. "Bolo, you and Azria clear the table. I'll have rice in the morning."

"Yes, Nana." Azria stood, glad to be excused from dinner when her stomach was bubbling with excitement. She stacked the bowls and plates, Bolo taking some of the dinnerware as well. She looked over her shoulder as Hiezh handed the bundle to Nana, her teacher not bothering to sit before he started opening his present.

"Your mother gives good presents," Bolo said, standing by her, arms crossed.

Azria smiled. "I know." She watched as Hiezh lifted the lid to the box and Nana untied the bow. The ornate fabric wrapping her present slid away, revealing a luxurious cream-colored silk robe. Nana ran the backs of her fingers against the smooth fabric, the pattern of leaves and flowers so vibrantly colored they looked real.

"Oh, Apzana," Nana said with a sigh, holding the robe so she could see how the fabric draped. "A perfect gift for a retired old woman. A robe to keep me warm on these cold nights."

"She got me a tiger beetle," Hiezh said, in a voice too excited for such a thing. His hands shook, holding the box and he put it down and closed it. "I've been looking for this type of tiger beetle for five years. It's the one!" He brought his hands to his head and pulled his hair, a grin spreading across his face. "It's the one!"

"Ocean take us, a bug," Bolo laughed.

"I wouldn't expect you to understand!" Hiezh griped. He looked to Azria, light in his dark eyes. "I wish you were staying to help me weave the magic with it."

"You'll be weaving your own magic on the *Hen & Chick*, Azria," Bolo said, draping an arm around her shoulder. "You'll be up to your armpits in ingredients for all kinds of weavings."

"Well, about that," Hiezh started.

"I'll never get to leave if I don't finish packing my bags!" Azria interrupted, her voice a higher pitch than she intended. "Nana, do you have that bag I needed?"

"Yes, hold on," Nana said, setting her cane down to help get herself out of the chair. "I think I might have one. Waxed canvas and all."

"Wait," Hiezh said, narrowing his eyes and closing the box. "Azria, you know you can't—"

"Leave till I have everything," she said with a nod, shooting him a look that made the older mage shut up. She walked towards her room, the floorboards creaking under her feet. "I have my winter garments and a belt and a knife. I'll bring my scrolls—"

"How much space do you think you're going to have on the boat?" Bolo asked with a laugh. "There's no room for books."

"These are small scrolls, Bolo," Azria explained. "They're already made, I swear, they'll take no space at all."

"Just bring a change of clothes, the knife you mentioned, and the scrolls," Bolo said, following her into the room. "You can buy what you need in the next port. The *Hen & Chick's* not a chieftain's ship but it has enough." He watched as Azria unrolled her dress to refold it, the jewelry spilling onto the bed. "Bring that though, in case you need to ransom yourself."

"That's what I was thinking!" Azria said. Nana came in with the bag and Azria set it on the bed, putting in her garments and the one jacket she had, her heart beating in her chest like waves on the shore. She was really packing. Azria picked up the jacket, her fingers showing through the thin fabric.

"You can sell it and put the money towards a better one," Bolo said with a shrug. Azria went to her shelf and opened a long ebony box, the black wood cool under her fingertips. She had an assortment of scrolls there, carefully written and woven together, waiting for the slightest bit of energy from her to ignite the working within. Each scroll was carefully rolled or folded and fastened with a waxed piece of thread. They were all unlabeled. She could tell what each one did by touching it. Would she have access to spell paper and ink on the ocean?

"There are a few things I should buy before we go," Azria said with a nod. "In Miz, I mean, not wherever we go next. I don't have much spell paper left. What if they don't have any in the next port?"

"Are you planning on using all of those between now and wherever?" Bolo asked, eyes wide.

"If I knew where wherever was, I could tell you," Azria said, taking a step towards him with the box. Bolo put his hands up and stepped back, eyes widening slightly. Azria cocked an eyebrow and wrapped the dark box with the coat and placed it in the bag.

"You'll know tomorrow morning when you're on the *Hen & Chick*," Bolo said, swallowing hard and returning to his previously cool demeanor. "Don't get too cocky making plans, Azria, there's only space for one pair of hands at the wheel. Learn this now before you start making trouble on the ship."

"Well, don't worry too much about me taking the wheel," Azria said, looking around the room for perhaps the last time. Her bed, messy and unmade, as she had risen and run to Hiezh's this morning. The clothes she was leaving, too thin for this new life, hanging white and clean on the rack. Dolls from every corner of the earth sat in a basket under the bed. Embroidered and painted shawls hung from a wooden rack suspended from the rafters. "I think I'm ready to see where the wind takes me."

"Spoken like a true sailor," Bolo said.

"More like an aimless fool," Nana said, appearing in the doorway. She frowned at Azria, clutching the head of her cane. Tears shone in her dark brown eyes but her face was brave. "But we all have our aimless fool stage, despite how our loved ones try to direct. Come here and give me a hug, Azria," Nana said, holding her arms open. "Promise me you'll use that brain of yours wherever those miscreants take you."

Azria put the bag down and walked up to Nana, embracing her. She felt the woman put her cheek on the top of her head, planting a dry kiss on her hair. Nana squeezed Azria so hard, the girl thought she might break something but eventually, the old woman released her and let her arms slip away. She took Azria's hands in hers. "Don't be afraid to come back. I know you don't believe me, but Miz is your home."

"If I come back, it'll be to see you, Nana, not Miz," Azria said, kissing the tops of her hands.

"But forget about your teacher, right?" Hiezh said, his voice coming from the sitting room. He still sounded upset but something told Azria Nana had said something to her teacher while she and Bolo had been busy packing.

"Oh, Hiezh," Azria snorted. She picked up her bag before she walked out of her room and smiled at her teacher, his expression humorless as always. "I'll never forget you. Thank you for everything you've taught me. I'm...I'm sorry to leave so soon," she offered, her face growing hot as she blushed. Azria could only imagine what Hiezh had said or done to get her the appointment. She realized just how much she had disappointed Hiezh in that day alone and it made a lump rise in her throat.

"I understand," Hiezh said softly. He cleared his throat. "I really do, Azria. Please. Understand that." Azria looked up but Hiezh was looking at the ground, avoiding her gaze.

"I hope to do you proud," Azria said, finding her voice.

"Not to be clichéd, but you already have," Hiezh replied with a nod. The faintest smile played on the corners of his mouth, his gaze still fixed on the floor.

"I look forward to hearing about all the things you destroy."

"You make me sound like a monster," Azria laughed. She didn't care if Hiezh bristled. She threw her arms around her teacher and hugged him, feeling his body stiffen and then relax. His warm hands patted her on the back and Azria let go of him before she made him feel self-conscious again.

"You are a monster," Hiezh laughed. "A good one. I'll miss you."

"Long goodbyes often turn into never leaving, so we'll be going now," Bolo said. "Nana, thank you again for all your hard work." He took her hands in his and kissed them, the unlikely pair exchanging warm smiles. "And thank you, Hiezh, for training her."

"Yeah, yeah," Hiezh said, crossing his arms over his chest. "We've done this already." He looked to Azria and sighed, nodding his head towards the door. "Go, catch your boat, girl."

"If you don't write me, I'll pay to have a curse put on you," Nana said.

"I'll write, Nana!" Azria said, walking towards the door, laughing.

"And send me news of your mother, when you do," Nana said, following them out. "Give an old woman some reassurance."

"I promise," Azria said. A cool night breeze was starting to blow through Nana's garden and the chirp of nighttime bugs hummed in the air. She walked down the stairs, shifting her bag on her shoulder. She was really leaving her home.

"And send me presents!" Nana called after them. "Just because I'm old doesn't mean I don't like presents!"

"Nana!" Azria said, halfway up the path. A grin was

splashed across her face but her deep brown eyes were filled with tears. Azria pushed past Bolo and ran back up the path, throwing her arms around the old woman once more. She felt the old woman put her cheek on her head, as she had many times before, hugging her with more strength than any old lady had the right to. "I'll miss you," Azria managed to say, hot tears finally rolling down her face.

"I'll miss you too," she heard Nana say. Nana kissed the top of her head again before she finally loosened her embrace. "Now go. Your momma's been waiting five years to see you, Azria. You have a lot of catching up to do."

"I know," Azria whispered, her chest aching as she held back her sobs. Finally, she pulled herself away from Nana and nodded another farewell to Hiezh. Hiezh put an arm around Nana and they stood in the doorway as Azria left down the path, trying to keep her eyes on Bolo to prevent more tears from falling.

"One more wave goodbye and then we have to go," Bolo whispered. Azria looked back again and waved, taking a final glance at the house she had grown up in and the two people who cared about her so much. One of the chickens walked across the path, clucking to herself as Nana and Hiezh waved farewell. Azria blew them a kiss and then put her arm in Bolo's.

"I will see them again," Azria said with a sigh. She knew Bolo heard it but she meant it for herself. Bolo pushed open the wooden gate and they walked down the dirt road away from the little house, the quiet clucks of Nana's chickens fading away as they continued down towards the bay.

Chapter 4
New Faces, New Life

Azria heard voices on the deck of the ship. She froze at the foot of the gangplank and stared up at the *Hen & Chick*, looming above her as it bobbed in the waves.

"Should I tell them all I'm Apzana's daughter?" she asked quietly.

"Them all, who?" Bolo asked. He followed her line of sight to the ship and chuckled, putting his hands on her shoulders. "The other crew members?" He snorted, pushing her towards the boat. "Azria, your mother has many secrets. You're not one of them."

Azria put one foot on the gangplank but didn't walk up, looking over her shoulder again as Bolo nudged her forward. "Are you sure she didn't just tell them she was getting a new mage, Bolo?"

"Very sure, Azria," Bolo said. "And once we get on that ship, it's Second Bolo, since I'm second in command."

"I thought maybe I could call you Uncle Bolo?" Azria asked, half-jokingly. Bolo took his hands off of her shoulders and stood up straighter, a smile brightening his face.

"Off the boat, yes, call me Uncle Bolo all you want," he said, obviously pleased. "But on the ship, you're the mage." He shooed her up the gangplank, Azria scurrying as she looked down at the blue-green water of the harbor below. "If someone says 'Mage,' you answer," Bolo continued. "And try to stick to Tradetongue on board, please," he added, switching over to the language spoken by almost all sailors and merchants on the Sapphire Sea. "I trust your Trade is good enough for the *Hen & Chick*?"

"Of course," Azria said, her heart beating harder the farther they walked up the gangplank. Mage. The thought of being referred to as 'Mage' brought a grin to Azria's face. In all of Azria's memories of herself, she was able to use magic. But that made her an Innate, not a mage. Her identity on the *Hen & Chick* wasn't tied to something she hadn't chosen but something she had forged herself, under the careful tutelage of Hiezh. The fact that the Guild hadn't officially bestowed the title upon her didn't matter, Azria told herself as she put one foot in front of the other. They would have. Azria had worked hard at learning to harness the power within her and followed the rules in regard to when it was appropriate to do so. Mage Azria. Azria sighed happily as she reached the top of the gangplank, setting a foot on the deck of the ship.

"So, this is our new mage?"

Azria stepped back, finding a strange face in hers. The stranger pulled away and Azria gasped, seeing the person in full. A citizen of the Skyward City. From the waist down, his legs were covered in shaggy brown hair, his backward knees and hooves making Azria grimace inwardly. Her eyes went wider as she saw the man stood by another of his kind. If it weren't for the slight difference in hair color, she would have thought them identical. The second one's hair was slightly darker and the hair that grew on the sides of his head was twisted into one pair of braids, not two.

They both wore breech-cloths, woven in gray, green and white, embroidered with what looked like a family crest. Their arms were hairy too, hairier than any other people she had encountered. Each of them wore bracelets made of silver and a white stone she couldn't identify. In truth, they reminded Azria of the goats people in Miz kept for milk and meat, but 'goat-people' seemed rude, since they were obviously more intelligent. She had heard of their homeland, the Skyward City which stretched up beyond the gray, wispy clouds, tens of thousands of homes, shops and fields ornately carved into the sheer, stone land.

Each of the Skyward men had a pair of horns atop their heads, each as long as their forearms, the gentle spiral design running up the horns majestic in their curvature. They gazed at her with amber-colored eyes, their long ears flitting in the cool ocean air.

"I thought she'd be taller," said the other man. Azria frowned.

"Sorry, I don't have horns on top of my head to make me seem bigger than I am," Azria said before she thought better of it, holding her belongings to her chest.

"Oh, a feisty mage! This should be an interesting jaunt, brother," the lighter-haired one said.

"Feisty?" Azria squeaked.

"Maybe we should not insult the mage as soon as

she gets onto the ship," Bolo said, irritation in his voice. "Mage Azria, may I introduce to you our riggers, the brothers Surefoot of Greyway Stronghold of the Skyward City."

"You make us sound so official, Second," the darker-haired man said. He smiled broadly at Azria, and she noticed the pupils of his eyes were more square than round. "I'm Brik," he said. "The older brother."

"I'm Brak," said the other, offering his hand to Azria for a shake. Brik looked to Brak's hand and frowned before he offered his hand as well, the pair of them waiting expectantly. "The younger brother. But only by three breaths and a push." When he smiled, Azria could see he had a slight underbite. It was a charming smile. She could tell it was genuine.

"I'm...looking forward to getting to know you better," Azria managed. She took both their hands in hers and shook them once, looking up into their bright, eager faces. The brothers looked to each other and nodded approvingly, as if satisfied with her hand shaking.

"I'm better to know than Brak," Brik said. "Really, I'm the more interesting twin."

"You are not," Brak laughed. "I'm better. You can ask Second, I'm the better jumper!"

"The serious man we're going to turn our attention to is Eixon," Bolo said, shooing the two brothers away. He put his hands on Azria's shoulders and turned her towards the figure standing off to the side. He wore black, baggy pants and a sleeveless tunic embroidered at the hem in red-black thread, a bright silk scarf painted orange and red draped around his neck. Curly hair was neatly trimmed to complement his long face and a bit of shadow on his chin and cheeks told Azria he had shaved that morning and would have a beard if he didn't shave for a week. He closed the small leather-bound book he had been reading and tucked it into his belt.

"A pleasure to meet you, Mage," Eixon said. He bowed at the waist to Azria, his long red-and-orange scarf sweeping the deck of the ship. Standing this close, Azria smelled his cologne, a light bouquet of red sandalwood, lemongrass and musk. Azria felt he was younger than Bolo and her mother but still older than her.

"He's our supplyman. In addition, if you're looking to learn another language while you're on board, Eixon speaks seven," Bolo said. "All of them well."

"All in the service of peace," Eixon said. His Trade was perfect, each syllable sharp and clear. Azria felt the hint of an accent he had was more because he wanted it, not because he couldn't hide it. He looked at Azria and while he didn't smile with his mouth, his eyes were bright. "More importantly," said Eixon, "if you need something which should be put on the ship expenses, let me know. I can even procure last-minute personal effects, as I always go to Final Night Market."

"What's Final Night Market?" Azria asked.

"It's the market set up before First Light, when most ships leave," Eixon said, obviously charmed he knew something Azria didn't. "For last-minute wares, forgotten items. The markup can be ridiculous but sometimes a thing just needs to be had. Oh, and you can read and write, correct?" Eixon asked, his thick brows furrowing.

"I'm a mage of Miz," Azria said, trying to keep haughtiness from her voice. "Of course I can write."

"I only ask that you submit all requests in writing," Eixon said. "I don't take verbal requests. If you feel kind, you'll help some of our less learned crew members with their lists." Azria watched as he inclined his head ever so slightly towards Brik and Brak.

"We can write, we just can't write Trade!" Brak said. "Maybe you should learn the writing system of the Skyward City!"

"If I devoted my time to learn every bit of syllabary, I'd have no time for myself," Eixon called to Brak. "Be warned," Eixon said with a wink, turning his attention back to Azria, "they have keener ears than most."

"We heard that," Brik said.

"See what I mean?" Eixon looked to Bolo. "I take my leave, Second. It was a pleasure to meet you, Mage of Miz. I look forward to meeting your needs," he said, giving another bow before he started walking towards the brothers.

"He's a Traveler, right?" Azria asked, taking her basket from Bolo.

"That he is," Bolo said. "We picked him up three years ago, in the Port-Of-Black. It's hard finding a Mudnebi who'll leave his family behind, let me tell you. I've only seen one other in all my treks across the Wet. And seven languages impresses even me!"

"How many languages do you speak?" Azria asked, following him over the deck. They walked past the room her mother had been in and Azria couldn't help but try to peer through the slightly open door, trailing behind Bolo as he walked in the opposite direction.

"Three. Goldtongue, Tradetongue, and Mizian and Buriqan halfway," Bolo said with a grin. "Tradetongue gets me far enough. That and my good looks."

"Your Mizian's not bad," Azria admitted with a nod.

"Probably a lot better than your Goldtongue." He smiled at Azria as he came to a door, pulling it open. "After you."

"But not before me," a voice called from below. Azria peered around the corner and saw someone running up the stairs. A woman stepped through the doorway, her brown eyes squinting even in the pink light of the setting sun. Her brown, wavy hair was plaited into two heavy braids woven with bright scarlet and indigo thread, and she wore a band of white cotton around her head. She wore the same bandeau-style top Apzana owned and shorts, though a leather belt full of tools was tied securely around her waist. "Need to get some light in my eyes before I'm back down below," the woman said. Painted white and black dots between her eyebrows and eyes adorned her face, and her lips were stained a pleasing shade of red. "Ah, the new mage is here!" the woman exclaimed as she set her gaze on Azria, her broad smile revealing small white teeth.

"Mage Azria, this is Hullmaster Onacá of Buriq," Bolo said, stepping aside so the woman could walk onto the deck into the light. Azria saw the threads woven into the Hullmaster's hair bled into her tresses, staining her hair with their color.

"You look so much like her!" Onacá gasped, covering her mouth with her hands. Her fingers were painted as well, more lines and dots and symbols Azria was unfamiliar with. "Especially the eyes. Not the ears though, which is to be expected." Onacá put her hands on her hips and nodded as she looked Azria up and down with a gaze that told her the Hullmaster didn't miss much. "You look like a better mage than the last *bobo* we had. You smell a lot better too!"

"Onacá is also responsible for the aesthetic of the ship," Bolo said, his words a bit tighter than usual.

"Just the colors and charms, Bolo. You know I had no say on the model," Onacá said. "No reason the boat can't be functional and beautiful. The wood from Buriq is the best for building ships like the *Hen & Chick*, Mage, don't let anyone tell you otherwise."

"But her construction was done on the Golden Isles, let's not forget that," Bolo quickly added.

"With a modified design!" Onacá exclaimed. "Who crafted the design?" She stepped up to Bolo, wagging her finger in Bolo's face. "Ediq, that's who got Apzana's money in the end!"

"Well, Golden builders realized them better than any—"

"I won't let you be the cloud on my face!" Onacá interrupted, throwing both hands in the air and turning away. "I hope you're less argumentative about ships than this one here," she said to Azria, pointing at Bolo. "And if you ever want to win a bet at a boat race, come to me first, Mage, not this deck walker!"

"She's just mad a Golden Island ship won last year's races," Bolo crooned, his confidence returning with his words.

"The sails and ropes were made in Buriq!" she shot back. She waved a hand at Bolo as she started to walk away towards the front of the ship. "It was nice meeting you, Mage. I look forward to your service here."

Azria watched as Onacá walked away before she turned to Bolo, seeing the look of exasperation on his face. He sighed deeply, as if relieved. "So that was Onacá and that's how we talk about boats," Bolo muttered, gesturing towards the stairs, the steps descending into the lower decks. "She was a boat builder for the head chief of her island. Her people have a...healthy rivalry with mine."

"That was very generous of you to put it that way," Azria said, placing her hand on the railing. Bolo just

grunted as he followed after her and Azria stifled a giggle as she walked down the steps.

Azria squinted as her eyes adjusted to the dim light
below deck. Down here she could feel the motion of the
boat, up and down on the waves slapping against its exterior. Somewhere within the hold, a high-pitched but
pleasant voice sang in a language Azria didn't understand.

"That would be Yabi," Bolo's said, his steps quiet behind her. "That first door on the right is the galley."

Azria walked through the streams of dying sunlight
pouring through the portholes. Doorways lined the hall
and Azria inhaled the aroma of salt, spices and rope
wafting through the still air.

"Knock first," Bolo whispered. Azria stopped short
and then stepped into the doorway, knocking on the
opened door.

"Oh!" The girl still jumped, spinning around. Azria
saw her grip the table behind her, her round face reddening with surprise. "Oh, I'm sorry! You startled me!"
Azria thought she was wearing a black cap on her head
but Yabi reached up and brushed at her forehead with
her fingers, her smooth, dark hair hugging her round
face. "I just get really lost in all the spices and potatoes!"
Yabi said with a nervous giggle. She started fussing with
the jars of spices on the table absentmindedly, looking
behind Azria at Bolo. "Is this the mage?" Yabi didn't
wait for Bolo to answer and stepped forward, holding
out her hand. "I mean, of course you're the mage, and
Apzana's daughter! I'm Yabi, the cook! But you can call
me Yabi, not Cook, if you like!"

Azria took Yabi's hand and shook it slowly. When
Yabi smiled, her whole face lit up and her eyes squinted.

Azria smiled back. "It's a pleasure to meet you, Yabi," Azria said, still shaking her hand.

"I didn't think you'd be so young!" Yabi said, her hand still in hers, her eyes wide. They were a deep brown and her long lashes and thin brows made her eyes look bigger. "I don't mean that as a slight! I know I'm young to be a ship cook, but I've had years of experience!"

"I think you're around the same age," Bolo said back. "Mage Azria turned sixteen a month ago and has been studying the ways of magic these last ten years."

"Ten years?" Yabi's eyes went big and her mouth opened in a round 'o' of surprise. "I haven't been cooking that long, so I'm sure you're a better cook than I am a mage. I mean, a better mage than I am a cook! Though, I am a good cook! Ask Bolo!"

"She's a good cook," Bolo said, a quiet sigh escaping from his lips. "You should let her know if any food makes you sick, Mage."

"No foods that I know of," Azria said, smiling and hoping this would make Yabi less anxious. She looked around the small supply room, the foodstuff all stacked and bagged. Bundles of herbs, familiar and unrecognizable hung from the ceiling. "Though I'm sure there are foods here I've never tried."

"Well, when you try a food for the first time, be sure you take a small portion and a small bite and wait to see if there are any ill effects," Yabi said, her face a mask of sudden seriousness. "Especially a scratchy throat. If you eat something and it makes your throat itch, tell me right away because it can suffocate you."

"What?" Azria squeaked with alarm.

"Alright, it was nice talking to you, Cook Yabi," Bolo said. He put his hands on Azria's shoulders once more and pulled her backwards slightly, urging her out of the room. "No plantain in my food, please."

"You can give me his portion," Azria managed, looking over her shoulder as Bolo pushed her out of the room.

"Good to know!" Yabi called. "See you at supper!"

"See you then!" Azria called back, walking out into the hall. Bolo let his hands slip from her shoulders and walked ahead of her back down the hall, clicking his tongue.

"There are two more crew members you'll meet but they're at our next stop," Bolo said. "I'll show you where the crew sleeps so you can choose your bunk."

"We don't each have our own rooms?" Azria's voice trailed off as she asked it, realizing there couldn't possibly be enough space for each crew member to get their own quarters. Ever since she began studying magic with Hiezh, she had slept in her own room, Nana's quiet snoring blending with the sound of nighttime insects.

"I have my own quarters," Bolo said, matter-of-factly. "As does your mother. Onacá insists on sleeping in the hull in one of her stupid hammocks. Everyone else has a bed and a small chest for their belongings." Bolo led her to another room, this one without a door. Portholes let in some light but several had thick, dark fabric pinned over them, dimming the room. "I told them to take those down before they left," Bolo grumbled, walking into the room.

Azria inspected the room. Three wooden beds were pushed up against the side walls, with four more beds pushed against the far wall. Each bed was bolted to the floor with heavy metal fittings. Loops of leather told her the mattresses were tied to the frames as well. At the foot of every bed sat a wooden box with a heavy metal latch. In the center of the room was a well-used table with benches, similarly secured, and the remains of someone's snack of nuts scattered across the worn, dark wood.

"I told those idiots, no food in the crew quarters," Bolo sighed, walking over to the table. "Pick an empty bed," he said, sweeping the shells into the bowl with his hands. "It should be obvious which beds are taken."

Azria looked over the beds, trying to figure out which bed belonged to whom. Seven were fitted with sheets. Two beds on the right had been pushed closer together. They probably belonged to brothers, Azria reasoned, noting the thin quilt on the bed and the bundle of flowers hanging from the rafters over it. To the left, the first four beds were claimed. The ornate, embroidered quilt on the bed closest to the door told her it was the Traveler's bed. Colorful depictions of caravans were stitched all along the border, while a prayer, ornately manipulated into a design, radiated out from the center.

The bed beside it was covered in furs. This couldn't be Yabi's bed, she thought. The next had a woven quilt done in shades of blue and gray, the weaving and colors looking strikingly like the sea. The third had a simple brown quilt, a satin border the only embellishment. Azria narrowed her eyes, seeing something poking out from behind the pillow. As she walked closer, she could see tiny feet, like those of a small doll. Someone was hiding a doll under their pillow. Azria stepped towards the empty bed beside the bed with the doll.

"I knew you'd pick that one," Bolo said, starting towards the door.

"What?" Azria said, spinning around quickly. "Why?"

"Right by the cook," Bolo said in a singsong voice. "She is pretty cute. You don't waste time, is that it?"

"What, she's just nice. And around my age!" Azria said in a voice louder than she had meant to. Her face felt hot as she tried not to look at the cook's bed, trying to brush off Bolo's accusation. "And I was just looking at the blanket."

"Her bed does look warm," Bolo said, winking. "Look, sleep where you want, Azria."

"I'll sleep here," Azria said, picking up her wicker basket and crossing the floor to the bed at the opposite corner. "This is the one I wanted anyway."

"The Kamerian's old bed?" Bolo said, raising both eyebrows. He nodded slowly and started towards the door. "Bold choice."

"It's just a bed," Azria muttered, putting her basket on the bed. "Mattress, blankets and pillows, same as the rest." Were the Skyward brothers' beds pushed closer to one another or was one just pushed farther away from the Kamerian? She looked to the wooden box which would hold her effects. Slowly she undid the latch and pushed the lid open, relieved to find the box empty when she peered in.

"Oh good, they did clean it out," Bolo said. Azria frowned, propping the lid as she opened her clothing basket. "If you dump everything out, I'll take your basket for you," Bolo said, holding his hand out. "I'll keep it in the stores."

Azria thought to argue, saying she would keep the basket here with her but she looked around, knowing there was no space in the crew quarters. With a sigh, she handed it over, Bolo slinging one of the straps over his shoulder.

"No eating down here," he said. "It attracts vermin.

You can eat in the galley, or on deck. Breakfast and lunch are cold foods, dinner is hot." Azria simply nodded in response, her gaze fixed down at her bed. "You okay?" Bolo asked.

"I am," Azria said, turning to look at Bolo. "I'm just...tired. It's been a very strange day," she murmured, rubbing her eyes.

"Well, get used to them," Bolo said with a smile. He put the basket down and stretched his arms out for a hug. "Come here, girl."

Azria bit her bottom lip but turned and leaned into Bolo, letting him embrace her. She put her head on his shoulder and hugged him back, though she swallowed hard to keep back her tears. Nana had been the last person to hug her but it seemed like so long ago. Bolo rubbed her back with his hands, a warm gesture which helped to steady her feelings.

"I'm glad you're finally here," Bolo said. She could feel his words in his chest when he spoke. "Your mother has been waiting for this day a long time. And I'm glad to see her happy."

"I'm happy too," Azria whispered. "It's just...everything has changed so quickly. It's hard to know what to expect."

"That's a good thing to admit," Bolo said. He gave Azria one more squeeze and let his hands drop, picking up the basket again. "Plan too much, you won't know how to react when the unexpected happens." He flashed her a grin and walked towards the door. "Come up on deck as soon as you can," he said. "I'm sure the other crew members would like to see you."

"I'll be up soon!" she said, trying to sound as enthusiastic as possible. Azria watched as Bolo left, listening to his footsteps grow further and further away. With a sigh she looked to the bed, realizing everything she owned in the world fit on that one mattress.

Carefully she folded the garments and put them in the box, wondering if she should hide her jewelry under the clothes or lay it on top to weigh the garments down. She felt fairly confident in the fact none of the crew members would steal from a mage. And, she thought with a sigh as she let the bag of jewelry fall into the box, they had probably seen things much nicer than her belongings.

Azria frowned and picked up the leather belt, feeling how heavy it was. She wrapped it around her middle, not sure if she should tighten it around her waist or let it hang on her hips. Azria had never worn a utilitarian belt before. With a few modifications, she could possibly fit her scrolls in it. It was the fashion for mages to wear bracers in Miz, the scrolls tucked away but close to the hands, where the mage could easily reach them. Azria had the feeling comfort would be more important than appearance over the next few months. Her scrolls would probably have to live in the box for now. Azria rubbed the smooth stone of her scroll case, laying it carefully on top of her few belongings. She'd have to think of a clever way to carry them on herself. Scrolls were of no use locked away.

Azria opened one of the pouches on the belt, surprised to see there was already something in it. What had Nana forgotten to take out of her belt? Azria reached in with two fingers and pulled out a three-sided metal coin. It didn't look like any money Azria had ever seen but she thought the engraving looked Mizian. Azria shrugged and dropped it back into the pouch. She'd ask her mother about it later.

Next Azria picked up the dagger, pulling it out of

its sheath to look it over once more. The blade was so strange. It wasn't of Mizian make. The hilt was made of bone, not wood and it was too long. Swirls in the metal looked like silver and obsidian had been melted together in a tentative marriage and forged into the peculiar weapon. It looked as if it still held its edge but Azria wasn't about to test the blade at the moment. Just holding it felt strange. Perhaps someone on the *Hen & Chick* could teach her how to use this weapon properly. She slid it back into its sheath before she placed the blade into the box besides the scrolls, latching the box securely before she exited the crew quarters, walking the now quiet halls of the ship by herself.

The deck of the ship glowed orange and purple with the dying sunlight of the long day. Azria heard the crew chatting and laughing, the roll of dice on the deck catching her ear. Nervously she tiptoed towards the front of the ship. Her mother sat on a chair, apart from the crew, watching over them as they played the game. Azria approached, not sure who she should stand next to. Bolo looked up from the game and caught the captain's eye, nodding. Her mother turned in her chair, meeting eyes with Azria before she rose to her feet. With a single clap of her hands, the rest of the crew grew quiet, all of them turning to look at Azria. Azria gulped.

"Come here, girl," her mother said, gesturing with a wave of her hand. Azria took a deep breath and walked over to her mother's side. Her mother put an arm around her shoulders, pulling her closer and Azria could see the happiness in her mother's mouth and dark brown eyes. The crew rose to their feet and stood before them, the air too still as they waited for either the captain or the mage to speak.

"I know all of you have met my daughter, Mage

Azria of Hitha, of Miz," Captain Apzana began, her voice loud and clear over the lap of the waves. "While she is part of our crew, she is just that. Part of our crew. I don't expect you to treat her any differently because she's my daughter. Are we all clear?" Azria watched as the crew nodded. She felt her mother squeeze her shoulder. "Since she's part of our crew, we'll welcome her in the way we typically welcome new crew members." She turned her face and finally grinned at Azria. "Hope you like coconut wine."

"I've only ever had a sip before," Azria whispered.

"Then Nana did what I told her to," Captain Apzana said with a laugh. She let her arm drop from Azria's shoulders and waved her hand at Yabi. "Cook Yabi, bring out the wine."

"Yes, my captain!" the cook yelped, scurrying off somewhere. Azria looked towards the crew, not sure what would happen now.

"Do you have anything to say?" Captain Apzana quietly asked, her voice warm.

Azria looked down at the deck as she tried to gather her thoughts, finding too many to choose from. She looked up at her fellow crew mates, expectation painted across their faces, all of them so different. What would they want to hear?

"I'm extremely pleased to join your crew," Azria said, trying not to let her eyes drift to the deck. She was never good at public speaking and speaking in Trade was making it harder. "And I know I bring a great many skills to this ship, which will prove useful." Azria winced inwardly, thinking of her words. She was making herself sound like a tool, not another colorful member of the *Hen & Chick*. What could she say to be like one of them? "I look forward to getting to know all

of you better. And…I'm sure we have a lot to learn from
each other!" Azria felt her face grow hot as the crew
politely applauded her less than eloquent introduction.

"Wine!" Bolo yelled. The crew all began clapping
more enthusiastically, Brak giving a *whoop* of approval.
Yabi carried the large jug with both hands, the cap sealed
with black wax. She heaved it up onto a stool next to
Azria and pulled a small wooden knife out of her belt,
prying the cap off with one quick motion.

"You get the first cup," Apzana said, pushing Azria
towards the wine with a gentle touch between her
shoulder blades. Azria stumbled forward, her stomach
already gurgling in anticipation of the drink.

Yabi smiled and handed her a metal cup before she
pried off the wax at the spout. Azria quickly put the cup
under the spout, watching the clear liquid stream into
her cup, its scent already perfuming the air. The drink
was cold, her cup cool in her hands and she wrapped
her fingers around it as she moved out of the way for
the next person to get their share. Azria watched, Bolo
and her mother getting their serving last. Her mother
raised her glass towards the sky, the rest of the crew
following suit. Azria raised her glass last, looking to
Yabi, her hands empty.

"To our crew, new and old," Captain Apzana said,
her voice loud and clear in the night air. A breeze blew
over the ocean, the smell of salt mixing with the fruity
perfume of the drink. "To the *Hen & Chick*, the greatest
ship to sail the Jeweled Seas." The crew cheered, clinking
their glasses together, a happy song which made Azria
smile. "And," Apzana said, turning her eyes to Azria, "to
the City of Peace, to trade and see the splendor of the
Winter Palace." Apzana raised her cup again before she
drank deeply.

"To the City of Peace!" the other crew members said, finally partaking of their drink. Azria looked around, expecting Nana to pop out and push the cup of alcohol from her hands. With a sigh, she brought the cup to her lips and took a sip, feeling the drink warm and then burn in her mouth. It was clean tasting but rich, the flavors of jasmine and creamy rice on her tongue. Azria felt her belly warm as the drink reached her stomach. The City of Peace, she thought. And the Winter Palace!

"Wait," Azria said, frowning, looking to her mother. "It's summer."

Chapter 5
When Secrets Surface

"If you use magic to get out of this, I'll throw you over-board."

Azria gulped. Her focus danced between the sharp pressure on her spine and the pain in her shoulder. She couldn't decide which was worse. Azria grunted, then winced as the wooden blade pressed harder against her neck, her blood bouncing just under her skin. Every breath she took flowed through her, pooling where it hurt most, waiting for her will to ease the pain, or even radiate out in a burst of angry energy. But Azria tapped her free hand on the deck of the ship. "I give up."

Bolo shifted his weight and stood, offering his hand to help her rise. Azria grimaced as she rolled onto her back before grabbing his hand. With one fluid motion, Bolo pulled her up, the deck of the *Hen & Chick* under her feet once more.

"You're getting better, Mage," Bolo remarked with

an approving nod. "I wouldn't have pegged you for a physical fighter."

"I've gotten into my share of scraps," Azria panted, adrenaline still surging through her. Back home, more than a few verbal altercations with fellow Innates had come to scuffles. Hiezh always advised her to walk away while screaming insults and Nana's advice was to ignore those with empty threats and emptier heads. Azria didn't always listen. Bolo taught self-defense after first meal every day and Azria found herself drawn to the physical exercise.

"I can tell," Bolo said, handing her a cup of water. "I can feel you trying not to fight dirty." Azria gulped the water, feeling her face grow even hotter with embarrassment but Bolo put his hands up. "I'm not judging! It's more important to get out of fights alive than to fight honorably. Besides, the ones left standing are the ones who get to say what an honorable fight is anyway." Bolo pulled out one of his daggers and started to flip it over and over in his hand, showing off his knife skills with tight flourishes and throws. Azria couldn't help but grin, even knowing he was showing off on purpose.

"I will point out, you didn't allow her to use her magic," Eixon spoke up, pulling his attention away from the scroll he was reading. "Had you allowed it, I'm certain that fight would have ended differently."

"Hey, if you throw magic at everything, you'll never learn how to throw a punch!" Bolo said, tossing the knife and catching it in his other hand.

"And mages are forbidden from fighting each other with magic on Miz," Azria chimed in, aware she may have been giving away her intentions with Bolo. "When do I get to train with the knife?" Azria asked.

"When I'm sure you won't stab yourself when I disarm you," Bolo said, spinning the knife one more time before slipping it back into its sheath.

"Fair enough," Azria said, bringing her fists together and bowing her head to Bolo in thanks for the lesson. Bolo mirrored the gesture, bowing less deeply, officially ending their session. Azria grimaced as she turned away, feeling the pains of their sparring settling in her muscles and joints. Her body ached and her stomach still felt queasy from the waves but Azria liked the way the activity got her blood moving and her spirits up.

"Port ahead!"

Azria looked up to Brik, stationed in the rigging, the Skyward man pointing off in the distance. She turned, listening to the *thump, thump, THUMP* of the two brothers as they leaped down from their stations among the masts and rigging, their hooves slamming into the deck of the ship.

"Is that the City of Peace?" Azria gasped. Beyond the shining bay stretched the myriad multicolored buildings and erratic spider web of roads which made up the city. Neat rows of emerald-leafed trees flanked the city, glowing under the golden sun. The roar of the waves and cry of seagulls muffled any sounds but Azria imagined the music drifting over the wind, coaxed from silvered strings and taut, bone-white drums. Wide, flat brown fields lay empty at this time of year but in winter would accommodate hundreds of colorful caravans, expanding the capacity of the city till bursting with people and merriment.

"That's her, alright," Bolo said, standing beside her. "Beautiful under all suns and all moons."

"What's that?" Azria asked, pointing to a large tower which stood by the shore, colors snaking up around the exterior in a beautiful rainbow pattern.

The top of the tower was fitted with the biggest glass windows Azria had ever seen, the head of the tower painted a bright red that reminded Azria of sunsets.

"The Beacon," Eixon said, standing beside her. "A lighthouse to guide those who seek the Silver Bay. Each color used on the exterior represents a different family of the Mudnebi. Every family sent a representative to lay one stone at the foundation, while the tower itself was built entirely by volunteers from every land on the earth."

"Why did volunteers build the tower?" Azria asked, wondering how anyone was able to organize that many diverse people. Miz was one people but even there, city planners argued over the best way to measure angles and which plants made the air the sweetest.

"Travelers are not to lay one stone atop another," Eixon replied. "As the Great Rider decreed it when they formed the first of us. But the Winter Sovereign of the 17th Winter saw the need for a lighthouse, for all those who sought refuge and respite in the City of Peace, so she decreed it. It took many years but in the end, it was built."

"It's beautiful," Azria said. Even from this distance, Azria could tell the City of Peace was different from Hitha. Miz was all about order. Engineers and architects consulted each other constantly, keeping the roads straight and the buildings functional and beautiful, built to maximize airflow, garden space and quiet. The City of Peace was all wrong by Mizian standards, yet Azria couldn't help but think it was charming, multi-hued and hugged by the lush green arms of the trees. If Hitha was a glittering gem, faceted by the most expert jeweler, the City of Peace looked like a raucous opal, glowing with color and patterns yet to be named.

"In early spring, the sweet perfume of the Gleaning Trees mingles with the salt spray of the Silver Bay, their petals like gleaming pearls floating on the water," Eixon said. The way he said it made Azria think he was reciting something from memory.

"Are you glad to be home?" Azria asked cheerfully. The supply master's thick brows furrowed, as if he didn't understand the question.

"The City of Peace is not my home, Mage," Eixon answered. "In my life I've visited it several times. Sixteen, to be exact."

"Oh," Azria said, wondering at the oddly specific number. "Well, I mean, are you glad to be among your people?"

Eixon stared out over the side of the *Hen & Chick*, a tightness in his jaw the answer to her question. In the blink of an eye, his expression softened and he took a deep breath, turning away from the sight of the city. "There is a bakery in the seventh district which serves strong tea and my favorite desserts. That, I am glad for. Now, if you'll excuse me, I must prepare myself to disembark," he said, bowing slightly before he walked away.

"Okay," Azria murmured after him with a feeble wave of her hand. She looked back to the approaching coastline, wondering what the people of the City of Peace were like. Were they all like Eixon? Serious and well-mannered, with a penchant for learning? Or the opposite, hence why Eixon wasn't too thrilled to be back home? Azria shrugged to herself and assumed the Mudnebi were like the people of Miz: different. There would be cultural quirks they might all have but people were people.

"I'm so excited to be at the City of Peace!" Yabi

exclaimed, popping up beside Azria. She clasped her hands under her chin, the sea breeze ruffling her smooth, dark hair. "I've never visited in the summer. Onacá, Jay and I are going to swim in the Jade Pools!"

"Who's Jay?" Azria asked, her interest piqued at both the mention of a new name and the idea of swimming. The ocean surrounded her new home but Azria hadn't been in the water for so long. She missed the feeling of hot, white sand on her soles, skipping to the ocean's edge to let the clear water wash over her brown feet. She missed the feeling of floating away in the arms of the sea and the taste of salt on her lips after a swim.

"She's the navigator!" Yabi said with a smile. "And my best friend. Besides Onacá of course. And my brother, though obviously he's not here."

"Oh," Azria said, trying not to sound hurt. She couldn't expect to be counted among Yabi's friends, Azria thought to herself. They'd only known each other a week and all their interactions were centered around meals, Yabi nervously chattering about the food and funny stories about the crew members. Azria never knew what to say to the cook and rarely got a chance to get a word in besides 'Thank you for the food.' Still, Yabi's words reminded Azria of how lonely she felt when she lay on her bed at night. "You have a brother?" Azria asked, trying to change the subject.

"Oh, yes! He's older than me and really tall. I hear he's handsome too. His name's Jido and he cooks, just like me! Learned from the best! My mom, of course." Yabi beamed, obviously proud of her family profession. Her mouth popped open as she stared at Azria, eyes wide. "You've never been to the City of Peace! You'll love it! I mean, the city is great but the orchards are beautiful and there's the Chariot to see! It's a huge rock, bigger than a house! They say it fell out of the sky, and their deity rode it to the earth. Oh, did you want to go swimming with us? We're all going to go, myself and Onacá and Jay! Not right away though! Onacá and I are going to go to the market. You should come with us too!"

"I would love to?" Azria said, not sure what she was agreeing to.

"Get ready to drop the anchor!" Bolo yelled. Azria listened to the flurry of activity behind her while admiring the bay, ships of all shapes and sizes along the coast. Sailors and dock workers walked back and forth in their myriad uniforms, chatting and calling to each other as they loaded and unloaded cargo. "Get ready to disembark, Mage," Bolo said. "And don't forget to give your supply list to Eixon."

"I have to get my list!" Yabi yelped, scurrying away across the deck. "I'll see you later, Azria! I mean, Mage!"

"Azria's fine!" Azria called, looking to Bolo. She felt her face grow hot as he smirked at her before he sauntered away, yelling more orders to Brik, Brak, and Eixon. Azria watched as they slowly pulled up to the docks.

"Welcome to the City of Peace!" the bare-chested man at the dock called up, squinting against the midday sun. His long dark hair was braided and tied into a bun, and he wore simple baggy trousers of blue and gray. His garments reminded Azria of the sailors back home in Hitha, their clothes made of tougher stuff than the linen and cotton dresses people like herself wore. The man who spoke wore a blue snail shell around his neck and he smiled with bright white teeth. "Where is your captain and your manifest?"

"I'm the captain, Apzana, and I have it," Azria heard

her mother call. Her mother stood beside Azria and held up a scroll case, her bamboo hat casting a shadow over her face. "You're new here," she called down to the man.

"I am," the man called up. "Took over for my uncle Yarix this spring. I'm Little Yarix."

"Well, that makes remembering your name easier," Apzana said. "Can you tell me if the *Storm's Eye* arrived?"

"Got here yesterday, as a matter of fact!" he said. With a clang and a bang, Azria watched as a gangplank was raised up to the boat, the anchor set by someone else on the *Hen & Chick*. "You got dealings with them?"

"Just expecting a few of their passengers," Apzana said. Azria watched as her mother walked down the gangplank first, handing the manifest over and placing a few coins into Little Yarix's palm. "You'll see our paperwork is in order. We'll be leaving two mornings from now."

"Two mornings?" Azria heard Brak grumble behind her. "Hardly any time to have fun."

"We expect the weather to hold out till then," Yarix said, looking over the paperwork. He handed it back with a wide smile, creases at the corners of his dark eyes telling Azria he smiled often. "May you enjoy your time in the City of Peace."

"I'm sure we will," Apzana said with a nod, turning her attention back to the crew as he walked down the dock to see to other business. "You heard him. Enjoy your time. And be back in two mornings or be left behind."

"I'm ready to soak for two days," Onacá said to Yabi as they walked towards the gangplank, past Azria. They had both changed into much finer clothes, Onacá's makeup fresh and bright, her colorful skirt fluttering in the breeze to show her mosquito-bitten legs. Yabi wasn't wearing her apron for once, though a white spot on her dark hair indicated leftover rice flour from the morning's breakfast.

"Yabi said I could come with you," Azria started as she followed after them, her voice somewhere between an excited whisper and a squeak.

"Oh no, you're coming with me," Apzana called up. Azria jumped, startled, trying not to blush as she heard Onacá and Yabi giggle to themselves.

"What?" Azria asked, walking after Onacá and Yabi, trying not to storm down. "Why?"

"Can't it wait, Captain?" Yabi asked, her voice pitched higher than usual. "I mean, you know best, you're the captain. But we're going swimming and I already told Azria she could come with us."

"I appreciate you and Onacá trying to keep my daughter entertained, but business first, then pleasure," Apzana replied. "I have need of her. There'll be time to swim later this evening."

"You can't be serious!" Azria exclaimed in disbelief. "You could have told me about this any of the days we were at sea. Besides, it's the City of Peace, not the City of Business."

"More transactions happen here than any other town," Apzana said, placing the manifest into her bag.

"Probably because you can't get stabbed for making a bad offer," Bolo added gleefully as he joined their group. "Remember, bloodshed of any kind is forbidden in the City of Peace. Drawing a single drop of blood will dishonor their deity. Don't get exiled," he said, giving a sly look to Onacá, who angrily wrinkled her nose at him.

"Worry about your own blades," Onacá snorted.

"I'd sooner die than get exiled from the City of Peace," Brak said as he trip-trapped past Azria, his brother and Eixon close behind. "I love it here. So many different buildings, so many different people! It's like a field of beautiful wildflowers, every color represented in one place, swaying in the breeze!"

"There is poetry in you after all," Eixon said, following behind them. Azria watched as they all left to scatter in the salty breeze. Yabi and Onacá waved a hasty good-bye before they too left to whatever relaxation awaited them.

Bolo yawned loudly as he stretched his arms over his head. "Well, I'm going to get a few hours of drinking in unless you need me, Apzana."

"I'll meet you at the Yellow Mango when we're done, Bolo," Apzana said.

"Sounds good to me," Bolo replied, already walking away. "Try to let Azria have some fun while we're here, Apzana. She'll get the wrong idea about us if you don't!"

Azria frowned as she watched him go, frustration making her face feel hot. "Even Bolo gets to leave?"

"All you've done these last few days is practice your fighting stance and duck your head when anyone looked at you," Apzana said, side-eyeing Azria as she started down the dock. "Sometimes we earn our keep off-ship, Azria."

"Hey, no one needed me for anything this last week!" Azria exclaimed, chasing after her. "And everyone already knows each other. I can't just go up to them and start talking about things!" Azria groaned inwardly. When she said it, it sounded stupid. But all week she had stood on the periphery of every discussion, not sure if her Tradespeak was bad or she just wasn't privy to dozens of inside jokes. A change of scenery hadn't made it any easier to make friends.

"Well, I hope when we get back on the *Hen & Chick*, you can navigate your way through a conversation a little better," Apzana said. "I'm sure you'll get some shared experiences over the next day or so. That always helps."

"Swimming is a shared experience," Azria pointed out. "And shopping."

"Stop," Apzana said, the slight hint of exasperation in her voice making Azria giggle. "You'll have time to do all those things, I promise."

"So where are we going exactly?" Azria asked, trying to keep up. Her mother's legs were longer than hers and her pace quickened as they approached the city proper. "And why are we in a rush?"

"Sorry," her mother said, slowing down. "Not used to that island pace you like to keep."

"The Golden Isles are islands," Azria quipped.

"Those people walk too slow too!" Apzana said with a laugh. "I don't have time to walk slow, girl."

"Slow to where?" Azria asked, annoyed. Was her mother avoiding her question? "Where are we going?" Azria stopped in the middle of the street, turning around in a circle as she gaped at all the buildings on the first street of the City of Peace. No two buildings looked alike. Two-storied stone buildings stood stiffly alongside colorful canvas tents and wooden huts with straw roofs. A building across the street looked like it was carved from a massive tree trunk, designs of animals carved into the smooth, striped wood. In the doorways and behind tables were mostly Mudnebis, selling and gesturing, trying to coax passersby into their shops in various tongues. Somewhere a band was playing, a drum and high-pitched string instrument, the lively tune in pace with the chaotic market.

"Keep moving, Azria," Apzana said, linking her arm in Azria's and pulling her down the road. "You're liable to get run over if you stand still in the street."

"Mother," Azria said in Mizian, annoyance in her voice. She slipped her arm out of her mother's grasp, taking a step back. "I'm not going anywhere until you tell me where we're going. I'm not suspicious, I'm just curious! Tell me something! We're in this amazing place but we're going somewhere specific, so it must be important. Where are we going?"

"Azria, don't cause a scene," Apzana whispered, holding her hands up. Her eyes widened and darted back and forth, as if to see who was watching.

"I'm not causing a scene," Azria shot. "I am just standing in the street, asking where we're going. You're the one not telling me what we're doing."

"Look," Apzana said, taking a step towards her. "Azria. Please. I'm sorry. I'm not used to...telling you things straight away. I've never lied to you!" Apzana said quickly. "But I do leave things out," she admitted, switching back to Tradespeak from Mizian. "It's just...it's something you learn to do."

"Please understand," Azria said, trying to think of the words in Trade. "I like to know things! I can...." Azria tried to think of the words to say. She knew the phrase in Mizian but she wasn't sure how to translate the idiom into Trade. "I can order the threads right...to make the right picture."

"You've been in Miz too long," Apzana said. Azria could tell she was trying not to roll her eyes. "Not everything can be ordered, Azria. Not everything can be tied down and placed in neat rows. Learning how to react when things get ruined, that's going to serve you better in this life."

Azria sighed.   She knew there was truth in her mother's words. But she would never admit information wasn't important. "So where are we going?" she asked, putting her hands on her hips.

"You're just like your father," Apzana chuckled. "Coconut for a head."

"You don't strike me as a palm frond yourself," Azria quipped back.

"Before you ask again and I get accused of stalling," Apzana said, "we're going to the Stone Vaults of the Mudnebi Bank."

"It's nice you think I know what that is," Azria said. Over her mother's shoulder she saw a figure walk out from behind one of the buildings, their face obscured by a deep hood on their red-brown cloak.

"It's a place people can keep things safe," Apzana said. "If they can pay. I can't carry everything I own on the *Hen & Chick* so I keep it there."

Azria watched as the figure slipped away before she looked to her mother. "Your belongings? Is this...are we going to see treasure?!"

"We're going to see all the items I can't bring on the ship," Apzana said, giving a sly smile as she offered Azria her arm again. Azria slipped her arm through hers, letting her mother lead her down the street past the myriad buildings and edifices.

"Treasure," Azria squeaked. Her thoughts turned to the small baubles and gems her mother had sent her over the years, knowing they would pale in comparison to her mother's belongings.

"Important items," Apzana said, leading Azria through the streets.   Azria looked over her shoulder once more before they turned a corner, not sure if the robed figure bent over a fruit stand was the person who had been watching them or just another stranger in the massive city. She frowned as she turned her attention back to the road, wondering what items would be revealed in the Vaults.

As they turned down another street, a huge building constructed from massive blocks of pink granite rose over the other structures, dominating the busy streets. Each stone block was carved with an unfamiliar symbol, some of them reminding Azria of the blanket Eixon kept on his bed. From where they approached, she saw one wooden door, twice as tall as she was and carved from a red, lustrous wood, set with mother of pearl in geometric designs. Azria gasped as they stood before it, staring up the building's rosy yet hard face. It may have been the biggest building Azria had ever seen, save the lighthouse. The lighthouse was taller but the Vaults were formidable with their mass.

Apzana reached into her jacket and pulled out a slip of pink paper, walking up to the two guards flanking the massive door. Azria looked them over while they inspected the slip of paper. They wore rounded metal helmets, the woman on the right's messy curls tucked into the heavy helm. Red-and-black uniforms fit snugly over leather armor and each guard held a large quarter-staff in their hands. Neither looked to have blades on them. Azria wondered if anyone ever tried to rob the Vaults. Just seeing the building was deterrent enough.

After both guards inspected the slip of paper, they wordlessly approached the wooden door. Gloved hands gripped the large door rings and with less effort than Azria thought would be necessary, they yanked and then pulled the huge doors open. Cold air rushed out to greet them and a strange blue light spilled past the threshold. Apzana pointed at Azria and said something to the guards with a smirk, who nodded with wide eyes, as if impressed. Apzana walked into the dark building and Azria scampered in behind her, the guards staring as she walked past.

Bowls of swirling blue light illuminated the long hallway all the way down to wherever it ended, the stone walls of the atrium carved with decorations which may have been writing. Azria gaped as she lingered after her mother, finally pulling herself out of the stoically decorated atrium and into the Vaults themselves. The walls were covered with rows of tiny doors, each one with a lock. As they continued on, the doors grew steadily bigger, some with several keyholes in the ornate faces. As far as she could tell, the doors weren't labeled in any way. "Who owns all these boxes?" Azria asked, squinting at them in the sparse blue light.

"Whoever has the money to buy one," Apzana said, her voice echoing as she continued down the cool, dim hallway. As they walked past the different repositories, Azria sensed pangs of power, locked away. There were magical things hidden away here and Azria sensed the different types of energy, working but waiting to be used. As she walked behind her mother, she couldn't help but reach her hand out towards them, trying to caress the magic the way Nana felt fabric at the market to tell its weave and fiber. Simple protection spells, familial magic, items waiting for the right word or condition to spring into activity. Something like hunger, sighing behind forged metal and intricate locks. Azria's stomach rumbled.

Apzana pulled a key out of her bag as she approached one of the doors. It was large, as if it were the door to a small chamber. "One day this will be your key," Apzana said, sliding it into the keyhole. She slipped another key out of her boot and placed it into the lock at the center of the door, giving it three clicks before she put her hand on the door ring and tugged.

Azria stepped into the doorway of the room and gasped. The small vault was neatly stacked with luxuries that made Azria ball up her fists to keep from touching all of them. Apzana locked the door behind her as Azria gazed about the room with wide eyes.

Rolls of fine silk and wool, richly dyed in bold colors. A chandelier of thick, metal rings hung from the ceiling, huge chunks of crystal illuminating the room. Alabaster jars held perfume, the pale white stone carved to reflect the scented oil they contained. A table of wigs, carefully combed and already set with ornaments. More than a dozen outfits, exquisitely embroidered and beaded, so perfectly cut there was no question as to who they were tailored to fit. A half-dozen chests made of wood and stone, gold coins scattered on the floor hinting at what was inside. The scent of amber, sandalwood and night roses wafted through the air. Azria put her face in her hands and looked from object to object, brimming with questions.

"Mama," Azria squeaked, excitement taking her voice. "Is this all yours?"

"This?" Apzana asked. She moved a few trunks aside, blowing a cloud of dust off her hands as she squeezed past a large ebony cupboard. "Yeah."

"Mama, this is so..." Azria couldn't find the words to speak. Where had her mother found all these treasures? Did Nana know about them? Hoarding items was frowned upon in Miz but Azria looked around the room breathlessly, wishing there was a way to tell Nana and Hiezh and all the people who had made fun of her about the exquisite items in her mother's vault.

"Here it is," Apzana said, interrupting Azria's thoughts. She bent down and grunted as she lifted something up, holding it to her chest as she stepped around several trunks made of teak and a white wood Azria had never seen before.

"Is this what we came for?" Azria asked, her mouth dry with excitement.

Apzana set the chest on a table, pulling out yet another key, this one hanging around her neck from a gold chain. Azria looked at the box. The chest was made of dark wood, carved with the images of the Sea Mother holding Miz in her hands.

"That is a Mizian box," Azria said, her brows furrowing with confusion. Holes were drilled in the box's lid, the edges ragged as if the person had made them in a hurry. Apzana took a deep breath before she lifted the lid.

Inside was a length of simple blue-and-green cloth. Apzana pulled out a clay tablet and a piece of paper, much like the paper Azria used at home for writing simple notes. Apzana held out the paper towards her. "Read this."

Azria took the paper, turning it over slowly to see the words written there. In a hasty hand was written in Trade:

To whomever finds my daughter, please take care of her. Her name is Zana.

"Who wrote this?" Azria asked, looking up at her mother.

"My mother," Apzana said. "My mother by blood.

The man and woman who took me into their family found me floating in the sea."

Azria's eyebrows furrowed, imagining the small trunk bobbing on the waves off of a foreign shore. "Mama, what do you mean?"

"What do you know about the Triumvirate?" Apzana asked.

"I know Nana always gets grumpy when we talk about them too much," Azria mused, looking at the box. "Wait," Azria said, several facts clicking together in her head. "Nana is not your mother?"

"No," Apzana said. "Not by blood."

"Do you happen to have a chair in here?" Azria said. "I think I should sit down."

"Actually, I do." Apzana walked to one of the glittering piles and pulled out an ornate wooden stool, upholstered in a shaggy fur.

Azria sat on the stool, trying to arrange her thoughts as she considered what her mother had just told her. "So Nana is not your mother and you were taken in by a family. From the Golden Isles, right?"

"Correct," Apzana said, leaning back on the table. "They renamed me Apzana. It fit better in Goldtongue."

"And the Triumvirate...their titles were The Wise, The Fair and The Innate," Azria said. "Though their names were Kish, Zaya and Iyzani. The rallied Miz under them to fight the Marauders who raided the coasts. They kept Miz safe and gave the people pride in our islands and our customs, something to fight for. Then one day, a great earthquake swallowed the island the Marauders congregated on, the Marauders' Island. Many Mizians say it was the will of the Goddess that swallowed it up."

"The woman who gave birth to me was The Fair and my father was The Wise," Apzana said.

"What?" Azria said, her mouth falling open. The Triumvirate hadn't been around in her lifetime but every Mizian alive knew about them. Two generations ago they had ruled Miz, governing from Gethe, the Old City in the north.

"And my aunt was The Innate," Apzana continued. "Since we all know she and Zaya were sisters."

"But wait," Azria said, bringing her hands to her temples. "Your parents went into exile after they turned on the mages. They wanted all mages to submit to them, to submit to rules The Wise made. Rules which would have stifled all mages. When the mages said they wouldn't submit, they left."

"They left because they feared for their lives," Apzana said. "As far as my mother and father could tell, Zaya placed me in this trunk and threw me into the ocean, to save me from the mages who came for them."

"Nana always said Iyzani betrayed them," Azria whispered, lost in the thoughts that surged in her mind. Her grandparents were legends. Her mother was the heir to three of the most important people in Mizian history. And mages had tried to kill her.

"I've heard the same," Apzana said, looking down at the item she held in her hands. Azria looked at her mother. This wasn't the same woman who swaggered on the deck of the *Hen & Chick*, who gave orders and smirked at every joke. Her head was bowed and her eyes glinted with the suggestion of tears as her long hair fell around her face. Apzana probably had no memories of her mother and father, and Azria couldn't help but wonder if her childhood was plagued with fear of the mages coming for her. Growing up in the Golden Isles,

Apzana had to know the people who took her in were not her parents by blood. When did Apzana learn of her true parentage and what had become of them? At least Azria knew her mother. A pang of guilt swept over Azria as she looked upon Apzana.

"Wait," Azria added, several thoughts coming together in her mind. "Nana...my Nana..." Azria said, the words catching in her throat. Memories of sitting in the front room, listening to Nana hum as she embroidered, the scent of Nana's soft skin when she would kiss Azria goodnight. If Zaya was Apzana's mother by blood, what did it mean for the woman who raised Azria all those years?

"She's your Nana, Azria," Apzana said, placing a hand on Azria's hand. "She's just not my mother. She cared for you, for us, like we were her blood, when she didn't have to. When I came to Miz all those years ago, alone, Nana took me in. I tracked her down to Hitha and she could have turned me away, put me away with the past she was trying to forget. But she didn't. She was loyal to my mother and father when they ruled and she protected us. She was my family when I didn't have any here. And Enza was gracious enough to take care of you when I had to go to sea, Azria, to learn more about all this."

Azria sat there, trying to take it all in. Nana, Enza, was not her grandmother. But Azria loved the old woman who walked her to Hiezh's in the morning, even when her knees ached. Azria had basked in Nana's care for so many years, her grandmother's love the balm on so many bad days. Apzana had left Azria in the care of Nana, while Apzana had been left to the mercy of the waves.

"I'm sorry," Azria said, wrapping her arms around

her mother. She felt her mother stiffen at first, but then soften in her embrace, laying her cheek on Azria's head.

"It's not your fault, Azria," Apzana said, her voice almost a whisper in the room full of treasure. "I'm glad you've avoided all of this bad blood. And the people who raised me, Papa Bapo and Mama Lila, were wonderful. I hope you can meet them some day." Apzana lifted Azria's head and kissed her on the forehead. Her deep brown eyes were shining, her face flushed as if the room was too warm. "But today, I need you to help me get a treasure."

"What?" Azria said.

"Take this," Apzana said, pushing the clay tablet towards her. Azria hesitated, looking at the object. There was writing on it in an old Mizian script, purple-black. The tablet read, 'Sealed by The Innate.' Azria's fingers shook as she reached out to touch it.

The tablet glowed as soon as her skin met the clay, another set of script blazing green on the surface under the ink.

"Down to the Gloomy Waters with you," Azria read. When she said the words, a sensation like a rock sitting in her stomach welled up within her, her skin tingling as the words escaped her lips. "By my hand and the power of Miz." A curse. Azria looked up at her mother, brown eyes wide with the realization. "The Goddess didn't destroy the Marauders' Island."

"The mages did it," Apzana said. "Iyzani did it. And you're going to undo it."

"How did they do it?" Azria asked.

"Same as they raised the Black Island from the sea," Apzana said.

Azria stood there, dumbfounded. The Black Island off the coast of Miz. She'd never seen it but Mizians

knew about the island of black rock which rose from
the sea. Shortly after the Triumvirate disbanded, it was
called up from the ocean by two elite mages, Ayozh and
Zosha. After the island was formed, they were never
heard from again. Magic didn't work on the island, so
mages avoided it. Nana had told Azria the day it rose
from the sea, the sky was full of light and smoke, the
smell of salt water and stone rolling through the humid
breeze.

"No," Azria said, shaking her head. "I don't...I don't
think I can raise an island." It stung to say it but Azria
rubbed her fingertips together, thinking about the
power it must have taken to affect land like The Innate,
like the elite. Such ability was divine in nature. The Sea
Mother had summoned Miz from the sea and the Black
Island's effect on magic was whispered to be proof that
humans should not try to do what deities did. "I...I'm
not powerful enough."

"You can," Apzana said, taking her hand. "The Marauders had a vast treasure on their island when the
mages sunk it. We can have the treasure all to ourselves.
The treasure of a thousand shores! The blood of Iyzani
runs through your blood, Azria. She's your great-aunt.
You can do it."

Azria put the tablet down on the table, the glow fading from its face. "I never knew her," Azria said. "And
I'm not like her. I could never even...think about sinking
an island." Azria gulped hard. The Marauders had pil-
laged the shores of Miz for hundreds of years, stealing
and killing. But to have their entire island sunk beneath
the waves, the surf gulping down the land as they tried
to escape? Knowing her fellow mages willed this made
her blood run cold.

"I know you wouldn't," Apzana said. She took a step

towards Azria and put her hand on her cheek, lifting her face towards hers. "You're not that cruel." There was an edge to her words, and Azria knew it wasn't directed towards her. Iyzani. How long had her mother planned for this?

"To say I'm asking a lot is an understatement," Apzana admitted. She still held the note her mother had written all those years ago in her hands. "But I wouldn't ask if I didn't think you could do it." She folded the note, looking down at it before she spoke again. "Hiezh has told me of your progress, your ability and your will. When I learned the truth of the Marauders' Island, when I knew it had been sunk by a mage's hands, I knew a mage's hands could lift it from the sea. Who better than you?"

"How can you be sure it was Iyzani who sunk it?" Azria asked. "And where did you get this tablet?"

"It was in the chest I was found in," Apzana said with a shrug which was meant to look nonchalant. Instead it looked sad. "And you read the tablet. 'Sealed by The Innate.' The Innate is her, Iyzani. I had other mages look at it, but their magic...it reacted, but not in any way that made them want to continue business with me." Apzana smirked. "Not that they could do anything besides look at it."

"Only Mizian magic can undo Mizian magic," Azria said, her eyes straying back to the tablet. She couldn't help but run her fingertips over the palms of her hands, wondering at the power it would take to undo what was done. How much power did Azria have within her?

"Is it a big treasure?" she asked.

"It will make this look like your supply box," Apzana said with a grin.

"By the Bright Waters," Azria said, putting her face in her hands and rubbing her eyes.

"Is that a yes?" Apzana asked. It was more than a simple question. There was a hope in her words that made Azria take a deep breath, exhaling sharply as she finally nodded.

"I'll do it," Azria said.

For a moment they both stood in the vault, saying nothing. Azria stared at the ground, one of the only bare spots in the room. Had she said it? That she would raise an island from the sea? She looked to her mother, the disbelief Azria felt dispelled by the excitement in her mother's face.

"We've got to see a man about a map then," Apzana said, putting the paper into the trunk. She locked it with the key and then lifted it up with one arm, looking around the treasure vault. "Oh, I guess you can pick out one thing from here for yourself."

It took a moment for Azria to realize what her mother had said. "Really?" Azria gasped. The thought her mother may have acquired some of these items less than honestly crossed Azria's mind, dampening her enthusiasm slightly. Still, there wasn't an item in the room that wasn't gorgeous, finely crafted or luxurious. Azria wondered what kind of items waited for her beneath the waves as she ran her hand over a pile of jewelry placed on a table.

"Just don't take too long, we've got places to be," Apzana said, already unlocking the door.

"I'm not going to get to go swimming with Yabi, am I?" Azria said, her gaze falling on a bracelet made of purple stones. Each one was as big as a mamon seed and roughly cut.

"At some point you might," Apzana said. "Did you pick something?"

"This," Azria said, holding her wrist up as she slipped the bracelet on. "Where did you get it? It's my favorite color."

"Who knows?" Apzana said with a sigh heavy with nostalgia and a hint of pride. She looked around the vault, a slight smile on her lips. This was the Apzana Azria usually saw. "I could always see another shore and use a little more."

"Is that your personal motto?" Azria asked, exiting the vault and stepping back into the blue-lit hallway.

"Something like that," Apzana said, closing the door with a thud and locking it behind her.

"So what do we do now?" Azria asked, walking alongside her mother.

"We get a map and we head to the Marauders' Island. Or at least our best approximation. We should be able to get what you'll need here. The City of Peace is well supplied." They exited the building, walking past the two guards before turning down the street.

"Could we maybe stay in the City an extra day?" asked Azria, trying not to sound too excited. "This isn't exactly the kind of thing I've trained for, Mama. I'll need some time to come up with a supply list and to figure out how I can—" Azria's word cut off. She didn't know what to say. Raise an island from beneath the waves? It didn't seem possible! But according to her mother, it had been lowered with the same power, and Hiezh had taught her to feel the weave of magic. If she could feel where the threads came together, in theory she could unravel it. Still, Azria gulped to think about the energy which had been wielded before her to do such a thing.

Was she strong enough to rip it apart? Or would she undo herself by tampering with their spell?

"Of course we can," Apzana said, hooking her arm in Azria's. "I'll tell the dock master. You may want to talk to Eixon once you get a supply list."

"Right," Azria said with a nod, pushing back the feeling of being overwhelmed down into her stomach. She could do this. At the very least, she could study the tablet and examine its role in the spell casting. Once Azria gleaned what magic the tablet had to give up, she could make more plans. There was no use worrying over a chaos of possibilities which probably wouldn't come to pass. *Don't worry about the soup before the firewood's gathered. That's what Nana would say.* "I might also need a place where I can work undisturbed. A quiet room where no one is going to knock on the door and bother me."

"That can be arranged," Apzana said. Her mother pressed her lips together before she spoke again. "One more thing," Apzana added slowly. "If you write a letter to Nana or Hiezh, it'd be wise not to mention any of this to them. They can't stop us of course, but I wouldn't want them to worry."

"Oh," Azria said, not able to keep from frowning slightly. Writing letters was as far from her mind as Miz itself, but the idea of not telling Nana and Hiezh any of what her mother had just told her? Azria felt as if cheated from a victory. All these years she had wondered about her mother; now that she knew a few things, she couldn't share them? Still, surely Nana knew some of it. Azria wondered just how much her grandmother knew. Mostly, Azria wondered when she would see her again. A wave of nostalgia hit Azria and she couldn't help but miss Nana, trying to imagine how she would respond to Azria's newest questions.

Azria's face darkened as a cloaked figured walked by. She was certain it was the same person she had noticed before. This time the person turned their face so Azria could see them. It was a young man, about her age, his hair and ears hidden within the hood of his cloak. But he was Mizian. Azria knew it. Recognition registered on his dark face and he narrowed his eyes at her before he hurried off. Azria leaned in close to her mother, tugging on her jacket sleeve to get her attention. "Mama, I just saw another Mizian."

"You did?" Apzana said. She looked over her shoulder and Azria turned as well, hoping to see him so she could point him out. "And they didn't say hello? I don't remember Mizians being so rude."

"He looked at me strangely," Azria said, still looking back over her shoulder. "Like he knew me."

"Well, if we see him again we'll find out if he does," Apzana said. Azria watched as her mother tapped the hilt of her sword more casually than Azria cared for.

"Mama, there's a law about spilling blood here," Azria said nervously.

"There's no law against threatening people," Apzana pointed out. "And well, there are no laws about spilling tears."

Azria gulped hard. Now she really didn't want to run into that boy again. She took a deep breath and prayed she wouldn't, for both of their sakes. Azria's eyes went to her mother's sword, noticing the shiny but well-worn hilt.

"Let's focus on the island, Mama," Azria said, not believing her own words.

"Good thinking," Apzana said, nodding up the street

towards a two-story wooden building with a porch
and a balcony. The outside was meant to be the color
of mango flesh but had been worn down over time
by wind and rain. The light from the windows was
cheerful enough, and Azria could already smell charred
meat and savory spices wafting through the air. "That's
where we're headed. Food and a bit more company. I
should warn you, Red can be a bit loud."

"Is Jay with him?" Azria asked.

"She better be," Apzana said, stepping up onto the
porch. "Though Red's more likely to jump ship than Jay.
He's got a husband and wife pining for him when he's
out sailing."

Azria peered in through the window. Round
wooden tables were set haphazardly throughout the
bar, spits of meat dripping grease into the fire. In
the corner a trio of musicians played for a handful of
people, the sound of their fiddle, drum and bells a lively
staccato tune. Bolo sat at a table with two other people:
a large man and a young woman, her hair wrapped in
a blue scarf. The thought of talking to anyone just yet
made Azria's chest feel tight, her heart thumping like
the drum in the bar. "If you don't mind, I think I'll stay
outside for a moment. Get some fresh air."

Apzana shrugged. "Suit yourself. Don't be too long."
Her mother turned to slip into the building but stopped
herself, turning to face Azria. "I'm glad you're here,
Azria. Not just because of the island. I just...it is nice,
to finally tell you some things." Apzana wrapped her
arms around Azria and embraced her, pulling her close.
Azria laid her head on her mother's chest, listening to
her slow, steady heartbeat, her mother's long hair tick-
ling her cheeks. Her mother planted another dry kiss on
her forehead, a kiss like Nana used to give. "We'll get

your hair done while you're here too," Apzana added, patting the top of Azria's head. "If you want."

"Sounds good," Azria said with a laugh, not sure why her mother's words made a lump form in her throat. Apzana waved once before she slipped into the bar, leaving Azria on the porch by herself for a moment.

Azria took a deep breath, rubbing her eyes with her fingers. The bar would be fun. And tomorrow she would have something to do, to help the crew. The thought loosened the knot in Azria's chest, knowing they would all be working together as soon as everyone else knew what they were doing. The Marauders' Island.

The flutter of a red-brown robe caught Azria's eye. Walking to the edge of the porch, she peered out over the busy street, trying to catch sight of the young man. Maybe she imagined the boy recognizing her, Azria thought to herself, turning towards the door. Maybe he was just glad to see another Mizian in the City of Peace.

Azria knew what relieved faces looked like. His wasn't one of them. Her mouth falling into a frown, she said a quiet prayer, hoping to wash unease from her mind. She would need all the focus she could muster, and she wouldn't let other people's dismay muddy her thoughts. It wouldn't be the first time her presence wouldn't be welcome and it wouldn't be the last.

Azria stood up straighter, taller, placing her hand on the door to pull it open. For once the thought of people dreading her presence made the corners of her mouth curl into a smile. If she could raise the Marauders' Island from the sea, she'd give people reason to stare, eyes as big as scallops. With a quick yank she pulled the door open, the feeling of being watched on her back but the thought of making jaws drop pushing her through the door.

Chapter 6
Spies and Suspicions

"So, this is the mage!"

Azria stopped dead in her tracks, hoping her expression didn't give away her unease. A large man clad in scarlet robes waved her over, his dark eyes glinting in the light of the oil lamp. Azria tried not to stare as she approached, not at the man's size, but his hair. The color of glowing embers, Azria had never seen hair that color before in her life. At first she thought his hair was dyed, but as she drew closer she saw stripes of gray, like ash, running through his thick locks. The man looked her over as well, his expression less impressed than hers. "I thought she'd be taller," he scoffed.

"I thought you'd be politer," Azria quipped back.

"That's the first time someone's said that about him," a young woman sitting at the table said, her hands wrapped around a thick clay mug. Her gray eyes twinkled as she smiled at Azria, a wisp of brown, wavy hair stylishly allowed to spill from her blue headscarf. "Not everyone is used to the boisterousness of Redlanders." The young woman smiled primly at Azria with big white teeth. "Please excuse my second father. He grew up yelling. Everything is far away from everything else, where he's from."

"Don't make excuses for him, Jay," Apzana said, waving her hand at her. "Red's just loud." The big man scowled at Apzana but the captain ignored him, unfazed by his expression. "Azria, this is Red, our weapon master and Jay, our navigator. This is in fact Azria, our new mage and my daughter."

"It's a pleasure to meet you both," Azria said, not sure if she should shake their hands or bow.

"Again, no one has ever said that to Red before," Jay chuckled, ignoring the older man's glowering face.

"Oh, to be trapped at sea with these rude young people," Red huffed.

Bolo drained his cup and slammed it down onto the table top. "Are we going or not, Apzana?" he asked, his voice cheerful with drink.

"Go?" Azria asked. "Where?"

"Just popping out for a moment, Azria," Apzana said, standing from the table. "Take the time to get some food and get to know Red and Jay." Azria must have given her a look because her mother laughed. "You'll know what I'm up to before the night's over, I promise."

"Trail's gonna get cold, Apzana," Bolo warned, already at the door.

"Order me a side of green beans and garlic," Apzana said, already walking after Bolo. Azria watched as they slipped through the doorway, back onto the street.

"She does that a lot, doesn't she?" Azria asked quietly, not sure if Red or Jay would answer her.

"She does," Jay replied.

"But she always comes back," Red added, pouring the contents of the pitcher into a cup. Azria slumped down into a chair, trying not to feel too dejected. "Here, have a drink," the man said, pushing the cup towards her.

Azria took the cup and looked into it, inhaling the aroma of the drink. It was the color of the sunrise and smelled sweet and yeasty. Azria took a small sip and wrinkled her nose as she swallowed, the drink cloying and heavy on her tongue, the burn of alcohol in her throat doing nothing to cleanse her palate. "Ugh, what is this?" she said.

"Don't like peach wine?" Red asked, filling his own cup. "It's the prized drink of the people here. Maybe you'd prefer the real thing?" Red waved a hand, summoning one of the barkeeps to the table.

Azria looked around the bar, so different from the food stands and drink stands of her home. She didn't go to drinking establishments in Miz but like most of the eating spots, they were fairly open, sometimes just bamboo posts with a palm frond roof. This bar had four walls and glass windows, the cold breeze that came in doing nothing to dissipate the aromas and din of the building. The crackle of boiling oil that emanated from the back heated unfamiliar but savory spices that made Azria's eyes water.

"I'd prefer a mango," Azria muttered. "Or some tea."

"Not a lot of mangoes in Yabi's stores," Jay said with a nod. "What has Yabi been feeding you these last few days?"

"White rice, dried fish and plantain stew. Seaweed soup. Beans," Azria said, trying to keep weariness out of her voice. She missed Nana's cooking pot more than she thought she would. The lush taste of fresh fruit and the nutty goodness of purple rice. Shrimp roasted in their shells, sprinkled with salt and spices. Nibbling on cilantro leaves after a meal. It made Azria's mouth water to think about the foods she'd rather be eating.

"I miss buckwheat porridge," Jay said with a sigh. "I never thought I would, but the smell of it cooking over the fire always makes me think of being safe and silly. My mother would make it in the morning, stirring it so it wouldn't get lumps. I always liked the lumps."

"An order of green beans and garlic, a bowl of peaches, soft cheese, whatever roast you have and bread. And another wine. And honey," Red said, shouting the last two items after the server. "You two should be glad you have food," Red muttered, taking a gulp of his drink. "Anyway, now that your mother is gone, why did she want me to get this map anyway?"

"What map?" Azria asked, almost taking another sip of the peach wine but stopping in time.

"Don't you play dumb, girl," Red grumbled, wagging a thick finger at her. "I know you know."

"Let me see it," Azria said, surprised at the brusqueness in her voice. The old man blinked before he reached into his robe and pulled out the map, looking around before he unfolded it and laid it on the table.

The yellowed paper was crisscrossed with the fibers of the reeds used to make it, brown lines running up and down and across. Azria reached out and laid two fingers on the edge of the brittle paper, trying to feel the energy poured into the object. It wasn't magical but she sensed the different hands of those who had made the map; the paper maker and the different artists. Each island had been drawn with pigment made from the island itself, a not uncommon practice meant to make the map more of a talisman than a tool.

Azria's gaze traced the line of the Floating Chain up, from Ultín to Miz, missing the Black Island off of the northwest coast. The map must have been made before it was summoned from the sea. Beyond the gentle curve of the chain, nestled between the Northern Continent and the Western was a small island, labeled simply: Marauders.

"The Marauders' Island," she whispered.

"The Haunted Sea," Red scoffed.

"Haunted?" Azria asked, trying not to gulp.

"When that many people die in one place, of course," Red said with a shrug that was too casual for Azria's taste. "Some say it was an earthquake, some say it was the judgment of your Goddess, finally stopping them from their violence. Still, to die in such a way. No wonder their souls are uneasy."

"Red is a priest, you see," Jay answered. "So he cares about people's afterlives more than most."

"Priest?" Azria said, furrowing her brow. She thought of the temple attendants back on Miz, gray-and-blue robes of the finest linen billowing in the sea breeze, praying for oracles, dancing the stories of creation, advising Mizians on the proper way to order their lives. She stifled a giggle as she thought of Red dancing on the beach, a crown of shells in his red hair.

"Don't look too surprised, Mage," Red said, suddenly seeming embarrassed, the faintest hint of sheepishness in his words.

"He's had ten wives!" Jay whispered loudly.

"You're just jealous!" Red said. "You haven't even had one wife! And it was a religious rite!"

"My mother and second father are enough for Red now," Jay said with a wink.

"Back to the haunting?" Azria asked, making a note to ask about the wives later, but more worried about ghosts at the moment. There wasn't a word for 'ghost' in Mizian, but there was in Trade. Mizians believed the spirits of the dead were all welcomed into the arms of the Goddess, regardless of how they died, but she knew other people didn't hold the same beliefs. Different deities demanded different things. And if there was a word for it... "What ghosts?"

"Many sailors have reported seeing wandering spirits, walking on the waves," Red spoke, his voice low as the lamp light threw strange shadows on his face. "Always there are voices on the wind, the sounds of crying and pleading. The sight of lights being extinguished."

"It's said the ghosts are in abundance when the Bloody Sword is highest in the sky," Jay said.

Azria shivered. She knew the constellation: an arch of stars called the Mage's Smile in Miz. On occasion a red glow appeared between the second and third star of the constellation, like a cloud far beyond the reaches of the sky. Hiezh had mentioned more than once: *Beware a mage who only casts when the smile is bloody.*

"What does your mother want with a map of a cursed place?" Red growled. The server came back and set plates on the table. A platter of roasted birds, the skin crispy brown and glinting with salt. A bowl of green beans, slivers of caramelized garlic brightening the plate. Flat bread studded with seeds lay beside a mound of cheese whiter than milk. And a bowl of what could only be peaches, the faint silvery down accenting their blushing curves.

"She'll tell you all soon enough," Azria said with a

nod. Something about having a secret made her want to smile. Was this one of the reasons her mother kept so much to herself? Azria smirked and picked up a peach, her smile melting into confusion. "How do I peel this?"

"You don't peel it!" Red laughed loudly.

"Look who's back," Jay said, nodding over Azria's shoulder. Azria turned in her seat, seeing her mother in the doorway, the sea captain waving her over. "We'll leave the peaches for you," Jay promised. "Won't we, Red?"

"We'll see," Red muttered, scooping up a chunk of cheese with the grainy bread. Azria rose from her seat, noting her mother was wearing a shawl over her shoulders.

"What is it, Mama?" Azria asked.

"I need you to come with me," Apzana said. Her mother's forehead was damp with sweat and she was panting. She had been running. "It'll only take a moment. You'll be eating soon enough. Believe me, I want to get to my green beans too."

Azria looked to the table one more time before she pushed back a sigh, ignoring her grumbling stomach. "Okay, lead the way."

Apzana closed the bar door behind her, Azria following her as she walked around the building, where a set of rickety wooden stairs crawled up the side to the second story. Azria held her breath as each step groaned under her feet, relieved to reach the small landing that led into the second floor. Wooden doors lined the hall, some opened and leading into small rooms, others locked, various noises coming from within. It smelled vaguely of sage and incense in the hallway, and Azria wondered if the owners of the inn burned it or if the residents did. Her mother stopped in front of one of the doors, knocking two times and then a third time before she opened the door.

Azria's mouth dropped open. "That's the boy who was following me!" He still wore the same cloak he had been wearing in the street, though his arms were tied behind him and his hood was around his shoulders. His thick, curly hair was pulled into a black puff behind his head, not neatly braided as was the fashion in Miz. Dark brown eyes were canopied by thick, bushy eyebrows and his chin sported the most scraggly beard she had ever seen. His wide mouth pulled into a frown. What stood out the most was his left leg. It was made of wood, discolored on the foot with wear. Bolo lay on the bed, tossing a knife up into the air and catching it, obviously bored with guarding.

"Well, that's confirmed," Bolo said. He sat up on the bed, tapping the boy on the chin with the hilt of his knife. "So, do you want to tell us why you were following the captain and her daughter?"

"I was only following the mage," the boy replied in Mizian. The notes and tones of his voice told Azria he was about her age.

"Not sure that makes things better," Apzana scoffed.

"Speak Trade, don't be rude," Bolo said.

"Why were you following me?" Azria said, balling her fists at her side.

"I won't tell you if they're here," the boy said in Mizian again.

"He says he'll only talk to me," Azria said.

"I got that," Bolo huffed. "Which makes me thinks we shouldn't leave."

"I can handle him," Azria said, standing up as straight and tall as she could. She couldn't let one boy scare her. Ahead of her lay a great magical feat and the uneasy dead of those wronged by her ancestors. The idea of being alone in a room with a boy who'd been following her seemed like nothing.

"Are you sure?" Apzana asked. Azria looked to her mother's hand, resting on the hilt of her sword.

"Of course," Azria said with a nod, rubbing her fingertips together. She could feel the boy's eagerness to talk but something was keeping him back. He seemed nervous, anxiety simmering just under the skin. It matched hers, though Azria was careful to keep her breathing steady, not to let her energy push her forward into something she'd regret. She was nervous for a different reason. She wanted to prove to her mother she could handle herself. Azria had voiced her concern about the boy and her mother had taken it upon herself to try and deal with it. Azria needed to finish it. "I'm a mage and he's just a tied up kid."

Azria saw her mother give her a look out of the corner of her eyes. "If you need us, we'll be right outside," Apzana said, placing a hand on her shoulder. "Just be careful." Her mother gave her arm a squeeze before she and Bolo left the room, closing the door behind them.

Azria looked down at the boy.

"I know Mizian isn't your first language," Azria said, kneeling down on the floor and leaning back on her heels. Surprise widened his brown eyes and Azria tried to keep her pleasure to herself, glad to have the upper hand for the moment. "Where are you really from?"

"Mizian's not your mother's either," the boy said. The corners of his mouth suggested the start of a smile. Azria rolled her eyes at him.

"You didn't answer my question. Where are you from?" Azria said. She thought about what he had said, how he had said it. "You grew up speaking Trade, didn't you? Your Mizian sounds like Big Island talk."

"I've never been to the Big Island but you're right," the boy said.

"What's your name?" Azria asked. "Tell me."

"Zesh," he answered, nodding his head in greeting. "Some people call me Zee."

"I'm Azria," she said. "But you probably already knew that."

"No, actually," he said, shaking his head. "I knew who you were and what I had to tell you. But not your name."

"What do you have to tell me?" Azria asked.

"You can't raise the island," Zesh said.

Azria felt her heart thump in her chest. How did he know about that? Azria had just found out earlier today. The only ones who maybe knew something were Red and Jay, and they hadn't guessed her mother's purposes with the map.

"Why can't I?" Azria demanded, sitting up straighter.

"Even if you can raise the island, no offense," Zesh said, trying to sit up, "my grandmother is going to stop you. If you continue down this path, you'll regret what's at the end. Keep the past where it is, below the waves."

"Is that a threat?' Azria asked.

"No, it's the truth." Zesh shrugged. "You're not so powerful."

"Meanwhile, you're tied up, talking to me," Azria said, unimpressed. "Why'd she send you, why not just stop me now?"

"Because she can't face you," Zesh replied. "She doesn't know what she would do if she was before you. Or your mother."

"Who is your grandmother?!" Azria asked, incredulous. "She sounds like a monster." Azria looked into Zesh's eyes, sucking in her breath as the realization glowed in her mind. "I know who your grandmother is! Iyzani!"

"Yes," Zesh said. "Iyzani, The Innate."

"I know all about her and what she's capable of," Azria said, her voice tight. Azria's gaze strayed to the door, wondering if she shouldn't get her mother right now and tell her who he was. If this boy was Iyzani's grandson, it would mean Apzana had cousins. Did that mean this boy was Azria's cousin?

"All about her?" Zesh said. Azria could hear something in his quiet voice, something sad and hurt. "More than me, who she raised?"

"I know enough," Azria spat. "And I'll know more once I spend time focusing on her magic."

"She didn't send the mages after your mother, or your grandparents."

"Right," Azria sighed. "Of course she didn't." Azria stood up and turned towards the door, ready to hand him over to Apzana and Bolo.

"We weren't there!" he exclaimed. "How could we know what happened?"

Azria spun around, annoyance pulling her mouth into a thin line across her face. "Why would my mother say Iyzani sent mages after her own sister and brother, if it wasn't true?" Azria asked. "Why?"

Zesh stared up at her, his expression blank, his mouth hanging open. "It's easier to slander someone who isn't around to argue, isn't it?" he said.

"Or it did happen, did you ever consider that?" Azria said, crossing her arms over her chest. Azria thought of her mother, tracking this boy through the street, the sword at her hip, the letters her mother had written over the years. "Sometimes the people we love do things we don't love. You have to know this."

"My grandmother loved her sister and her brother-in-law. She would never have hurt them," Zesh said.

"Sibling rivalry is a thing," Azria said.

"I'm not saying my grandmother didn't make mistakes," Zesh said. "But things aren't what they seem. You don't know the whole story."

"I could say the same about you." Azria looked the young man over.

"Why are you raising the island?" he asked. "Why dig up the past?"

"Treasure," Azria said. When she said it, it didn't sound as impressive. Zesh hadn't seen her mother's trove. He looked like he hadn't seen anything nicer than a wooden comb in his whole life, to be honest. "A treasure my mother wants." Azria thought about the treasure. Did she care about it? It wasn't just the treasure that tweaked at the corners of her mouth, made her hearth thump. It was the magic involved. Her mother's desire. The story. "And as a mage of Miz, I am up to the challenge of undoing this magic."

"So of all the treasures, in all the world, you feel the need to dig up this one?" Zesh said. He cocked a thick eyebrow at her.

"Yes," Azria said smugly.

"Well, I can't stop you," he said. With a shrug, he brought his hands forward, setting them down on his lap, along with a thick length of rope.

"Wait, I thought Bolo tied you up," Azria said, taking a step back.

"He did," Zesh said with a nod, rubbing his wrists with his hand. "Tight, too."

"Not tight enough," Azria said. She lifted her hands and aimed her fingers at his wrists, pushing him back. Zesh's hands flew up, his hands by his head as if he were surrendering. His mouth fell open in surprise.

"Hey, I wasn't going to do anything," he said, probably sounding more worried than he meant to.

"Oh, I know you weren't," Azria said, focusing her energy into one hand and letting the other drop to her side. "What are you, some kind of thief?"

"No, I just know how to get out of things," Zesh said. He looked up at his hands, gritting his teeth as he strained against Azria's hold. "Though there are obviously limits to my skill."

"What were you supposed to do after you told me not to raise the island?" Azria asked, still holding the young man there. "Assuming you could ever convince me."

"I don't have to convince you," Zesh said. "I just had to suggest not raising it as a possibility. You have to convince yourself."

"That seems pretty wise, coming from a boy like you."

"My grandmother trusts me," Zesh said with the slightest shrug. "She tells me things."

Azria narrowed her eyes at him slightly. Was that meant to be a dig? Azria thought back to just earlier today, before the idea of raising the Marauders' Island was even an idea in her head, talking to her mother in the street. Trying to pull facts out of her.

"Untruthful things," Azria said.

"Everyone lies," Zesh said, his eyes fixed on the floor. "Because she's a person, just like you and me. Not a monster."

Azria loosened her spell around his wrists, drawing

back until he was completely free. She couldn't help but think about the two guards at the Vaults, the looks on their faces as she walked past them. She wasn't a monster. In Miz, she was just another Innate, trained and ready. But here, out among others, in different cities and among different people...she remembered the way everyone on the ship talked about the Kamerian, always with raised eyebrows and smirks and rolled eyes. Did they talk about her like that when she wasn't around?

"You're not going to get what you want," Azria said.

"Well, all I want right now is for you to help me up." Zesh flashed a smile at her. Azria could tell it was a smile which wasn't often returned, his big brown eyes looking helpless enough for two. Azria sighed and stepped up to him, offering her arm to help him.

"No funny business," she murmured, pulling him up. On his feet, she noticed he stood strangely, as if slightly off balance. "Are you alright?" Azria asked. "Did Bolo and my mother hurt you?"

"No, I actually surrendered," Zesh said, sounding not a bit embarrassed. "I don't take chances. And I don't do much running these days." Zesh bent down and knocked on the side of his shin, a loud, hard sound popping as he rapped his knuckles against his wooden leg.

"How did you...?" Azria's voice trailed off. She wasn't sure what to ask. Her face grew hot as she considered she shouldn't have asked at all.

"An earthquake destroyed my home while I was in it," Zesh said. "I was young when it happened, probably three or four. My parents were killed. My grandmother was away. When she came back, it was...too late." Zesh just shrugged. "She took me in after that. It's been just us ever since."

"Does it hurt?" she asked quietly.

"Sometimes, yeah," Zesh said. "Sometimes I dream I've got two feet and when I wake up, I can still feel it. I can wiggle my toes. It feels like...my leg is made of centipedes. Alive. Crawling and biting."

Azria made a face, the idea of a pile of centipedes sending a shiver through her. Zesh just stood there in the room, watching her face for a moment before he asked, "So, can I go now?"

"No," Azria said quickly, not sure why she said it. "I mean, not yet."

"I'm not going to tell your mother anything else," Zesh said, his face darkening as he narrowed his eyes at her. "Or anyone else. So, you should just let me go."

"Let you go where?" Azria asked. "Is your grand-mother supposed to meet you somewhere?"

"Yes, as a matter of fact," Zesh said. "Not in the City of Peace, though."

"I'm not going to let you go just yet," Azria said, a bit too quickly.

"You...can't really keep me prisoner," Zesh said. "What purpose would it serve?"

"I don't know!" Azria said. "Just...wait here!" Azria knocked on the door, her eyes fixed on Zesh, a mixture of confusion and mild panic starting to settle on his features. "Mama, let me out."

The door opened a crack and then Bolo opened it just far enough, Azria slipping through the doorway into the hall. Apzana and Bolo looked at her, expectation bright in their eyes.

"He's Iyzani's grandson," Azria said.

"Iyzani?" Bolo said, mouth falling open. "THE Iyzani? Is she here, in the City?!"

"Calm down, Bolo," Apzana ordered, her words sharp. "She's not in the City, is she?"

"As far as Zesh will tell me, no," Azria said. "He came to tell me not to raise the island."

"Another person who doesn't think it's wise, Apzana," Bolo muttered.

"Stop," Apzana said, raising her hand to stop Bolo from talking.

"He said his grandmother sent him to talk to me, to dissuade me from doing it," Azria said.

"What do you think we should do?" Apzana asked.

Azria heard Bolo suck in his breath. She looked up at her mother, her arms crossed over her chest, just as Azria had done when talking to Zesh. Her mother wanted her to do it. Azria wanted to at least pursue the possibility and research the spell.

"I don't want to just do what he says," Azria said. "I want to study the tablet."

"Why didn't The Innate come here herself?" Apzana asked. "If she knew we were here?"

"I asked that too," Azria said. "He said she didn't come because...she didn't trust herself to face us."

Apzana's lips parted slightly, as if to say something but she stopped before any words left her mouth. Bolo put his hands on the sides of his head. If he had hair there, he might have pulled it.

Bolo broke into another language Azria didn't speak, his rapid words intoned with what seemed like fear. Apzana answered back in the same language, speaking slowly, just a few short syllables Azria couldn't understand but which she could guess at. "Speak Trade," Apzana added, her scowl apparent in the darkened hall.

"I don't want that witch coming after us, Apzana!"

Bolo exclaimed. "Why can't we go after an easy treasure? I heard the Black Cockle is leaving Ultín with a cargo of pink pepper and cinnamon! Ilipo won't even be expecting us!"

"You'll have to excuse Bolo," Apzana said to Azria. "He's got a fear of magic."

"Dying by magic," Bolo quickly added. It was meant as a correction. "And I have every reason to be afraid. I know what magic can do."

"And she doesn't?" Apzana said, tilting her head towards Azria. Bolo's mouth fell open, stammering over his words. "Get your head out from under your wing."

"I don't think Iyzani will kill anyone," Azria spoke up, trying to sound as confident as she could. "When I talked to Zesh, he was trying to convince me she wasn't a monster. Maybe she didn't come herself because...she's ashamed. Maybe she was afraid she would break in front of you." If Iyzani hadn't killed her sister, she may have still felt responsible for her death. Maybe The Innate thought she could have prevented their deaths. Azria thought of the map downstairs and the ghosts that wandered the surface of the sea. What if Iyzani regretted the sinking of the island, her guilt heavier than the weight of the sea?

"We'll see what's broken in the end," Apzana said. "We're bringing that boy with us."

"What?" Azria asked. "Why?"

"Yeah, why exactly?" Bolo asked. "She'll definitely come after us if we have her grandson! Apzana, you haven't even told the crew what we're doing!"

"He's coming with us and that's that." Apzana turned to leave, pushing past Bolo towards the stairs. "Bolo, guard him. Azria, come with me."

"Apzana!" Bolo called after her.

"You're welcome to stay here in the City of Peace, Bolo," Apzana said, looking over her shoulder. Her expression was touched with a hint of sadness.

"Never that, Apzana," Bolo replied, his face reddening from chin to forehead. "Where you go, I go."

"I'll inform the crew," Apzana said, nodding her head. "And we'll make plans to cast off as soon as Azria is ready."

"Can I talk to Zesh?" Azria said. "I want to be the one to tell him he's coming with us. Since...well, he actually talks to me."

"Make it quick," Apzana said. "Meet me downstairs when you're done."

"Yes, Mama," Azria said. She watched her mother leave, avoiding Bolo's gaze as she opened the door to the room and stepped in.

He was sitting on the edge of the bed, fiddling with the rope in his hands. Azria couldn't help but think his expression looked hopeful. "Can I go now?" Zesh said.

"No," Azria said. "You're coming with us. To the island."

Zesh blinked before he laughed, a high-pitched giggle that was more nervous than anything else. "You're messing with me," he said.

"I'm not," Azria said. She watched as his smile dropped and his eyes widened, panic settling into his expression. "Hope you don't get seasick."

"My grandmother will come for me," he said.

"I think my mother is counting on it," Azria said quietly. Azria wasn't sure how she felt about meeting Iyzani in person. What was the woman like? What would she do if she came for Zesh? Would she land on the ship and fly away with him? Or would she appear in the blink of an eye and then be gone, the air hot with the energy of her spell?

Azria took a deep breath and looked to him. "Bolo will be watching you. If you need something, ask him."

"Alright," Zesh replied feebly. He just stared at the floor. Azria opened the door, expecting him to say something in response or even try to rush her and try to escape. Instead he didn't move as Azria slipped out, not even saying anything as she closed the door behind her.

"He's all yours," Azria said to Bolo.

"You're sure he's not a mage?" Bolo asked.

"Yes," Azria said. "Though apparently he's good at getting out of knots." She looked at Bolo, the tenseness he now held in his shoulders, the angles of his jaw set hard. "Are you afraid of me, Uncle Bolo?"

"What?" Bolo asked. His face scrunched up, confused. "No, why would I be?"

"Because I'm a mage." She watched as something like fear and then embarrassment crossed his features.

"No, Azria, I'm not afraid of you," Bolo said. "I know you wouldn't do anything to hurt me. Or hurt anyone. Even though I'm training you to kill people."

Azria laughed. Her thoughts wandered to her magic. She hadn't used it while on the *Hen & Chick*, not in any way the other crew members would have noticed. She still meditated in the morning, performed her morning exercises as Hiezh had trained her to do. She couldn't help feeling the energy in the still sheets, the breaths of everyone in the room, the roll of the sea under the ship. Magic was a part of her, but she still hadn't figured out what that meant on the *Hen & Chick*. Did it make her more dangerous than Bolo? More formidable than her mother?

"Just leave the killing to me and your mother," Bolo added. Azria's smile faded, thinking of the way her mother had tapped the hilt of her sword. The way her mother had spoken about The Innate. Was she going to use Zesh to lure her to the *Hen & Chick*, to try and kill her? If Iyzani confronted them, there was a chance Iyzani would try to kill her mother. What would Azria do? She couldn't have her mother taken from her, for good. The possibility of having to face another mage in a fight...Azria had never dreamed it would come to that, let alone that her first fight might be against one of the most infamous mages of Mizian history.

"Right," Azria managed, walking away from Bolo and towards the stairs. She walked down the stairs lost in her thoughts, the scents and sounds of the restaurant below barely registering to her senses. Pushing open the door, she stepped into the bar and blinked, surprise popping her mouth open.

The crew of the *Hen & Chick* was there. A quick glance around the room told Azria everyone else had cleared out of the bar. Only the barkeep remained, lighting the candles set on each table. So many sets of eyes were on Azria, she couldn't help but gulp.

"Oh good, you're here," Apzana said with genuine pleasure. "Now I can tell everyone the good news."

Azria walked over slowly, resisting the urge to run out the door. She steadied her breath, looking over the faces of those who would be counting on her. Brik and Brak, their bearded faces bright with curiosity. Onacá looked slightly annoyed, as if she had been dragged from something fun and was upset to have been interrupted. Yabi waved, oblivious to the tension in the room. Eixon was calm as always but Azria saw his eyes dart to a paper on the table and then back to her, his eyebrows rising ever so slightly. Red looked a bit drunk. And Jay looked pleased, her hands folded primly in front of her. Azria wondered what her own face looked like and hoped she was masking her panic sufficiently.

"Where's Bolo?" Brak asked.

"Detained," Apzana said. "Don't worry about Bolo, he knows what I'm about to tell you."

"Of course he does," Brik said, sounding a bit annoyed. "He knows everything the captain does."

"Stop talking, let the captain tell us why we're all here," Onacá said.

"I've called you all together to tell you about our next stop," Apzana announced, her voice loud without yelling. She had their attention. Azria stood by her mother again, wondering what their reactions would be. She couldn't help but look at Yabi, who was staring back at her, catching her in a blush.

"With our mage now on board and a map procured by Red, we can now take on an adventure worthy of our great crew," Apzana began. "The Marauders' Island is known by most of you, and all of you have heard tales of how it was swallowed by the sea. Many of you know the sea where it once stood is haunted. When the island was pushed below the waves, a great treasure went with it." Azria watched as realization swept across the faces of the crew members, showing in different ways. A bushy raised eyebrow, the corner of a mouth curling, a snort. "Azria, a mage of Miz, will raise the island. We will be the first to set foot on the island in a lifetime, the treasure free for us to take. The treasure of a thousand shores will be ours!"

There was no doubt the possibility of having the treasure all to themselves was exciting. Even Azria couldn't help but think about what riches lay below the waves, waiting for her hand to just reach out and grab them. Still the excitement trying to rise up among the crew was tempered by something. She could feel them sizing her up.

Azria's gaze strayed towards the ceiling and the second floor where Zesh waited, thinking about his role in all this. Dragged along on this mission. Putting the rest of the crew in danger.

"This quest will be dangerous," Apzana continued. "There are perils we know about. There are perils yet unknown." Azria watched as her mother's face turned so slightly, looking every person in the eye. "Those of you who don't wish to take on the danger, you are free to remain in the City of Peace. I'll end your contract with me, no hard feelings, as long as you swear yourself to secrecy regarding our quest. But this is the best crew I've ever had and this is a treasure you all truly deserve, so I hope you will all remain with me. So, who's with me?"

Azria held her breath, looking to the crew. Several of them looked at Azria before they directed their focus back to the captain.

"You have us both," Brik said loudly.

"You always answer first," Red snorted.

"It's because we're the bravest!" Brak said.

"If you say so," Red chuckled, shaking his head. "I'm going. After everything I did to get this map, I want some of the treasure."

"You'll need me to get there," Jay said nonchalantly, though Azria could see the excitement shining in her eyes.

For a moment, no one else said anything. Azria looked to those who hadn't spoken yet. Onacá's face darkened, her lips a thin line on her face as she pondered. As for Eixon, Azria could almost see the various thoughts he had about the whole situation written on his brow. "You three?" Apzana said.

"That sea is haunted," Onacá spoke up.

"I know," Apzana said.

"And I don't think taking the treasure is going to put those souls to rest," Onacá added.

"I have never cared about the souls of the dead, Onacá," Apzana said. "I've never said I did. And even if I did, the Marauders are not the ones I would care about. This is about treasure, not reconciliation. If you want some of it, come with me."

"I guess you will need food," Yabi chimed in.

"I've got a big appetite for many things," Apzana said.

Onacá sighed. "If Yabi's going, I'm going. Someone needs to keep an eye on her."

"Someone will need to help her count her treasure," Apzana said, winking at Onacá. Onacá didn't smile back. The captain turned her attention to the supply master. "Eixon? Last, as always."

"I wouldn't miss this for anything," Eixon answered, a brightness in his eyes Azria hadn't seen before. "To see our mage perform such a feat? I'd be a fool to leave now."

"Then it's settled," Apzana said. "We have our crew."

"Plus one," Azria blurted. Apzana turned her head sharply to Azria, her eyes narrowing slightly.

"Who is it, Captain?" Jay asked. "Another deck hand?"

"Not quite," Apzana said slowly, looking towards the crew again. "A prisoner, actually."

"What?" Yabi exclaimed. "Who?"

"A spy," Azria said. "With connections to the island. While I research the island and ways to raise it, I'll be asking him questions." Azria looked up at her mother and gave her a sideways glance. That was technically true. Azria didn't feel right, concealing the whole truth from the crew, especially if Zesh's presence might be a danger. At the same time, Azria didn't want to anger her mother. Perhaps with a careful wielding of the facts, Azria could stave off dangers that were only threats for the moment.

"A spy?" Onacá frowned slightly. "From where?"

"Miz," Azria said quickly.

"There are some who will try to stop us," Apzana said, lifting her hands to quiet the crew. "The Marauders' Island is not completely forgotten and the idea of getting any of the treasure will set many after us. That's why it's important no one speaks of our quest. Our secret weapon is Azria, who will be doing the bulk of the work. If she asks you for anything over the next few weeks, I suggest you provide it. Are we clear?"

"Yes, Captain," everyone said. Apzana nodded at them all and Azria watched as she smiled, her expression softening as she looked over the crew.

"Alright, you're dismissed. We won't be leaving for a while. Check in with Bolo and me every evening at dinner. Now, get back to whatever you were doing." Apzana waved them away. Brik and Brak left first, followed by Onacá and Yabi, Yabi looking over her shoulder to Azria, whispering something to Onacá before they got to the doorway.

"Captain, if you don't mind, I'll leave with Onacá and Yabi," Jay said. "We had plans."

"I dismissed you," Apzana said, her voice suddenly

sounding weary. She sat down and put her booted feet up on the table. "Get out of here."

"Want to come with?" Jay asked Azria cheerfully.

"I think I'll stay in tonight," Azria said, thinking about the clay tablet. "I've got a lot to do."

"Right," Jay said, disappointment creasing the corners of her eyes. "Well, maybe tomorrow. Can't work all the time! See you later." She waved a quick goodbye to Apzana and Azria, giving Red a quick kiss on the top of his head. The old man grimaced and waved her away as she giggled.

"I'm at your disposal, Mage," Eixon said. "Anything you need to perform this great feat, I am sure I can procure."

What did Azria need? She wished she felt how she had in the Vaults, after agreeing to go along with her mother's plan. Exultant, heart racing, the magic of the tablet still glowing in her mind. She needed to know she could keep her mother safe from the secrets Apzana was trying to expose, from monsters of the past who were broken people in the present. Azria thought about Yabi blushing when she looked at her and Zesh locked in the room, their looks of surprise. She wanted to know she could raise the island. If the mages of Miz knew she was doing this, what would they say? Azria shook her head inwardly. This test of her magic was harder than anything the Guild would have thrown at her back home.

Azria looked to Eixon, his typically calm expression brightened with his enthusiasm for the adventure to come. She wanted to know their desires wouldn't be dashed upon the rocks of her failure. She wanted to know they'd be safe from Iyzani's wrath and the ghosts who haunted the waters above the island. All of this she wanted.

"Thank you," was all she said to Eixon. Eixon waited there for a few moments, as if expecting her to say something. When she didn't, he turned towards Red and asked him something, the old man exclaiming in response. Azria sat there, ignoring the food and conversation, lost in her thoughts. Tomorrow she would focus on the tablet and start them down the path to the Marauders' Island. With a hand steadier than how she felt, she grabbed her glass of warm peach wine and took a gulp, swallowing a mouthful down. Magic wasn't for the fearful, she told herself, taking another sip.

Magic was for the bold.

Chapter 7
Sanguine Study

Azria placed her fingers on the edge of the circle, the ink crackling before it began to glow. Illuminated by the magical light, the room her mother had rented for Azria to inspect Iyzani's clay tablet felt smaller. Taking the vial of ink and brush in her hand, she took a deep breath before focusing her gaze on the tablet, set before her within the circle.

It had taken them two days to get all the supplies needed to examine Iyzani's tablet. None of the other crew members had complained about a few extra days on land, happy to play while the mage worked. A raw silk rug rested under Azria, the off-white fibers soaking up the deep blue ink made from clay and dried snails. Eixon practically glowed as they traveled the markets together, obviously in his element. The supply man slipped into languages the way other people changed shoes, gesturing wildly as deals were made. Azria

pulled her thoughts from the acquisition of the tools
and turned her attention to her task. Focus would be
needed.

The bristles of the brush drank the ink in the vial,
the darkly pigmented liquid wrapping itself around each
individual hair. As the ink rose up the bristles, Azria
breathed the spell into her tools. Lifting the brush out
of the ink, she drew part of a circle around the tablet,
painting symbols at four points. These were variations
of symbols Hiezh had taught her when she started her
training, standard characters each mage made their own
with a curve here, a flourish there. Azria smiled as she
painted the familiar runes, admiring her careful lettering as the magic shimmered on the ink.

She then painted a path from the circle around the
tablet to the circle she sat in, both of them within a larger
circle painted to contain the power of the spells cast. At
the neck of each circle, Azria carefully painted warding
signs, magical doors she could open and close at will to
control the flow of energy.

Azria placed the brush in the ink vial, careful not
to upset both before she set them on the floor, off of the
rug. Gazing over her line work, she reached out with her
right pointer and middle finger, barely pressing her dig-
its onto the still damp ink before she let the spell swirl
around in her belly, breathing it out into the ensorcelled
circles.

The circles glowed brighter, glittering lavender
light illuminating the room as Azria's magic circu-
lated through her workings. The energy of the spell
throbbed gently with every breath she took, as if it
were breathing along with her. In a way, Azria knew
it was. The young mage watched as the energy found

its way through the circles, flowing along the path she had carefully drawn in the deep blue ink.

Azria inhaled deeply, drawing her magic up into her chest. As she brought her power from her lungs to her heart, the rhythm of the light shifted in time with her heartbeat, a joyous thrum of amethyst luminescence. The magic in the tablet shimmered, effervescent as Azria's magic surged around it.

Azria regarded the tablet. Her hands rested on her lap but as she regarded the object with her magesight, she could feel the contours of the white clay, the grooves in the physical face of the object melting away as the magic became more prominent. Azria recalled the curse on the tablet. The old script still blazed across the face, laid over the green magic of the thing. "Let's see what this seal is all about," Azria whispered to herself, shifting slightly within the circle as she pushed on the magical doors, allowing her magic to wash over the tablet.

The magic glowed in response to Azria's, green and vibrant as the leaves in Nana's vegetable garden. The power in the object scintillated under her gaze, still alive with the intent of the caster. Her brows furrowed as she watched the flow and colors of the tablet's magic. Something about it was off. Azria had the impression of rubbing a cat the wrong way, and how the cat felt under your hand, its annoyance under the skin. Azria followed not the uneasy feeling in her hands but the feeling in her chest. There was more to this seal than what had first revealed itself.

The weave on the spell was tight, words and intent overlapping and knotted artfully to cause new action, miraculous and awful. Azria watched as the green tendrils of magic swelled before her eyes. With a start, the green magic unfurled, spreading through the circle. It crawled towards Azria so quickly, she almost recoiled and broke the circle she had drawn.

With a snap, she closed the door, severing a tendril of magic. The shred of green light wriggled before it dissipated, overcome by Azria's own spell. She gulped as the emerald glow of the tablet's magic swirled and surged, pushing at the confinements Azria had placed around it. Azria felt her heart thump in her chest as she watched the lavender light of her own magic pulse in time with her life, surrounding the tablet. The strange magic still reached out for hers and Azria felt a tightness in her throat and chest, as if something was coiling around her.

Azria blew out her breath, snuffing out the magic of the tablet and her circles, taking the light with it. The sudden darkness in the room made her blink as her eyes tried to adjust, the late afternoon sunlight less dazzling than the magic. Wiggling her toes before she stood, Azria walked to the windows, opening each one wide to let the air circulate in the room. Sounds of sea birds mingled with the smell of the salty wind and the burning spices of the City of Peace. "Back to the air," she murmured, lifting her hands towards the sky. "Back to the land, back to the sea, back to the soul," she continued, reciting the old closing Hiezh had taught her for magic workings of this magnitude. Azria sighed in the dark, weariness growing in every muscle of her body. The light dappling the hardwood floor was stretched thin, as if it were late afternoon. How long had she spent on the spell?

A timid knock on the door spun Azria around. "Is it safe to come in?" came the high-pitched voice.

Azria's face grew hot as she smiled. "Yes," she called loudly enough for Yabi to hear. The door creaked on its hinges as it opened, Yabi's brown eyes wide as she poked her head in.

"It's dark in here," Yabi whispered, pushing the door open. She held a tray of food in her hands, and after she had entered she closed the door behind her with a well-placed nudge of her foot.

"Sorry about that," Azria said, going to the candles Apzana had left her. With as little effort as was needed, Azria lit the candles, their yellow light flickering on the plaster walls. Azria heard Yabi suck in her breath as the flames rose up from their wicks, whispering something under her breath. From what Azria could guess, it was some charm or exclamation from her homeland. Azria watched as black smoke wafted off of the orange flames, the smell of beeswax already scenting the air. "Not a lot of magic where you're from?"

"Not really," Yabi squeaked. She held the tray out towards Azria, the bowls sliding forward slightly. "I hope you're hungry! I figured you would be. The magicians who performed in the palace would always ransack the kitchen after they performed for the Sovereign."

"So there's at least some magic," Azria mused. She sat on the floor and patted the space next to her, gesturing for Yabi to sit beside her. "What kind of mages do you have in Bol-Haybi?"

Yabi handed the tray of food to Azria, frowning as she thought over Azria's question. "The magicians get their power from the deities," Yabi said, sitting down as Azria looked over the food. Circles of grainy bread and two pats of tangy butter. Grilled fish, the white flesh stained orange, black and yellow with fire and spices that tickled Azria's nose. Salty and sour slices of lemon brightened the plate alongside the roasted green beans and garlic her mother favored. Golden and blush chunks

of peaches studded with rock salt sat in a bowl alongside the white cheese Azria wasn't fond of. Before she
could ask, Yabi pulled a small bottle of cold tea out of
her pocket and handed it to her. "They dedicate themselves to one or the other. In exchange, the deity be-
stows the...miracles, I think is the best word to use."

Azria tore a piece of bread in half, scooping up a
chunk of fish. "So they're priests."

"No, no, no!" Yabi said. "Our priests look for signs
for the future, try to read the past. They make sure the
deities are properly understood. Not only through their
favored mages, but through signs."

"The world is so big and magic makes it even
bigger," Azria said, shoving the food into her mouth.
Her stomach grumbled as the food hit her tongue,
her hunger growing inside of her. She chewed and
swallowed, watching Yabi fiddle with the ends of her
tunic. "I grew up knowing other lands and other people
had different powers and magics than us. But being the
first mage of Miz some people have seen...it's strange."
Azria sighed, not able to collect her thoughts. She
looked up at Yabi as she scooped up another chunk of
fish with the bread. A thought that had been nagging
at Azria since she boarded the *Hen & Chick* rose to the
surface of her thoughts and she stared at her food as
she asked the question. "Are you afraid of me?"

"Of course not!" Yabi said. Even without looking,
Azria could see the warm smile on Yabi's face. "I know
you're kind. And good. Maybe a little shy. But I'm not
afraid of you!"

"But you're afraid of my magic," Azria said, looking
up. Yabi blushed and tried to smile, her eyes squinting
as she tried to avoid Azria's gaze.

"Well, magic is strange and powerful!" Yabi said. "You can make fire with your thoughts!"

"But that's just it," Azria said quietly. "They're my thoughts. Mine. Magic is a part of who I am, Yabi. If you're not afraid of me, then why would you be afraid of my magic?"

"When my mother made a fire in the fireplace, I couldn't put my hand in it just because she made it," Yabi said.

Azria's mouth fell open to speak, but she couldn't think of anything to say. Not anything worth saying, at least. She sipped on her cold tea and looked at the clay tablet. It still sat on the rug, inert. She remembered the tightness in her throat and chest, the binding sensation. The green tendrils...that magic must have been Iyzani's. It had been untouched for decades. Mizian magic reacted strongly to the magic of other Mizians, wanting to join creative forces. But there was Mizian magic which was destructive. Should Azria be so quick to put her hand in the fire stoked by Iyzani?

"Well, what did I miss while I was inspecting the tablet?" Azria asked, picking up green beans with her bread.

"Well, everyone else is pretty happy to spend time in the city!" Yabi offered, trying to sound cheerful. "Your mother keeps reminding us we'll have to leave at some point. Eixon isn't back from clothes shopping for you. But he did find me the incense I was looking for."

"I'll be glad to have warmer clothes," Azria said. The City of Peace was colder than Azria was used to, and even her rainy season garments didn't keep her from feeling chilly all the time. The hot food Yabi had brought made her feel happy however, and the spices warmed her up.

"Are you going to eat your cheese?" Yabi asked.

"You know, I don't really like it," Azria said with a laugh. "I do like the peaches though!" Azria picked up the plate with the cheese and offered it to her. "You can have it if you like."

"Oh no, I can't," Yabi said, her face pale as she wrinkled her nose. "When I was a little girl, someone paid my brother with cheese and I ate a piece as big as my fist. I got so sick, he thought it was poisoned! He had to trade the rest to a doctor to make sure I wasn't dying."

Azria couldn't help but laugh at the story, trying to imagine Yabi as a child and her brother frantically taking her to the doctor over a gross but simple misunderstanding. Yabi eventually laughed too, their laughs fading to awkward giggles in the dimly lit room. Azria ate the rest of her food in silence, glancing over at the tablet between bites. There was something about it which hadn't been revealed.

In the dark ink of mages, someone had written *Sealed by The Innate.* Azria could only assume it was in fact Iyzani and not some other mage. Impersonating mages was not something commonly done in Miz, and the greatest mage of their time probably was not someone to be crossed. In addition, regardless of the inhumanity in sinking the island, the fact it had been done...it was something only a great mage could do. Iyzani was the great mage.

Azria took a sip of her tea as she thought, finding it surprisingly sweet, a hint of citrus keeping it from being cloying. Nana had told stories about spells cast by old mages, unwitting fools who broke spells and were changed forever, transformed into strange beings or transported to strange lands. Several books in Hiezh's library mentioned magical seals, calling them 'spells that sat' as opposed to 'spells that ran.' Most Mizian magic was done for the moment. Her scrolls were basically like a sentence that fell off before it was finished, waiting for her to say the last words so they could affect the world. Different things broke those seals, just as different mages cast spells in different ways. Magic was personal. By inspecting the seal and Iyzani's magic, she would get to know Iyzani. Iyzani, her great-aunt. Iyzani, whose grandson was locked away on the *Hen & Chick*, bobbing in the harbor.

"Do you think you'll be able to...do...undo her magic?" Yabi's words were quiet but the question filled the room.

"We're both trained in the Mizian ways," Azria answered.

"That's...that's not a yes," Yabi whispered. "It's a big undertaking. A huge undertaking. Probably the biggest task I've ever heard of that wasn't a story my mama told me before I went to bed."

"All stories come from somewhere," Azria said, finding herself agitated by Yabi's words. Yabi doubted her. Did Azria actually believe she could raise the island? Looking at the tablet, still lying on the rug, Azria realized she did. She didn't feel like there was any choice in the matter. Azria was going to do it. "I've studied magic all these years, Yabi. I know if I study her magic and the spell used to sink the Marauders' Island, I can undo it." Azria smiled to herself. She wished Nana and Hiezh were there to hear her speak those words. "Just give me time, Yabi, and your trust. And your cooking."

"I think I can do that!" Yabi said, blushing. Azria smiled sleepily, the bowl of food feeling heavy in her hands. "You look exhausted," Yabi interjected, taking the bowl from her. "I can't imagine how much energy this must take."

"This sort of spell does," Azria admitted. Even her clothes felt heavy on her. "If I was just writing a spell or taking the salt out of sea water, it'd be fine. But magical appraisal takes a lot of time and energy, especially something like this." Yabi offered Azria her hand to help her up, pulling Azria up in one motion. "Thanks."

"Don't mention it," Yabi said, holding the food bowls. Azria picked up the tablet, looking over its green glow again. She ignored the sound of Yabi drawing in her breath in surprise.

"I think I might take a nap," Azria said, stifling a yawn. "I'll have evening meal with you all and try to get a few more hours of study in before I go to bed. I'd like to have some information for us by tomorrow night at the latest."

"That soon?" Yabi asked, opening the door. Azria smirked, crossing the threshold and walking into the hallway. Red sat on the chair positioned right outside the door, and he just nodded at the two of them as they walked to the room Apzana had rented for sleeping.

"We have to leave the City of Peace sometime," Azria chided, giggling at Yabi's disappointed expression. "Don't you want to have more adventures on the ocean? See a ghost?"

"No, I do not want to see a ghost!" Yabi exclaimed. "Why would I want to see a ghost?"

"Are you trying to scare sweet Yabi, Mage?" Red called down the hall. "Don't do it." He pointed at her in what was probably meant to be a menacing manner. Azria just rolled her eyes.

"I'm just joking, Red," Azria said.

"Ghosts are nothing to joke about," he called. His eyes fluttered shut and he folded his hands in his lap.

"I'm going to take a nap," Azria said, opening the door to the room.

"So am I," Red said, not bothering to open his eyes.

"Old people," Azria muttered, shaking her head. Yabi giggled behind her, following her in. No one else was in the room. Four beds and four chests were the only furniture, Brik and Brak's various belongings spilling out from under their beds. Azria had brought some of her belongings from the ship and enjoyed the feeling of sleeping in a bed not rolling on the ocean waves. Right now, the small bed with the blue and orange blankets looked like the most beautiful thing in the world.

"I'll probably just read while you sleep," Yabi said, going over to her bed. Azria made a sound in an attempt to acknowledge she heard her before she kicked off her sandals, not bothering to get undressed before she crawled under the sheets. The top quilt was scratchy but the sheets were cool and soft and smelled like hay and lavender, an herb the Mudnebi believed helped sleep. Azria tucked the clay tablet under her pillow, by the knife Nana had given her. As her eyes drooped, she watched Yabi, sitting quietly on her bed, reading from a book. Azria tried to make out the title but just as she realized the words were in a language she didn't know, she drifted off to sleep.

Azria's eyes fluttered open. Her limbs felt like bags of wet sand. Was this a dream? Azria often dreamed of being back in Nana's house. She was sitting at the kitchen table, the same table where she had eaten her last meal in Miz. A pile of flowers lay in the middle of the table, red and purple, still wet from morning dew. Early morning shadows stretched across the clean, swept floors, the merest hint of morning sun starting to glow at the edges of the windows.

"You must be Nana's granddaughter."

Azria turned and looked. Sitting across from her at the table was a woman she had never seen before. Her skin was smooth but the deep lines at her mouth and nose told Azria she was older than Nana, her lips almost the same color as her skin. Her hair, wild and white, billowed around her head in a way that made Azria think of a fair weather cloud. Behind the old woman's left ear was a single calabaza blossom. The flower was so bright and yellow, it hurt Azria's eyes.

"I am," Azria said. Her mouth felt strange, as if stuffed with cotton. "And who are you?"

"A friend of Nana's," the woman said. Her voice reminded Azria of honeyed peppers, sticky sweet but fiery on the tongue. "I'm waiting for her. I haven't seen her in a long time."

Azria rose from the table, moving the chair without feeling the smooth wood under her grasp. Soundless, she walked through the front door, leaving the old woman behind her. "This is a dream," she said, trying to reassure herself it was.

"It's dark. Will you light a lamp?" the old woman asked. Azria turned to face the house, but the old woman was still behind her somehow. Dreams were strange in that way, Azria thought to herself. She stood on Nana's porch, overlooking her grandmother's property. All along the ground grew the thick emerald vines of the calabazas Nana used in her stews. Blossom buds wriggled, pale green among the deep green leaves.

"Nana!" Azria called. The sea roared close by, much

closer than Azria remembered it sounding. "Nana! It's me! Azria!"

"Azria, I'll help you find Nana," the woman said, behind her again. "Light a lamp and we will find her. She is probably in her garden somewhere."

One of Nana's chickens flapped across Azria's path, its fluttering wings kicking up a wind that made her wince. "How do you know Nana?" Azria asked. As she walked down the steps, she couldn't help but feel like she was floating.

"Friends from a long way back," the old woman said. "Very long ago."

"Nana?" Azria called again.

"Light a lamp," the old woman said, handing her a lantern. Azria took the lantern from the old woman, the coconut oil shimmering in the clay bowl.

"Azria?" a voice called from within the garden. Azria walked through the garden, under the jasmine trees and past herb bushes, trying to see Nana. Azria had recurring dreams about losing Nana in the market. She wondered if this dream would be the same, panic starting to rise in her chest.

"Nana?" Azria called, her voice sounding so quiet in her ears. "Nana, are you here? Nana! Nana, I need you!" Azria's eyes stung, oncoming tears made her face feel tight, as if anticipating the weariness of sobbing. She couldn't see her but Azria could tell the old woman was still behind her.

"Azria?" It was Nana's voice. Azria ran through the dim garden, trying not to trip over the thick vines crawling over the path, the fresh smell of leaves being crushed underfoot thick in the air.

"Nana, it's me!" Azria ran towards where she thought the voice was coming from. Another chicken flew up from the vines, squawking. Its feathers brushed Azria's face. Azria ran, knowing she should have reached the end of the garden already, the neat, painted fence Nana built and maintained. "Nana!"

"Light the lamp, Azria," the old woman said, her voice in Azria's ear. Azria whipped around, screaming. The old woman's breath was hot on her neck. She looked down to her hand, surprised to see the lamp was still there, full of oil.

"Azria?" Nana's voice came. "My girl?"

"Light the lamp so you can see your grandmother," the old woman said. She stood at the end of the path. Azria watched as the pumpkin vines started to climb up around her in the dark, the vines creaking.

"Nana!" Azria shouted, her heart thumping in her throat. The creak of the growing vines grew louder. "Nana, we have to get out of here!"

"Azria?" Nana's voice came, closer.

"Light the lamp, Azria," the woman said. Azria stepped back as the vines tightened around her feet. The rough flesh scraped against her ankles.

"Azria! The knife I gave you!" Azria looked over her shoulder, only to see Nana standing off in the tree-shadowed light. A cold wind howled through the grove, shaking the leaves of the trees like rattles. "The knife, girl! Kill her!"

Azria looked down to her hand, expecting to see the oil lamp. Instead, her hand gripped the hilt of the knife Nana had given her. Her fingers traced the carvings in the ivory handle, reading the words carved into it.

For Iyzani, a wound only time can heal.

Azria stared into the garden, the trees growing thicker. Their branches crisscrossed, a ceiling of leaves and wood to keep out the sky and stars. The harsh wind whipped over the foliage, the fleshy leaves of the calabaza vines scraping against each other. The figure of the old woman stood off in the distance, floating above the ground.

"Are you Iyzani?" Azria called, her voice still too quiet, her words devoured by the wind. Was she still dreaming? Had Iyzani infiltrated her dreams? Azria gulped hard, anger flaring inside of her like a flame. "How dare you come into my dreams and try to disgrace my memories!" In Miz, dreams belonged to the dreamer, a surreal creation of the mind. Mages only dealt with dreams if given permission by the dreamer. The trees pressed in closer, the wind growing colder as Iyzani's silence answered Azria's question.

"Iyzani!" Azria shouted. The air around her swirled. The leaves rattled on the trees as the branches scraped against each other. It was her dream. Azria could do what she wanted. "Iyzani, stand before me!"

Iyzani flashed into existence before her. The same woman who had sat at the table, asking for Nana. Her wild, white hair framed her face, her deep brown eyes full of surprise. The yellow flower tucked behind her ear faded. "I am here, Azria," Iyzani said, her voice far off and echoing though she stood before Azria. "What do you want from me?"

"Kill her!" came Nana's voice behind Azria. "Kill her! She deserves it!"

"Don't!" Azria looked beyond Iyzani's shoulder. A silhouette made its way through the dark grove. Azria blinked. It was Zesh. He leaned against a crutch. Azria couldn't see his face but she could taste the salt of his tears on her tongue. "Please!" Zesh cried out. "She's all I have."

This was just a dream. Azria drew in her breath as

she lifted her hand. Her hand ached from gripping the knife.

"Kill her!" Nana screamed behind Azria. "She took everything from so many."

"You're stalling," Iyzani said to Azria.

Azria furrowed her eyebrows. As she held the knife, ready to strike, she stared into Iyzani's eyes, wide and brown. They reminded Azria of her mother's.

"You are stalling," Azria said. "You are trying to buy time. You...you don't know what to do."

Azria watched as Iyzani's eyes filled with tears, the way a bowl filled with water. Tears streamed down her face, a torrent of sobs as a cold wind screamed around them. Azria heard Zesh and Nana calling to her, their pleas swallowed by the wind.

Azria turned around, away from Iyzani. Despite the influence Iyzani had at the moment, it was still her dream. Hiezh had taught her about dreams, the tenuous magic which operated there, usually sourced from different soils. Azria drew in her breath, knowing it was just her dream body. There was still truth in dreams. If she could remember parts of the dream, she could glean knowledge from them. Perhaps something about Iyzani.

Azria closed her eyes, intending to wake herself up. A piercing shriek from behind spun her around. A pale figure rushed towards her. Clad in rags, its red eyes glowed like fire. The stench of salt water and death washed over Azria. The trees withered as the blasted, pale apparition screeched past them, shrieking.

Azria screamed, throwing her hands in front of her face.

"Azria!"

Hands on her shoulders pushed her away. Azria

flailed as she fell back, landing on something soft. Her grip on whatever was in her hand loosened as she let it fall.

She was on her bed, on her back. Azria blinked and sat up, still feeling exhausted. Her eyes turned to see what she had been holding. Nana's knife lay on top of the sheets. Red blood glinted on the blade.

Azria looked up. Eixon had his hand on his face, blood seeping through his fingers. "Eixon!" she said. "Are you okay?"

"I'm alright!" he said, standing back. He said it not to Azria but the other people in the room. Yabi and Bolo stood back, their mouths hanging open. "It's just a scratch. It was an accident."

"What happened!?" Bolo demanded.

"She stood up from the bed," Yabi squeaked. "I didn't want to wake her. So I got Eixon to watch her with me."

"I was just dreaming," Azria sighed. She blinked as she realized it wasn't true. She'd had the knife in her dreams, and in her waking life.

"Why did you grab the knife?" Bolo asked, his voice strained.

"I just..." Azria didn't want to explain the knife. But she had to. "I grabbed it in my dream."

"What did you dream about?" Yabi asked, the tension in the room making Azria feel on edge, like her skin was crackling. Should she lie?

"I dreamed of Iyzani," Azria said, the truth easing some of the tightness in her chest. She looked up at Eixon, his face still bleeding through his fingers. "I dreamed she was before me." Azria thought about her dream, the knowledge it was more than a dream making the hair on the back of her neck stand up. She had to remember all the details.

"Iyzani, The Innate?" Bolo said, his dark eyes widening. "Azria, do you think it was actually her?"

"I...I think we should try to see to Eixon's wound first," Azria said, her eyes on the floor. Her embarrassment made her stomach feel warm as she looked up at the man. "I'm so, so very sorry, Eixon."

"It's just a scratch," Eixon said. He tried to smile warmly at her but winced, pain in his eyes. "I hope you aren't too tired to heal me, Mage." His words were laced with the slightest amount of worry. "There's no bloodshed allowed in the City of Peace."

"But," Yabi said before Azria could protest herself, "it was an accident!"

"I know it was an accident," Eixon said. "You know it was an accident. However, if any of the Mudnebi see this, they'll know I was cut. We must not tell anyone of this. They may not understand what happened."

"Are the Mudnebi that strict about their laws?" Azria asked quietly. She could feel the presence of the knife behind her, lying on the bed.

"It only takes one of them to take it more seriously than the others," Eixon said, pulling his hand away from his face and looking at his palm. It was more than just a scratch. The gash ran up his left cheek, deep enough that it made Azria's stomach turn. His well-trimmed beard was soaked with his blood, thick and wet. "I hope you can heal this quickly."

"Of course," Azria said, stepping towards Eixon. She was relieved to see he didn't flinch from her touch. She saw Yabi watching as she placed her hand on his face. Pushing her weariness aside, Azria spoke the healing words she had spoken many times before, a lavender flush glowing on her hand. The spell faded and she pulled her hand away, the spilled blood gone as well.

Azria's eyes widened as the gash on Eixon's face re-opened, blood flowing down his face. Eixon pressed his fingers to the wound, confusion knitting his dark brows together.

"Why is he still bleeding?" Apzana's voice made Azria jump. Azria spun away from Eixon, facing her mother in the doorway. Her mother looked as if she had hurried there, her calm exterior barely holding over a growing agitation. "Make it stop."

"I already tried," Azria said, dread creeping into her stomach. The knife lay on the bed, the blood already darkening, soaked into the blue sheets. She thought of the words on the hilt, her skin reading the inscription on the ivory.

A wound only time can heal.

"I can't heal it," Azria said. "The knife. It makes wounds magic can't heal. I..." Azria looked up to Eixon helplessly, her stomach knotting as the realization set in his dark brown eyes. "I can't."

"Bolo, get her out of the city," Apzana ordered. "Yabi, get Onacá."

"Mama," Azria huffed. "I can still help."

"Go," Apzana said. It was an order. Azria blinked, her mother's tone cutting into her.

Azria meant to mutter under her breath but couldn't think of anything to say, instead reaching under her pillow for the clay tablet. Bolo took a step towards her, Azria rolling her shoulder away from his grasp. "I can make it there myself," she spat, avoiding everyone's gaze as she left the room.

"Follow her," she heard Apzana say to Bolo.

"Don't you dare!" Azria shouted, holding her hand up to the door. With a burst of light she slammed the door closed, the force making the entire building rattle. Azria took a step back, listening to everyone in the room curse in various languages. The doorknob rattled as someone tried to open it.

"Azria!" she heard her mother shout. "Let us out of here!"

Azria bent her fingers up, her hands trembling as she stood there, frozen. It was an accident. It wasn't her fault. She could fix this. Running to the end of the hallway, she gestured towards the door to release it before running down the stairs, holding the tablet to her heart. She could unlock the secret of the tablet on the *Hen & Chick*. She would do it herself, with her magic, and no one would get hurt in the process.

Azria would figure out Iyzani's secrets. If Iyzani wanted to come for her, Azria would face her. If anyone's blood was spilled as Azria searched for answers, it would be her blood and hers alone.

Chapter 8
Faith and Practice

Azria felt every cobblestone underfoot as she sprinted over the streets of the City of Peace. Clutching the tablet to her chest, she rushed past the stares of the people trying to buy fruits, vegetables and other foods. Her heart pounded against the tablet as she ran, her breath trying to soothe the tingling in her legs.

Azria had done her fair share of running. Hiezh had made her run as part of her training, to feel her breath and body, the way her arms and legs and lungs all worked together. Nana would tell Azria to run while she could, while gripping the crab-claw handle of her cane. Azria had put their advice to good use and run from quite a few problems in her life. Speed was important but also stealth. Her legs were short, which meant she couldn't cover as much distance as some, but it made hiding in crowds much easier. At least it was in Miz. Azria cursed to herself as she ran past two Mudnebis in their blue-and-black clothes. She stood out here in her white linen garments, her dark hair freshly braided and wrapped in bright strips of cotton.

Azria turned a corner down a street with more buildings, slowing her pace to match those of the market-goers. More buildings meant more places to hide. She hurried past three alleys before she ducked into one, slipping behind one of the many crates stacked behind the business. Azria knelt on the ground, the street here made of hard packed dirt that felt gritty against her skin. She peered through the rough slats of the crate, watching the street for any suspicious movement. Had they chased after her?

A blur shot past the alley. As quick as they went, Azria still recognized Bolo. She waited to see if he doubled back or if any one else ran down the street. After what seemed like an hour, Azria sat on the ground, her back against the building, drawing her knees up, still hiding. She was safe at the moment. Why did she feel like crying? Azria stared at the tablet, her heart still thumping in her chest, the alley feeling small around her. Why had she run?

She ran because she was ashamed.

Azria swallowed the lump in her throat as she recalled Eixon's face. Wide brown eyes under thick eyebrows. Red blood. Her mother's demand. Yabi's mouth, fallen open with fear.

Azria fought back her tears as she stared down at the tablet, the faintest of green glows emanating from it. Had she done something to enable Iyzani to come into her dream? Had putting the tablet under her pillow been her mistake? Dream magic wasn't something Mizians often used, and if they did, they didn't use it against people. Surely she hadn't been wrong not to suspect it. Controlling people...Azria's hands began to shake, the reality of what had happened sinking in.

Iyzani had controlled her body. She had used a type of magic not used by Mizians, not gifted by the Goddess before she went to sleep beneath the waves. Acid rose in her throat. Azria remembered the cold feeling in her nerves as the blood began to pour from Eixon's wound a second time. Knowing her magic had failed her.

Her magic hadn't been disabled by Iyzani, she told herself. No, Iyzani had wanted to see her magic. Still, Azria's stomach went cold, the thought of her magic not working like ice in her gut.

Her magic still worked, Azria told herself. She had gusted the door shut and locked it. The tablet still glowed green under her touch. Was some remnant of Iyzani still with her? How had Iyzani been able to use her like that? Azria gulped as the question floated to the forefront of her thoughts. Had the elder mage's incursion caused her fellow crewmates to distrust her? She remembered her mother's order to Bolo. *Follow her.* Azria gritted her teeth in the alleyway, screwing her eyes shut against tears of frustration.

Something brushed against her leg. Azria jerked back, surprised to see a black-and-gray cat rubbing against her. The small beast purred loudly as it bumped its head against her shin.

Azria blinked, pulled from her anxious thoughts. Tentatively, she reached her hand out, her fingertips barely brushing against the cat before it nuzzled her hand, continuing to purr.

Azria chuckled at the cat, petting its soft fur. The cat opened its big green eyes, licking its paw as Azria stroked it, the small gesture calming her down. "I'm not alone," Azria murmured. "I can still do something."

Her magic still worked, Azria told herself. She could feel it. One failure didn't soak up all the ability she had cultivated over the years. Iyzani was the cause of all this trouble. Azria couldn't let her cause any more. Azria rose from behind the crate, giving the cat one more scratch behind the ears. "Thanks for snapping me out of it," she whispered, the cat mewing sweetly in response. Taking a deep breath, Azria walked up the alley and back onto the street, giving a quick glance up and down the road before she jogged across.

The southern road would take her to the docks. The *Hen & Chick* was moored at the eastern end of the Silver Bay. Azria ignored the myriad stores that faded into the covered stalls and open air blankets of the city. She wanted to get on the *Hen & Chick*. It was where she was supposed to go, anyway.

A man lit a streetlamp as Azria walked down the street, the cold wind blowing off the sea smelling both familiar and strange. The aroma of salt and fish reminded her of home but it mingled with the forests and hills surrounding the City, as well as the odors both pleasant and otherwise of the marketplace. Azria crossed the street, hoping she wasn't too far from where the *Hen & Chick* was moored.

Azria walked north along the street, quickening her pace as she saw the *Hen & Chick* in the distance. Dock workers coiled rope and loaded and unloaded crates, big boats being towed off in the distance. One of the dock workers waved at her and she waved feebly back, not sure if she should remember him or not. Azria breathed a sigh of relief as she arrived at the gangplank heading up to the *Hen & Chick*. The setting sun colored the whites of its sails orange and purple, and more than ever, her mother's ship looked beautiful. Azria walked up the gangplank, wondering who was guarding Zesh.

Azria glanced over the deck, listening for anyone on board. The only sounds were the creaks of the ropes and the waves lapping at the sides of the ship. If anyone was here, they would probably be below and they would probably hear her footsteps. Azria considered casting a spell to quiet her steps but she didn't want to spend her energy right now. She might need it later.

The yellow light of a lantern illuminated the staircase. "Hello?" she called down. She wasn't in the mood to be surprised. "Anyone down here?" Footsteps approached, making Azria stop halfway down the stairs. She breathed a sigh of relief as Jay walked into the light, her face dark with the shadows of the lamplight.

"Azria?" Jay said. "Is that you?"

"Yeah," Azria said, continuing down the stairs. She considered making up an excuse as to why she was here but something like anger began to simmer as she thought of the boy in the brig. Did he know something about this? "Is Zesh around?"

"What do you think?" Jay asked with a smirk. Azria walked past her, heading back to the brig where Zesh was being kept. When she walked in front of the barred door, he was already looking up.

"Your grandmother should be drowned," Azria spat, holding the tablet against the bars to the brig. Her hands trembled but Azria fought back her anger. It was tempting to take it out on Zesh. Zesh just frowned, still holding the scroll of paper he was reading from.

"What?" he said, his bushy eyebrows furrowing. "Why?"

"She broke into my dreams," Azria said. "Like a foreign witch. And her magic on this seal is all wrong."

"How do you mean?" Jay asked.

"This tablet is a seal, but I haven't figured out its role in the sinking of the island," Azria said. Zesh stared at her. Something in his expression told her he was more lost than she was.

"No, the dream thing," Jay said. "What do you mean?"

"I took a nap after casting a spell on the tablet," Azria began, looking down at its pale glow. "Iyzani came into my dream. She spoke to me. She tried to get something from me." Azria hated how vague her words sounded. She hated the uncertainty of the situation. She hated the way Zesh was looking at her, eyes wide, unkempt hair uneven. She wanted him to help her, to win him over to her side.

Jay said something under her breath. Azria glared at Zesh. "Mizian mages don't do such things. They don't enter the dreams of others, combing their thoughts for information. And they don't..." Azria didn't want to say it. She didn't want to admit what had happened in the room.

Azria's narrowed her eyes. Zesh had something around his neck. With a flick of her wrist, her magic lifted the pendant from where it was tucked into his shirt, the small trinket floating in the air.

It glowed gold.

"Hey!" Zesh said. "What are you doing?"

Azria moved her fingers back, untying the leather cord the pendant was on before she willed it to snap into her hand. "Give that back!" Zesh demanded, approaching the bars.

The pendant glowed in her hand, a soft, warm orange color. It reminded Azria of the spicy pumpkin soup Nana made. Her thoughts wandered back to

Iyzani standing before her, the flower in her hair, glowing in the same hue.

Iyzani's magic was hidden under the green, sprawling magic of the seal. It was in there, somewhere, under the weave of someone else's.

"Azria, what is it?" Jay asked.

"Iyzani gave you this pendant, didn't she?" Azria asked Zesh, fixing her eyes on him.

"Yes, it was a gift from my grandmother," Zesh huffed. He reached through the wooden bars, palm up as he glared at Azria. "Please give it back."

"For a prisoner, he's real polite," Jay said.

Azria held the tablet in both her hands, looking at it, focusing on it. The magic that manifested when she looked at it...it was not just The Innate's. It was someone else's.

Azria couldn't help but wonder how Hiezh would see the tablet, if he inspected it. Azria experienced magic as colors and sensations, while Hiezh experienced sounds. Perhaps if Hiezh was here, he would have heard the harmony of the tablet instead of seeing what Azria saw. Then again, as Azria concentrated, what had felt off about the tablet before tingled in her fingers, a swirl of colors before her eyes.

The magic of three people was at work here.

Who had helped Iyzani? Azria looked to Zesh. "Did your grandmother ever mention any friends?"

Zesh just glared at her, still holding out his hand. With a sigh, Azria placed the pendant in his hand. Zesh fastened it around his neck and sat back down before he spoke.

"Of course she did," Zesh said. "She wasn't a monster. She had friends."

"Who is Iyzani and what do they have to do with all this?" Jay asked.

"She's a mage," Azria said, her eyes still on Zesh. "And a traitor." She hoped the glare she gave would make Zesh keep his mouth shut.

"A traitor?" Jay asked, her thin brows rising in her face. "Who did she betray?"

"It doesn't matter," Azria said, turning away from them both. The sound of footsteps, quick and heavy on the deck, made Azria cringe. Someone was running. Probably looking for her.

"If it doesn't matter, why am I in the brig?!" Zesh shouted.

"Because you're a spy," Jay said. "We don't want anyone to stop us or get a head start on us."

"I'm here because your mother thinks she can use me as leverage when Iyzani comes for me," Zesh called after her. "I'm here because she believes a lie."

"Ignore him," Azria said, catching herself. She sounded just like her mother. Same commandeering tone. Curt. She turned around to see the hint of surprise in Jay's dark eyes.

"Yes, Mage," Jay said with a nod of her head.

"Are you going to blast us off the side of the ship?" came Bolo's voice from around the corner.

"No," Azria huffed. "Not today at least."

Bolo poked his head around the corner before he stepped into the hall. "So, any reason why you tried to give us the slip?" Bolo looked past her down the hall-way, to Jay.

"I don't need a babysitter," Azria said. "I can handle myself."

"When you stab people and run away, it doesn't really make people think they should let you out of sight," Bolo said. Azria scowled at him but the man didn't flinch.

"What's this about stabbing?" Jay asked. "I'd like to know about the stabbing."

"I didn't stab anyone!" Azria said, her voice pitched with anger. "You know I didn't! It wasn't me. It was Iyzani!"

"Until we know what happened and that you're safe, we need to stick together," Bolo said. "We can't let news of this get out, Azria. You know what could happen."

Azria nodded somberly. Prison. Or banishment. Eixon said the officials might not accept their account of what had happened. Blood was blood. "Is Eixon going to be okay?" Azria asked quietly.

"What happened to Eixon?" Jay said.

"You tell her," Bolo said. Azria's face grew hot, but she knew Jay would find out anyway. It'd be better if she found out from her. She turned to face the navigator, but kept her gaze on Zesh, who was watching from the small brig.

"I cut Eixon with a knife," Azria said. Jay's face darkened with confusion, but her eyes grew wide as the realization hit her. "No one in the City knows I drew blood," Azria assured her. "But how and why I did it..." Azria faltered in her words, not sure what to say. She looked to Zesh again, wanting to see his face when she spoke. "Iyzani came to me in a dream and made me take up a blade. I was sleepwalking because of her influence. Eixon got too close, and I cut him."

"Why didn't you just heal him?" Zesh asked before Jay could.

"I tried," Azria said. Her words sounded so small. "But my magic won't work on this wound. The knife, it's...strange. It wasn't made with magic, but it makes wounds magic can't heal." Azria thought of the inscription on the hilt. In her dream, Nana had screamed for Azria to kill Iyzani. When Nana had given her the knife, she said the blade was for 'some woman I used to know.' The hole in the story of Nana and Iyzani gaped in Azria's thoughts. Azria realized just how much she didn't know about her grandmother, and the thought loomed larger than the threat of the knife itself.

"Onacá is seeing to his wound," Bolo said. "He'll have a scar but he'll be fine, Azria."

Azria puffed out her cheeks, giving a sigh of relief. "I'm glad to hear it. If I can help in any way, please, let me know."

"You can keep working on the tablet," Bolo said, nodding his chin towards it. "The longer we stay here, the more likely we're going to get in trouble. If Iyzani is coming for you, it'll be harder for her to get us out on the open water."

"Well, she can probably fly," Azria said.

"Of course she can fly," Bolo said, rolling his eyes. He shook his head and exhaled, the weariness in his eyes tempered by the shrug he gave. "Your mother is in her quarters. She wants to see you."

"Why didn't she come down here herself?" Azria asked, not able to dampen her accusatory tone. Bolo raised a brow at her and pointed up the hallway.

"Just go, Azria," Bolo said.

"Please tell your mother I said hello," Zesh called after her.

"Don't tell me what to do," Azria called back, not bothering to turn around. She skipped up the steps, still holding the tablet in her hand.

The sky glowed shades of darkening blues and purples, the first few points of light glimmering against the lingering sunset. Azria stared up at the sky as she collected her thoughts, leaning against the wall. Staring at the stars from the deck was something she liked about being on board the *Hen & Chick*. Tracking their movements and trying to find the constellations she had learned about back home. Sometimes she'd ask one of the other crew members what they called the same constellation. Brik and Brak always had the strangest answers. Yabi always wanted Azria to go first. For now, though, the deck was empty. Azria took a deep breath before she headed to her mother's quarters.

The door was slightly ajar but Azria knocked anyway, pushing the door open so she stood in the doorway. "I'm here, like you asked," she said, managing to keep her voice even. Her mother sat on a chair, her hands wrapped around an ornate wooden cup.

Apzana looked up, as if roused from deep thoughts. She gestured towards the chair next to her with a nod of her chin. "Sit," she said, her voice considerably calmer than the last time Azria had heard her speak. "Close the door behind you."

Azria hesitated before she entered the room, shutting the door as her mother had instructed, and walked past the table to the chair. She couldn't help but look at the books on the table, as well as the blue glass bottle half full of liquid, the cork on its side. The books were in some language Azria couldn't read, as well as the lettering on the bottle. Golden Isle script. Azria settled down in the chair, smiling uneasily as she sank into the cushions that smelled of sage and smoked salt.

"Do I need to lock you up too?" Apzana asked. It was a serious question. "Tell me the truth, girl."

Azria thought about what she wanted to say. The room was strangely quiet and Azria smelled the clean, floral aroma of her mother's drink, mingling with the candle wax. She stared down at her own hands, still holding the tablet. "If you want to lock me up to keep you all safe from me—"

"That's not it," Apzana interrupted. "Never that." Apzana leaned towards Azria, the light of the candles throwing strange shadows on her face. "Azria, I'm not so stupid as to think you cut Eixon on purpose. I'm not scared of you. And I won't let anyone who is afraid of you on this ship."

"Except Bolo," Azria said.

"Bolo's not afraid of you," Apzana said, rolling her eyes. "I'd kick him off the ship if he was."

"I know," Azria said, slumping down in her chair. "What do you mean, then? About locking me away? I mean, how am I supposed to take that?"

"Can I keep you safe?"

Azria looked up at her mother. She could see the worry in her dark face, the creases of her mouth and eyes. Her mother looked old, and tired. More than anything, she looked like she needed an answer.

"Eixon's the one who got cut, Mama," Azria said.

"I know," Apzana said. Her mother leaned forward in her chair and took her hand. "Azria. I know finding the treasure is going to be dangerous. I do dangerous things." Her mother gave her a smile Azria assumed was meant to be reassuring. "But you're my daughter. And a mage."

"You think I can't handle myself," Azria said.

"No!" Apzana said. "I just...I didn't realize how much I was afraid of losing you again."

"You never lost me," Azria said. "You just...went away for a while."

"If something were to happen to you, Azria, I would

lose myself," Apzana said. "I didn't think Iyzani would come after you, not like this. Eixon bled, but she attacked you."

"I'm fine, Mama," Azria muttered. Her eyes stung, and the same tears which had threatened to fall in the alley came again. That was how she felt. Attacked. Her mother's words softened the pain in her chest. They weren't accusatory or distrustful. They were full of concern. Her mother was still behind her, not because Azria could do something she wanted. Apzana cared. Azria thought back to the dream, the knife and how she had held it over Iyzani. The indecision that lingered in the air, still, as Azria considered their path. "In the dream, she was there, but I was in control."

"But you picked up the knife, Azria, and you didn't even know it."

"But I did know it," Azria said, sitting up in the chair. "I had the knife in my dream. And Iyzani was before me." Azria tried to recall as much of the dream as she could, worried at the uncertainty that had already slipped in. "She just waited there, before me. I raised my hand to strike her but...I couldn't."

"Because she wouldn't let you?" Apzana asked.

"Because I didn't want to," Azria said. That was the truth. "Even with Nana telling me I should. She was in my dream too."

"Azria," Apzana said. "Do you believe me when I say I thought she'd come after me?"

Azria looked up into her mother's face. There was something in her expression that made Azria gulp. Her mother wanted Iyzani to come for her. It wasn't jealousy. It was defiance.

"I do," Azria said.

"Good," Apzana said, taking another drink from her

cup. She turned to look at Azria again. "Now, I'll ask you this again. And answer me straight, girl. Can I keep you safe?"

"Mama, no." Azria sighed. She looked down at the braided rug on the floor. "We've already started down this path, unraveling this magic. Even if you sent me back to Miz right now, which I don't want, Iyzani knows about me. I'm sure she knows what we're up to. When you asked me to join the crew, you offered me danger and I took it, Mama. But I'm a mage of Miz. The cataclysm of creation runs through my veins. That's what we say, at least. My life was going to be trouble no matter what. I want to see this through." Azria looked up at her mother, trying to think of something to say that would reassure her. "I'll do my best to keep everyone safe from Iyzani, including myself. But don't get in my way." Azria blinked, taken aback by her own words.

Apzana took a sip of her drink and looked ahead, her eyes on the door. She swallowed before she handed the glass to Azria. "I guess we do have that in common, girl. Give us a taste of something, we want the whole thing." Azria sniffed the drink before she took a sip. Coconut wine, just like back home, though this one tasted grassy and sweet. "Can you promise me something?"

"Depends," Azria said, wondering if she should give back the cup but not wanting to.

"Promise me you'll look out for yourself, first and foremost," Apzana said.

"Mama—" Azria started.

"Please," Apzana said. "Please. Everyone else is capable on this ship. They can take care of themselves. Don't worry about them."

"Alright," Azria said, not sure if she believed her own words. She wanted to become friends with the others on board the *Hen & Chick*. Vowing not to help them if they were in need didn't seem like a step towards building relationships. Not that her mother said she couldn't help them at all. Azria took another sip of the drink, trying to swallow the lump in her throat.

"I did want to say," Azria offered, "I think I should be able to figure out the tablet and its tie to the island. Something from the dream and Zesh, of all people, have given me a clue. I think there's more than one mage's magic at work here."

"So we're close?" Apzana said, leaning forward again. Azria recognized the look on her mother's face. It was the same as in the treasure vault. Gold hungry.

"I'm close," Azria said. "I think I can have something by tomorrow."

"I can't wait to get this hull bucking," Apzana said with a laugh, holding her hand out towards the cup. Azria pulled it back and narrowed her eyes, smirking.

"I've had a taste," Azria said.

Apzana laughed out loud, Azria chuckling with her. Her mother grinned, pulling out another cup and pouring herself a drink. "See to the tablet. Sort it out. I want someone watching you when you cast. And Onacá and Red will see to your sleeping."

"What's that mean?" Azria asked, frowning.

"Charms," Apzana said with a wave of her hand. "Nothing as serious or involved as magic but charms which should help to keep Iyzani away from you."

Azria wanted to refuse the workings of Onacá and Red. But she couldn't help but be curious as to what they would do. Plus, if it would make her mother feel better about the whole situation, Azria didn't think it could hurt. "So you're going to tell the rest of the crew about Iyzani?"

Apzana frowned and narrowed her eyes at Azria, her answer apparent without speaking. "Mama!" Azria said. "Bolo knows. So does Eixon and Yabi. And Jay. Don't you think you want your capable crew to know what exactly they'll have to go up against? Since we know?"

Apzana exhaled slowly. She didn't want to tell the crew about Iyzani for some reason. Her full mouth was pulled in a frown, her gaze set on the books on the table. "Mama," Azria started. "Your crew trusts you. You having a personal stake in the Marauders' Island shouldn't muddy the waters. There's still a lot of treasure for everyone! And no one would think you were doing this for Miz. They know where your loyalties lie."

Apzana gave her a glance Azria couldn't decipher. Her mother simply nodded and took another sip of her drink. "I'll tell them about it tomorrow."

"Sounds like a plan," Azria said. She couldn't help but feel a bit smug, knowing her mother was going to follow her advice. Azria was right about telling the crew. Was her mother worried they'd get scared off? Finding a new crew would take time they could be spending heading towards the treasure.

"Take it easy tonight," Apzana said with a sigh, placing her hand on Azria's. "Eat a good meal, have a good rest. Tomorrow might be the biggest day of your life. At least until we actually get the treasure."

"I think I'll have the soup at the inn," Azria said. "It's probably the best thing they have there." Apzana gave her a sideways glance and gulped her drink, a guilty look painted across her expression. Azria frowned, disappointment making her shoulders droop. "I'm not going back to the mainland, am I?"

"Not until this is over, not to the City of Peace,"

Apzana said quickly. "We can't risk you getting banished because of some witch's doings."

"She's not a witch," Azria said.

"What?" Apzana said.

"She's not a witch," Azria repeated. She remembered her own words below deck, to Zesh. She hadn't called Iyzani a witch, not exactly. But accusing her of using witch's magic...it was basically the same thing. Azria pushed her own allegations from her thoughts. "She's a mage of Miz, just like me."

"She's not just like you, Azria," Apzana said. "Not at all. I'll have one of the other crew members bring your belongings to the ship."

"Including the knife?" Azria asked, cocking her head to the side.

"Yes," Apzana said, much to Azria's surprise. "If that knife makes a wound no magic can heal, I want you to have it. If Iyzani comes for you, you'll know what to do."

"Right," Azria murmured, looking down into her cup. "I'm actually hungry so if someone could bring me some food, I'd like that."

"What would you like?" Apzana asked.

"Nothing with cheese, please. Something with rice, if they have rice here," Azria said.

"I'll see what I can get Bolo to find," Apzana said. Azria nodded and rose from her chair, setting her cup on the table before she walked towards the door, about to push it open. "Are you sure you don't want to just...sit and talk for a while?" her mother called after her.

"I'm not really feeling like company at the moment," Azria said with a shrug, feeling awkward.

"Oh," Apzana said. Azria winced inwardly, hearing

the sadness in her voice. Her mother drained her glass and set it on the table. "That's fine. I'll just go find Bolo."

"We can sit, it's fine," Azria said quickly, knowing it was already too late.

"No, you need some time to yourself," Apzana said with a wave of her hand. Apzana rose from her seat and started towards her, her shoulders drooping as if she was carrying a heavy load. "Once we get out on the sea, we'll have so much time to talk. We'll get sick of each other."

"Alright, Mama," Azria said, feeling a knot in her stomach for refusing her. Her mother leaned over and kissed her on the forehead, giving her a quick squeeze that made Azria wince with embarrassment. Before she could say anything else, Azria turned and walked out of the room, ignoring the feeling of her mother watching her and listening to her footsteps as she slipped below deck.

The lights of the City of Peace glowed yellow, points of brilliance within the chaos of the city. The beacon in the lighthouse shone bright and steady, the bright colors of the facade swallowed by the darkness of the chilly summer evening. Azria didn't think she would miss walking the streets of the City of Peace. Not being able to made her want to be there. Azria laughed at herself, resting her elbows on the side of the ship and her face in her hands. Isn't that just how it was?

She'd be back, she told herself. After the trouble was over. After she raised the island from the sea. She'd return with a bag of money and no cares. Azria smiled as she closed her eyes, imagining the fun she would have, once she put this and Iyzani behind her.

Azria set the tablet in front of her. She glanced up at

Eixon, sitting on the cushion he had asked for. His face looked uneven with the poultice applied to his cheek, secured with wide, white fabric that kept his hair back. The medicinal herbs Onacá mashed gave the air an astringent scent which stung Azria's nose. She had seen Onacá's stitch work. It was clean and even, the stitches enough to close the wound and no bigger. It would leave a scar. When Azria had asked for a volunteer to watch while she cast her spell, Eixon had eagerly volunteered.

"Are you ready for me to begin?" Azria asked, trying to sound strong.

"Yes, Mage," Eixon said, sitting up straighter on his cushion.

"You can call me Azria, Eixon," Azria said. "I think we're past formalities."

"Fair, Mage," Eixon said with a smile. He wasn't wincing when he smiled anymore, which was good. "I mean, Azria."

"Thank you," Azria said, trying not to chuckle. There was something nice about hearing him call her by her name. "I'm going to begin."

"I'm still not entirely clear what I'm watching for, Mage," Eixon said. "I mean, Azria. My apologies."

"It's fine," Azria said. "Well, it's my mother who wants me watched at all times. Just sit there. Nothing strange should happen."

"Except all the magic you are about to do, correct?" Eixon asked.

Azria opened her mouth to argue with him but stopped herself, nodding her head with a sigh. "Right, magic."

"It's difficult, isn't it?" Eixon asked.

"What is?" Azria asked.

"Creating a new normal for yourself," Eixon said.

"Especially when in doing so, you must accept you are the outsider, and work your way in."

Azria looked down at the tablet, trying to think of a way to answer him. "I've always been on the outside, Eixon," she said. "Even in Miz. Rumors will do that."

"I can relate," Eixon said, nodding. Azria gave Eixon a sidelong glance. Something told her they were at the edge of a very long conversation, one which could press on till the sun went down. Eixon, for all his politeness, was intrigued by Azria's magic and until now, Azria had never really wondered why.

"Maybe we can talk about it after this is over," Azria said, not sure if she was asking or telling.

"I think I would like that," Eixon said with another of his charming smiles. "I do know of a good bakery where we could have a cake and a pot of tea," he said. A glint in his dark eyes told Azria he was referring to their conversation back when they had first approached the City of Peace. It seemed so long ago.

"I'd like that," Azria half-whispered, her face growing warm. She blinked her embarrassment away and cleared her throat, shifting her weight on her legs. "Anyway, I'm going to start. If I look like I'm in trouble...run away?"

"Pardon?" Eixon said.

Azria drew in her breath and exhaled, enclosing herself and the tablet within a dome of magic. The rest of the small room melted away, Eixon's figure blurred by the glittering amethyst of her will. Under her legs she could feel the rock of the ocean, familiar and strong, the *Hen & Chick* giving in to the lull of the waves. Still, Azria steadied her mind and her breath, looking at the seal before her.

Reaching out with her hands, Azria extended her

fingers, flexing them towards the power that hummed greener and stronger under the vault of her will. Azria felt along the weave of the spell at the surface, trying to feel where it overlapped and intertwined. The green glow pulsed, meeting the violet light of her own, rubbing against each other like scales. Vibrations ran along her skin as the magic of the tablet scintillated, meeting Azria's influence. Azria ran her fingers up and down the magic which swirled around her, trying to touch what her instincts told her was there. The sensation of vines wrapping around her arms returned and she recalled the calabaza vines in her dream.

Azria gasped, trying to keep her triumph under control so as not to disturb the spell. A flash of gold. "Show yourself to me," she whispered. Letting her magic wash over the tablet, ripples of purple poured over it, exposing the threads of the spell. They sparkled and under Azria's watchful eye, she saw there were two shades of green. Close in energy, they wove together almost seamlessly. Whoever the mages were, they must have worked together intimately, close enough to emulate each other's magic.

She had been right. Three people's magics were at work here. Azria took a deep breath before she exhaled, pushing away at the weaving. Under her will, the threads frayed ever so slightly, tightening at first. Still, Azria summoned her power, flecks of gold showing themselves to her desire. The tight sensation in her throat and chest grew, as if thick vines were wrapped around her arms. Azria gritted her teeth and pushed against the weave harder, feeling where it was weak and digging the tips of her fingers into it.

Azria gasped as the clay cracked. A seam popped into the face of the tablet as the hard surface gave way.

The green magic split into millions of brilliant motes.
They spun around Azria, a cloud of emerald, enveloping
her in their verdant illumination.

It floated before her eyes. Golden bright, it sparked
red and yellow. Its power crackled like lightning. The
heat reminded her of the warm Mizian sun on her face.
Azria's mouth fell open, her hands trembling slightly as
she held it in her will.

The spell Iyzani had cast. The will of Iyzani, turned
into raw power. The working that sunk the Marauders'
Island.

Azria had found it.

The green light began to pulse and fade, the magic
which had kept Iyzani's intent tied up and contained.
Azria felt the sensation of vines falling away from her
limbs, freeing her. The soft glittering purple of her
magic shimmered more brightly as the jade winked out,
the colors coalescing like glittering opals all around
her. Azria saw where her magic began and theirs ended
but separated from the gold of Iyzani's magic, it seemed
to falter.

Azria had to do something with the spell. Cupping
her hands around it, the energy of the spell made her
heart pound in her chest like hurricane waves. Her own
will poured out of her as she exhaled, keeping the energy moving, trying to feel the workings of the magic.

The spell felt sharp in Azria's hands, despite its
spherical manifestation. The longer she held it, the
hotter it grew, like a knife being heated in the flames.
Azria bowed her head, keeping her hands steady and
she breathed in and out, her will and Iyzani's mingling.
There was anger in this spell, emotions which had
been put under pressure for years and years. Carefully

manipulated until it could be contained no longer. Unleashed with precision.

Azria opened her eyes. This was a part of the spell. Part had driven the island down, below the crash of the waves. The energy displaced by the spell, the will of whoever had caused the island to rise in the first place...Azria held it in her hands. Iyzani had bound it and sealed it away.

Moving her fingers and speaking under her breath, Azria willed her own magic around the sparking orb, around and around and around again. It spun, throwing violet and gold light all around. Her own magic grew brighter to meet the golden power of the orb. Her own power surged through her body, the beat of her heart encasing the orb till not a shred of gold was visible.

Azria exhaled, letting the orb settle into the palms of her hands. It was still warm, and touching it, she sensed the angry energy swirling within the new containment. It was purple, much like the stones in the bracelet her mother had given her, faceted irregularly but strong enough to hold it.

Her protection spell melted around her, the room coming into view. Azria looked up, her eyelids feeling heavy. Eixon stared at her, his mouth open in a stupor.

"Get my mother, please," Azria managed to say, weariness welling up within her.

"I know how to raise the island."

Chapter 9
On The Horizon

Azria clutched the rigging of the boat, feeling the metal rungs against the soles of her boots. The cold sea wind washed over her face, biting at her ears and cheeks. Long silk socks kept her legs warm under the wool wraparound skirt, the socks fastened around her thighs with shell buttons. A linen undershirt kept the rough fabric of a thick brown tunic from irritating her skin. Azria had left the thick fur coat and silk-lined cowl in her stow box. She couldn't imagine the weather required for such heavy garments. For now, she enjoyed not feeling cold as the wind streamed past her. With the force of the gales bending around her, fluttering her garments, Azria could easily imagine flying over the sea, her magic willing the air to keep her aloft as she sped over the waves.

Her mother shouted something from the deck. Azria looked down. Even from this elevation, she could see the worry on her mother's face, the disapproving frown with the furrowed, worried brow.

"She asked if you've had enough!" Brak said. Azria grinned, feeling how dry her lips were from the blustering wind.

"I had to make sure these clothes were warm enough," Azria said, knowing she wouldn't have to shout for him to hear her.

"You look plenty warm to me!" Brak said. He smiled a toothy grin, squinting against the wind. Azria wondered how he and his brother didn't get their horns caught in the rigging when they were leaping about, but the Skyward men seemed to be aware of every inch of their bodies, turning their heads to look around just so, their hoofed feet never missing a rung or getting caught on a rope.

"It's a nice feeling!" Azria said. She didn't realize just how chilled she was until she put on the new garments. The City of Peace had been warm but dry, with cold nights which made it difficult to sleep. A thick quilt for her bunk would make sure that wouldn't happen aboard the *Hen & Chick*.

"You should just grow some fur like Brik and me," Brak said with a hearty laugh. "I'm sure it wouldn't be too much trouble, for a mage such as yourself."

"Now why didn't I think of that?" Azria said, laughing as well. The thought of growing fur made Azria giggle. Back when she had studied with other Innates, they would often take turns, spinning simple glamours to change the shape of their mouths or eye color. Azria had grown her hair a handful of times, when an occasion called for longer hair and no other style would satisfy her vanity. Hiezh would chide her, telling her not to waste her abilities on such frivolous spells. Fur would keep her warm but Azria didn't think she'd be spending energy on that just yet.

Azria looked down again. Her mother had warned her about looking down. Some were easily dizzied by heights but Azria didn't find herself disoriented up on the mast of the *Hen & Chick*. She watched as her mother waved, trying to get her attention before gesturing for her to come down. "I should probably get back on deck," she said with a slight sigh.

"Come back any time," Brak called, climbing higher up the mast. Azria kept her eyes on the rungs as she turned and began her descent, the wind biting at her skirt and legs. When she was a few strides above the deck, she jumped down, landing on the deck with a thump.

"Do you need me, Mama?" Azria asked, cheerfully.

"I need you to be on deck, not up in the sky," Apzana said, her words tight with worry. "And that's Captain Mama, girl."

"I had to make sure my new clothes were warm enough," Azria said, grinning as she spun around to model them. "Can't be cold when I'm casting." The new clothes, along with the approaching quest, had Azria in high spirits. The City of Peace melted behind them into the Silver Bay and the high winds carried them towards the Marauders' Island. Excitement bubbled in Azria's stomach.

"Do you approve of them?" Eixon asked. "I had no doubt Onacá would follow my instructions to the letter. But it pleases me that they suit you." Eixon had been quarantined to the small room above the restaurant, Onacá having to do all the supply runs on his behalf, including a new set of clothes for the mage. Tales of an upset stomach had satisfied most of Eixon's contacts.

His face was still bandaged but Onacá had simplified the dressing to a square of fabric placed on the wound with honey.

"I do, Eixon, both their function and form," Azria said with a nod of her head. She was fairly certain the beautiful details of the garments were more Onacá's work than Eixon's. "My thanks to you, and Onacá of course."

"My pleasure," Eixon said.

"Your hair's all messed up," Apzana huffed, interrupting their niceties.

"There're no Mizians here to judge the state of my hair, Mama," Azria said with a laugh. Her mother cocked an eyebrow at her and Azria smirked. "I mean, if anyone's hair needs to be set, it's yours."

Apzana started to scowl at Azria but the corners of her mouth curled ever so slightly. "If Nana could see you now," Apzana sighed.

"She'd tell me my hair was a mess and not to talk to you like that," Azria said.

"If you're done playing in the rigging, we can talk about what's going to happen once we get to the island," Apzana said. As if on cue, the door that led below decks swung open, Onacá, Yabi and Red stepping through the doorway. Apzana brought her fingers to her lips and let out a shrill whistle that summoned the rest of the crew. Azria tried not to grin, standing among the rest of the crew.

"Alright, we've put the City of Peace behind us," Apzana said. "As always, we're moving forward. Little Yarix said the fine weather should hold out for the next phase and Jay agrees, so we should be at the Marauders' Island in five days at the most.

"I know we haven't done a straight treasure grab in

a while," Apzana continued. "So I'll remind you, we load up until Onacá says we can't carry more. Grab the best items and that means most valuable, not most bulky. If you have a question, ask Bolo or Eixon to do a quick appraisal. For most of us, this'll be the easiest haul we'll ever pick up. Azria's doing the heavy lifting," Apzana said with a smirk.

"And we have a guarantee the island will be lifted?" Red grunted from the back. Azria resisted the urge to spin around and give the man a dirty look.

"Our mage says it'll be done. I doubt she'd let us waste the trip," Apzana said.

"It'll be the most difficult thing I've ever done," Azria said, turning to face the crew. She could read the doubt on some of their faces. She focused on the shining eyes and hopeful smiles of those who knew it would be done. Brik and Brak. Eixon. Jay. "But it'll be done. I understand the magic used to sink the island."

"We won't need to rush this job," Apzana said. "We'll be the first ones there in two generations. Only the fish have picked over the loot."

"Will we return to the island after we unload the ship?" Jay asked.

"No," Apzana said. "We'll get there first and we'll get the best. Whoever wants to pick over the bones is welcome to. When we're done, everyone will know the *Hen & Chick* was there first." Apzana smiled at Jay. "I'll give you time to get a good map drawn of the island, Jay, don't worry. And we'll be there at least one evening, so you can chart the stars." Azria saw Jay smile broadly, her real concern addressed by their captain.

"What should we do if the witch shows up?" Yabi asked, her words spilling from her as if she'd been holding them back this whole time. Apzana had told the crew the truth about Iyzani the day before they left the City of Peace. Most of the truth. Azria felt her stomach turn as she remembered Iyzani's face in her dream. Her eyes, so red. The tears in her eyes.

"Tell me so I can kill her," Apzana said with a casualness that bothered Azria more. "We're not going to let her stop us." Azria gulped, swallowing all the words she wanted to say. Her thoughts about Iyzani were so muddled, but it wasn't time for discussion. Not now. Azria tried to keep her expression calm, hoping her face didn't give away the thumping of her heart. "We'll be wealthy as sovereigns after this," Apzana continued, her voice rich with the same tone as in the vault. Gold. "I hope you'll all stay on afterwards," she added. Azria could hear the slightest hint of sadness in her voice. "Just because you're rich in gold doesn't mean you should be poor in adventure."

"Let's get that treasure in our nests before we plan our next flight," Bolo said, interjecting before the mood could turn melancholy. "You heard the captain. We'll be there in five days at the most. Let's all get back to work and get there as fast as we can."

"Yes, Second," the crew said in a chorus, scattering across the deck. Azria smiled timidly at Yabi as she waved in response, blushing. Onacá rolled her eyes before she grabbed the cook by the arm and dragged her towards the stairs.

"Azria, I want you to work with Jay on the navigation if you can, before you get back to your...spellcasting," her mother said. Her mother turned and looked towards the horizon, back where they had come from. The City of Peace hadn't been in view since morning meal but her mother still looked back occasionally, sniffing the air. As Azria's excitement mounted, she could feel her mother's unease grow, as if she anticipated something.

"Do you still think Iyzani will show up and try to stop us?" Azria murmured. It seemed like the most opportune time to ask, the rest of the crew busy with their work. Azria knew her mother wouldn't appreciate her bringing it up in front of the others.

"I don't see why she wouldn't," Apzana said. "First the boy, then the dream. She'll come," she said, something like apprehension tight in her voice.

"I thought that was what you wanted," Azria said. Her mother eyed her, narrowing her eyes slightly.

"I want to face her, yes." Her words were an admission, and Azria saw the defiance in her mother's expression, the tightness in her jaw, the slight pout of her full mouth. "I still worry about the rest of the crew." There were still words left in her mother's thoughts, but her mother didn't speak them. Not now, under the shining sun, the cold sea wind blowing past them. "This is my fight."

"But you're not alone, Mama," Azria said, not sure if she was volunteering to join her mother's fight or not. "Even The Innate didn't sink the island all by herself."

"You'll be raising the island by yourself," Apzana countered, her eyes ahead as she walked to the wheel of the ship, Bolo holding it steady.

"That's not entirely true," Azria said. "I'm working with a spell already cast by another mage. And the rest of the crew has helped me in all sorts of ways." Azria clasped her hands behind her back and looked out over the *Hen & Chick*, feeling content for the first time in a long time. She had the crew of the *Hen & Chick* behind her. She held Hiezh's teachings and Nana's wisdom in her heart. And while the task of raising the island loomed before her, having a purpose tying her to her fellow crew members made Azria smile. For the first time in a while, she didn't feel lonely.

"I definitely helped," Bolo said. "I helped a lot."

"Shush," Apzana said, shaking her head at him. Her mother looked to Azria, the faintest of smiles playing on her lips. "I'm glad you finally feel like a part of the crew, Azria. But know, not every problem can be solved by a group of people. Your friends can't always be there for you. And sometimes, they shouldn't be there."

Azria just nodded, not sure how to respond to her mother. Azria felt like she had already faced so much alone. She thought she was moving past that. Hadn't her mother told her to make friends with the other crew members? Now that Azria had, her mother was warning her against them. She recalled the conversation they had in the City, after her accident with Eixon. She looked to Brik and Brak in the rigging and Eixon and Red, tying things on deck. Yabi and Onacá below. If Iyzani came and threatened them, could she ignore their pleas for help?

"Go talk to Jay, Azria," Apzana said, interrupting her thoughts. It was an order.

Azria just bowed her head to excuse herself from her mother's presence before she walked away. Jay had set up a table on the deck with various instruments used for navigating. Rolled out on the center and secured with large, flat stones was a map, freshly made for their journey by Jay's own hand. Her handwriting was perfectly blocky, making it easy to read the names of islands and seas she had inscribed there. A length of orange ribbon on a small post fluttered in the wind. Jay smiled at Azria as she approached, her hazel eyes squinting as she did. "With the wind bearing southwest as it is, we may get to our destination more quickly than we thought! We'll have to be sure not to pass over it."

"I've got that covered," Azria said, tapping one of the pouches on her belt. The newly crafted spell sat tucked away in the leather pouch, wrapped in a square of silk. "As we approach the island, the spell will react." If Azria concentrated, she could feel the spell pulling towards the island, like a lodestone. The pull was ever so slight but it was there. If her weaving had been done well enough, it would grow stronger the closer they approached as well.

"Your map is lovely," Azria said. It was a perfectly square piece of linen paper, bleached as white as could be. Fat, empty borders waited for Jay's expert notes about the various locales and a blank spot waited for her steady hand to paint the dimensions of the Marauders' Island, to join the rest of the islands in the Floating Chain.

"Thank you," Jay said, pride obvious in her tone. "I'll admit, Mage, I'm excited to be the first map maker to include the Marauders' Island in decades. The last map that included it was made fifty years ago, as far as I can tell. When it's revealed that mages sunk the island and not your Goddess...I can't imagine how the news will spread."

"Right," Azria said with a nod. Her gaze drifted back to the map, her eyes focusing on the empty borders. So many maps didn't even bother to mention the island which had sunk into the sea. Now it would be back. Would her name be written in those borders, as the one who undid the spell? Would she and Iyzani be linked on atlases for ages? Would the mages of Miz be judged by Iyzani's actions or hers? Azria gulped, placing her hand on the pouch of her belt, feeling the magic of her spell swirling just beyond her touch.

"Do you mind if I ask you something?" Jay asked. She looked up at Azria, stray brown curls slipping from her headscarf.

Azria hesitated before she nodded. "Not at all," she answered, not sure if she should try to meet Jay's gaze or not.

"It's just," Jay started, putting her hands on the table. "I know your mother and you say that Iyzani is a traitor. That she betrayed Miz. But...how?"

"Does it matter?" Azria asked.

"It kind of does," Jay said. "I've got a special interest in traitors."

"You've been talking to Zesh," Azria said. She frowned at the thought of the boy in the hold. A part of her had hoped they would leave him in the City of Peace but her mother had kept her word and brought him along. He spent most of his time reading and napping, as far as Azria could tell. She avoided him, in truth. Azria felt guilty for him being there.

"Well, I've had guard duty more than a few times," Jay admitted. "And I can be chatty."

"Iyzani..." Azria hesitated again. Why? She remembered Nana's face whenever the Triumvirate came up in conversation, the way the knife had felt in her dream. "She betrayed Miz."

"I don't know if you noticed this or not, but your mother doesn't really care about Miz," Jay said, adjusting one of her instruments.

"What do you mean?" Azria said. "Of course she does. It's where she's from."

"Captain Apzana of the *Hen & Chick* is not of Miz," Jay said quietly. "Captain Apzana is...Captain Apzana.

She doesn't have loyalty to Miz. She has loyalty to those she loves. Her crew. Her ship."

"Jay," Azria said, trying not to sound exasperated. "What's your point? I know my mother wasn't in Miz with me. I was there, you know."

"I'm just saying," Jay said. "I know a little something about traitors. There are people in Miz who would call your mother a traitor. I left my home because they called me a traitor."

Azria pressed her lips together, trying to fight back memories of fellow Innates saying Jay's words but in crueler tones. They were more than just words. They colored how they saw Azria, and how they treated her. "You betrayed your homeland?" Azria asked.

"Not my home, and not myself," Jay said. "The Church." Jay adjusted her headscarf, looking towards the map. "My mother and people knew who I was. I knew who I was. But when our city-state joined Haran to avoid war, the Church said I wasn't a woman. They said I was a traitor to the Holy Family, to the Father and Son, for rejecting the body I was born with, and commanded me to join the army. So my mother and others and myself...we left. We got in the sturdiest fishing boat and left Haran. Your mother found us on the sea and took us all to the City of Peace and I joined her crew. She didn't care if Haran saw me as a traitor. She knew who I was meant to be."

Azria looked at the borders of the map, their emptiness louder than the waves. What would they say about her, and Iyzani, and Miz? Azria wanted to raise the island, for treasure, for her mother. No mage would argue and say it was nothing less than a great working. But what would they say about it? What would sailors say about Mizian mages, once the island was raised?

"All I'm trying to say is one person's traitor is another person's hero, Azria," Jay offered quietly. "When we feel betrayed...we don't always think about why the other person did what they did, what it meant to them. We just feel the pain. And react."

"My mother, and a lot of people besides her, think Iyzani killed her parents," Azria said, her words slow and measured. Her face felt hot despite the cold wind and she wanted to turn and walk away just then and there. "Zesh said she didn't. And maybe she didn't. I wasn't there. It was a long time ago. But...my mother thinks this. I don't think anyone can sway her from it." As the words left Azria's lips, she drew in her breath, the truth of her words sitting in her stomach like a stone that would drag her down to the bottom of the sea.

"Oh." It was all Jay said for a while. They both looked at each other for a moment and Azria smiled nervously, not sure what to say. "Well, the nice thing about revenge, it's often very simple," Jay murmured, shrugging her shoulders. "At least with this revenge we'll all get rich."

"Right," Azria said, chuckling because she didn't know what else to do. Azria took a deep breath before she put her hand on her pouch, feeling the pull of the stone before she pointed off in the distance. "We need to adjust our course, starboard, right there," she said.

"Will do, Mage," Jay said. She adjusted one of her instruments and looked to Azria. "Azria?" she said quietly.

"Yeah?" Azria said, her anxiety starting to grow again.

"If you ever need someone to talk to, you know we're here for you, right?" Jay offered. "Me and

Yabi. Even Onacá. Especially if you need makeup tips, Onacá."

"Yabi only talks about food," Azria said with a laugh, looking down at the deck. Her face grew hot with a blush. Jay's words were meant to be comforting but Azria couldn't help but feel embarrassed by her kind offer.

"Yabi does talk a lot about food but..." Jay's voice trailed off, her eyes darting to the side as she considered her words. "You make her nervous, Azria. But, we're all on this boat together. We have to look out for each other."

"Right," Azria said, nodding her head and clasping her hands behind her back. "And I hope if you ever want to talk to me, you do," she said stiffly.

"Wow, that was pretty sad, Azria," Jay said with a laugh. "You sound like a doctor saying I can come over if I need a poultice."

"I...this is not my thing!" Azria exclaimed, waving her hands in front of her face. "It's just not."

"We'll work on it," Jay said. "I'll tell your mother to adjust our course. Please check in with me if we're veering off. I think if the winds hold up, we'll get there sooner than anticipated."

"Will do," Azria said, not commenting on how soon they'd arrive. It would be days but so much could happen. At the end of it all was the island. She nodded her head to Jay in goodbye before she turned and walked across the deck towards the stairs. Before she walked through the stairway she gave one more glance up at her mother at the wheel, her hands on the spokes. Her dark brown eyes stared out at the horizon, the wind blowing at her hair.

Her mother looked behind her. Azria sighed and

ducked her head as she entered the dark hold of the ship. She had work to do.

Azria looked over the words of the spell she had crafted. Several pieces of dark brown paper were scrawled with different versions of the spell in silvery graphite, drafts as she tried to craft the correct words to go with her intent. The finished version of the spell was written in neat script, her spellwriting penmanship clean and dark.

Azria pulled out the length of pale yellow ribbon purchased for her in the City of Peace. Single use spells could be written on the special paper made in Miz, set off with a bit of intent. But for the casting for the island, Azria knew a spell engine would be best. An endless loop of ribbon, the spell written on it, to circle the main spell and enhance it. Azria carefully measured the ribbon along her words, trying to remember the method Hiezh had taught her.

Azria pulled out a small sharp knife and cut the ribbon, twisting the ribbon before she brought the ends together. Using the least amount of energy needed, she pressed the ends of the ribbon together, knitting the fibers. As she breathed, the ends smoothed out till it was seamless. Azria gave a slight sigh of relief. Hopefully she wouldn't need to do too many.

The hold was quiet, save the intermittent singing of Yabi in the galley, getting hot food ready for evening meal. Azria looked over her inks and brushes. For a brief moment she missed the Snail Quarter of the market back in Hitha and the various items people sold to Innates. Nana had taken her there many a time, the pride evident on her face as she followed Azria down the streets. Azria chuckled as she thought of all the arguments Hiezh had gotten into, haggling for herbs and metals. She wondered what they were doing right now. Nana was probably stirring a stew, the clean, nutty smell of rice drifting through her garden. Hiezh was most likely looking through his cupboards, cursing himself for not having food in the house.

What would they say if they knew what she was doing? Azria picked up one of her brushes, feeling the cold wood under her grip. Yabi's singing stopped abruptly and Azria glanced up, looking to the doorway. In the distance she could hear the cook talking to someone. Azria listened as light footsteps approached the room.

"Still hard at work?" Apzana said, walking through the doorway. She looked happy but tired. She and Bolo were taking shifts at the helm, sailing through the night. Azria guessed she was about to go to bed but wanted to check in.

"Yes," Azria said. "Just about to make a spell engine."

"A spell engine, eh?" Apzana said. Her mother looked around the room, gazing from bed to bed. Azria couldn't tell if she wasn't interested in what she was doing or if she just had no clue what she was talking about.

"Yes, it's a way of enhancing a spell," Azria said, picking up her paper. She looked over her words again, the lettering. "It should make the raising of the island go more smoothly. And take less out of me." Azria set the paper down and picked up the paintbrush again.

"Smooth is good," her mother said. "I just wanted to see if you needed anything before I went to bed," she said.

"Actually," Azria said, putting the brush down. She brought her hands together on the table, trying to think of the best way to bring up the topic which had been pressing on her mind. "I wanted to ask you something."

"What is it, Azria?" Apzana said. Her mother smiled warmly, her weariness making her expression soft. It reminded Azria of her memories of her mother, when she was younger. Azria took a deep breath, keeping her eyes on the table as she spoke.

"I was just wondering, what do you think people in Miz will say after all this?" she asked, her voice higher pitched than she intended. Her mother's expression melted, annoyance pulling at the corners of her mouth.

"After all this what?" Apzana asked, leaning against the doorway.

"After the island is raised?" Azria said. She asked it as if it were a question.

"Are you starting to think you can't do it?" Apzana said, her eyes narrowing. "Azria, don't doubt yourself. I know you can raise the island. You're a smart girl, and an Innate."

"It's not that," Azria said.

"Then what is it?" her mother snapped. Azria paused, taken aback by her mother's tone.

"It's just..." Azria began, her voice trailing off. "People think it was the Goddess' will that sunk the island. But when I raise it, it could get out that Iyzani sunk it." Azria paused, trying to gather her thoughts about the island, trying to make sure she was voicing her own concerns.

"Good," Apzana said before Azria could speak again. "Let everyone know what Iyzani did. She destroyed an island. She killed all those people."

"She didn't do it alone," Azria said.

"Are you saying we should go after those mages too?" Apzana asked.

"No!" Azria exclaimed. "No. I am trying to say..." Azria took a deep breath, hoping her mother wouldn't interrupt her again. "I am saying, once it gets out that mages sunk the island, Mizian mages, what if people think we're capable of things like this?"

"Well, aren't you?" Apzana's expression was one of confusion. Azria's mouth fell open, not sure how to respond.

"No!" Azria said. "We aren't! I mean...technically, yes, but no one is going to know why Iyzani sunk the island." Azria frowned, realizing the entire story as to why Iyzani had sunk the island was still untold. "They're just going to know Mizian mages can do and undo things like this. People might start to fear us, Mama."

"Azria, do you want to raise the island or not?" Apzana asked, exasperation heavy in her voice.

"I do, I really do!" Azria said. Her words were more insistent than she felt. "But I just worry about Mizian mages, how people will see us."

"It's not your job to protect the reputation of the mages of Miz," Apzana said. "They're all their own people."

"You know that doesn't matter, Mama!" Azria said. "I mean, it does matter. But people still do consider our reputation, not just in Miz but elsewhere. And," Azria added, "I do care what the mages will think of me, when I return to Miz."

Her mother stared at her for a moment, as if she hadn't understood what she said. Perhaps, she just didn't want to hear it. "Who cares what they think?" Apzana said finally.

"I do," Azria said, trying to keep her voice calm. "I'm one of them. I want to be able to go home and be avoided less than I was when I was just a student. It's kind of a goal of mine. And not just the mages. Other Mizians, other people in Hitha."

"Azria," Apzana said, bringing her hands to her temples. "I love you. You're my daughter. You're also a mage of Miz. But as my daughter, you need to believe me when I say this. People will always believe the worst about you. So you might as well get some money while you're at it."

Azria sat there, her mouth hanging open. She saw the slightest hint of a smile in her mother's eyes, triumphant in Azria's silence. Azria frowned before she stood up. "So that's it. You didn't care if Miz hated you, and kept you from me these last five years. As long as your hold is full of gold."

Suddenly Apzana's face lit up, her eyes wide. "That's not fair."

"Nothing is," Azria said. "Believe me, I know. I can't believe I spent all these years training as a mage so you could burn it all to the ground." Azria thought about her last day on Miz, her failure to gain her commission and the disappointment. It was nothing compared to the anger she felt right now.

"Azria, when you do this, it's not going to matter—"

A flash of light glowed in the room, a peal of thunder rolling through the air. Azria and Apzana stared at each other, disbelief on both their faces.

"I thought we were supposed to have fair weather," Azria managed.

"We were," Apzana said. Azria looked to the doorway, already hearing the thumps of Yabi running from the galley.

"Captain!" Yabi exclaimed. "Was that thunder?"

"Get back in the galley," Azria said, rushing to store her items.

"Don't order my crew around," Apzana said. She turned to Yabi, nodding to Onacá who popped up behind her. "Yabi, get to the galley. Secure every barrel of water, every grain of rice, every bean. Onacá, secure the hold. Get Eixon above deck."

"Yes, Captain!" they both shouted, both of them disappearing down the hallway.

"Come with me," Apzana said, already heading through the door.

"We're not done arguing," Azria said as she followed after her, feeling as if they weren't going fast enough.

"Oh, I know it," Apzana said. They both hurried up the stairs, trying not to trip over each other as they rushed.

Azria ran past her mother towards the back of the ship. The sky was a clear, beautiful blue, save a path trailing behind them. A pile of gray-green clouds as big as an island followed behind them. As Azria squinted, she saw a streak of orange-yellow lightning crackling through the clouds, the thunder booming over the boat.

"Iyzani," Azria whispered. "It's her."

"Captain, what is happening?" Bolo yelled, his voice pitched with fear.

"It's Iyzani," Azria shouted, turning around. "She's coming."

"Red, bring up the weapons fit enough to take down a witch," Apzana said. "Bolo, get Brik, Brak and Eixon to secure this ship. I don't want it blowing over."

"You heard her!" Bolo shouted. Brik and Brak scurried across the deck, Eixon popping out from below deck. "Bring down those sails, secure the rigging!"

Bolo continued to shout orders in Trade. Azria stopped paying attention as she gazed back at the clouds.

Azria clutched the side of the boat, the wind the coldest she had ever felt. Water sprayed up from the sea, splashing on her face as the clouds loomed behind them.

Azria wanted to say Iyzani wasn't a witch. She wanted to say Iyzani wasn't a mage who had hardened her heart against others and used her magic only for selfish reasons. But the words stuck in her throat, her mother's accusations rolling through her mind. Iyzani sunk the island. She killed those people. Another sliver of lightning cut across the sky and when it flashed, Azria saw the small figure within the clouds.

Iyzani.

"She's a mage. Like me." Azria gulped, not believing her own words. One of the greatest mages of Miz to ever live was following them. Could Azria be like her? The cold wind blew past her, the same wind she thought she could fly on just earlier the same day. Iyzani willed the same air to carry her aloft as she pursued them. Azria wrapped her arms around herself, the gales biting at her face.

Azria couldn't be like Iyzani. She didn't want to be. She remembered the anger in the spell sitting in the pouch at her belt. Azria never wanted to be that angry. She didn't want to harden her heart.

Azria bolted across the deck, her boots thumping against the wood. She ignored the brief stares of her friends as she turned sharply, clambering down the stairs and bolting into the cabin.

Azria's hands shook as she snapped open the box with her ribbons and inks, pulling out the paper with her spell. She shook the bottle of ink, feeling the dark liquid bouncing within the glass vial.

"Azria, what are you doing?"

Azria looked behind her. Yabi stood in the doorway, her eyes wide. Her normally smooth hair was a mess and her eyes were wet with tears that threatened to fall.

"I'm going to keep everyone safe," Azria said. Another flash of lightning illuminated the hold, the thunder louder than before. She popped the cork of the vial and dipped her brush into the ink before she carefully but quickly wrote her spell.

> *Unsunk, Undone*
> *Unloosed, Unspun*
> *Through sea, to air*
> *Dry land, laid bare*
> *By my hand, and the power of Miz*
> *I break the curse and summon you.*

Azria breathed her intent into the spell, the ink drying as she wrote, her hand as steady as her breathing. The ink glowed as she inscribed, pulling the ribbon along. She came to the end and carefully painted the symbol linking the beginning to the end of the spell, a glyph of motion and power. Azria took a deep breath as she lifted her brush from the ribbon and tossed it to the table, not bothering to close the ink before she looped the ribbon around her wrist.

"Yabi, don't worry," Azria said, her heart thumping in her chest.

"I don't know what you're talking about," Yabi said helplessly, looking Azria up and down. "What are you going to do?"

"It's not smart but—" Azria didn't know what to say. She threw her arms around Yabi and hugged her, feeling foolish and awkward but her face feeling hot with excitement anyway. Azria pulled herself away, not sure what to do with her hands. "When this is over, will you spend time with me? Not around food?"

"Sure," Yabi said, confusion on her face as she nodded slowly. "Of course." Yabi blushed before she smiled. Another flash of lightning made them both jump.

Azria leaned forward, kissing Yabi on the cheek, half-regretting it as she pulled away, seeing the surprise on Yabi's face. Azria pushed past her and stepped into the hallway.

"Zesh, I'm sorry about all this," Azria shouted as she ran down the hallway back to the stairs.

"Azria!" Yabi called after her. Azria took the stairs two at a time, the spell engine on her wrist, her hand holding the pouch that held the spell against her hip. She ran across the deck past the rest of the crew. Wind splashed cold water on her face.

"I can't be heartless," Azria thought as she reached the bow of the ship. Her mother shouted something behind her. "Reckless maybe, but not heartless." The clouds loomed above, closer. The next lightning bolt boomed with thunder. The storm was almost on top of them.

The spell in her pocket pulled towards the island. Azria climbed up on the prow. The air was cold but sweat popped on her brow, her skin hot.

"Azria!" her mother shouted. "Girl, what are you doing?!" Apzana ran towards her.

"I know what Iyzani wants," Azria shouted into the wind. "And it's not the *Hen & Chick*."

"Get down right now!" her mother ordered, frozen

before her. Her brown eyes were wide, the rest of the crew all running to standing behind her.

"Jay, keep on the course I set," Azria said, her words almost swallowed by the wind. She looked up at the gray-green clouds before she looked to her mother again. "Mama. I'll see you at the island."

Azria took a deep breath before she pivoted on her heel and stepped off the side of the boat.

The cold wind and salt spray rushed up to meet her. Azria inhaled as the air engulfed her, screwing her eyes shut as she willed the air about her.

Azria opened her eyes. The amethyst glow of her magic emanated from her, her feet just a hand's width above the churning ocean. Azria grinned.

"Come and get what you really want," Azria whispered, staring at the clouds. She looked back at the *Hen & Chick*. Apzana stared over the side of the ship. Was it horror or disbelief on her face? Azria didn't have time to find out. Closing her eyes and concentrating on the pull of the spell, Azria flew over the surface of the water. Thunder rolled behind her, speeding her along. Despite the uncertainty looming before her and the storm behind her, Azria couldn't help but grin. Caught between the two impossibilities, she was still flying.

She would get there first. She would face Iyzani. Iyzani was the stronger mage. But Azria's desire to keep her mother and the rest of the *Hen & Chick* safe was as strong as her own magic. Azria just hoped it would be enough to carry her through the trials which lay ahead.

Chapter 10
Clouded Judgment

The surface of the water flashed gold, reflecting Iyzani's lightning. Thunder rumbled behind her. Azria felt the sound roll over her, rippling over her damp skin. Sweat popped on her forehead as air surrounded her, keeping her aloft. Azria sped over the surface of water, the taste of salt on her lips. Cold wind washed over her face as she willed herself forward, as fast as she could.

Her mother wanted to face Iyzani. Azria felt the power chasing after her, the image of her mother's hand on the hilt of her sword springing to mind. Zesh had tried to convince Azria Iyzani had had her fill of bloodshed but if provoked by Apzana, what would The Innate do? Azria didn't know and she didn't want to find out. All possibilities of a battle between Apzana and Iyzani turned her stomach. Azria couldn't have her mother raise her sword to protect her. And she couldn't have the crew swept up in their clash. The faces flashed through her memory as she accelerated in the direction of the pull of her spell, hoping to put as much distance as she could between herself and the *Hen & Chick*. She would try to reach the island first but her mother's order to put herself before the crew melted away as she sped over the waves.

Her hair stood on end, a strange thrumming filling the air. A bolt of lightning crackled so close to Azria, her cheek burned with the heat. Azria screamed. In her fear, she veered off course slightly, spinning in the air. Thunder sounded behind her, shaking the surface of the waves. Azria pushed her will to steady herself and placed her feet on the water, willing the water to hold her up.

In the distance the *Hen & Chick* cut its way through the waves, gray-green clouds looming overhead. Azria saw the sheets of rain falling from the clouds, imagining the fat rain drops bouncing on the deck, soaking the crew as they worked the sails, her mother and Bolo barking orders. At the front of the clouds, like the figurehead of a ship, floated the small figure of Iyzani. Her white garments fluttered in the breeze, orange-gold magic floating around her.

Azria's heart thrummed in her chest like a bird trying to escape its cage as she watched, trying to steady her breathing. She gulped down her terror as the *Hen & Chick* darkened. The full, billowing mass of the cloud floated above the ship, casting its massive shadow. Azria took a step back, her foot slipping just slightly below the surface of the ocean, soaking her toes. Azria caught herself, willing the water to hold her up as she watched the clouds roiling, the ocean waves cresting white underneath them.

Azria gazed up at Iyzani, still riding the front of the

cloud, heralding the storm. It was hard to tell how fast the squall was moving and Azria squinted, trying to see if it stopped over the *Hen & Chick* or rolled over it. The ship bucked in the sea like a goat. Guilt made her face hot, knowing she wasn't there to help stabilize the ship. But the *Hen & Chick* wasn't the true target of Iyzani's plans, was it? It was Azria who had been attacked in the City of Peace. Azria took a step forward on the waves, trying to keep steady as the surface rippled more and more, the crests of the waves whitening. She could get back to the *Hen & Chick* if she had to.

The shadow over the *Hen & Chick* lightened, the dark silhouette passing over the ship. Azria exhaled in relief, only to jump with surprise as yet another bolt of lightning zigzagged right off the bow of the *Hen & Chick*. Her cheeks stung and the wind whipped up as the waves rose ahead of her.

The clouds poured across the sky towards Azria.

"By the deep, I do not think things through," Azria said through gritted teeth, taking a step back. Her feet tingled, a strange sensation vibrating through her. A sequence of lightning bolts careened between clouds and sea, orange light blinding her. Azria put her hands up to shield her eyes, her feet sinking below the surface of the churning waves.

Azria pushed off of the water, darting forward on the air. Thoughts of how amazing it was to fly mingled with her growing terror. Iyzani was chasing her. For now the crew was safe but Azria was out in the open. Could she appeal to the more powerful mage? How long could she fly? As the younger person, she had more energy but Azria was certain Iyzani had more magical stamina.

"Keep it together, Azria," she whispered to herself. "You left the *Hen & Chick* to protect the crew. Get some distance and then try to talk to her." She would fly until she couldn't see the *Hen & Chick* anymore and then address Iyzani. She had given Jay the course. She could find them again. "You can talk to her."

Another flash of lightning, this one farther from her, sent its peal of thunder across the ocean. Azria sped forward, feeling the pull of the spell in her pouch. The water was gray-blue under her, her reflection in its surface. A streak of lightning bounced off the water and Azria's hair stood on end.

Azria spun around again, hovering above the water as she gazed up into the clouds. The clouds had gained on her. She had put distance between herself and the ship but there was still more to cover if she was to get Iyzani clear of the boat and the crew. The hungry ocean stretched before her, free of landmarks save the ship, the clouds speeding ahead of her as the winds Iyzani conjured caught up with them. The sun shone high in the afternoon sky, occasionally obscured by Iyzani's storm. The wind was colder than before.

How fast could she go? If she sped up, she could give better chase and draw Iyzani away from the ship. But she risked exhausting herself, with no land to rest on.

Azria thought of the crew on the *Hen & Chick*. The expressions on their faces as they put their hands to the work Apzana and Bolo demanded of them. The sound of boots on the deck. Yabi's eyes, wide with terror, the strained calm on Eixon's face. Her mother. Azria sped forward, putting the crew farther behind her. She'd see them again. And when she did, they'd all be relieved, all grins and laughs.

Azria grit her teeth as she pushed herself forward, her magic growing hotter in her belly and limbs, her breath circulating through her. Orange lightning cracked around her but each bolt just edged her speed, the fear in her heart fueling her magic. She looked down at the sea.

Iyzani was directly above her.

Azria brought herself to a stop, willing the air to hold her aloft, hovering over the surface of the sea. Billowing clouds blocked the sun, cool shadows making Azria shiver as she looked up at the mage.

Where was the *Hen & Chick*? Azria looked around and found herself alone, save her fellow Mizian. While it was what she wanted, it still made a lump form in her throat. Azria gulped it down as she stared up at Iyzani, wondering what her next move should be.

"She is the greater mage," Azria said. What would she do if she was home? Azria pushed aside thoughts of what 'home' really meant and remembered the other mages of Miz. Their formality and stoic pride in their discipline. Their colorful stoles draped over their bleached white garments. Azria, as a student, had always bowed her head to more senior mages. She had gotten away with ignoring her fellow Innates but the opportunity for ignoring had been destroyed at this point. Azria took a deep breath before she willed herself aloft, higher and higher above the sea, towards the clouds.

Iyzani descended from the clouds, hands flexed at her sides, the wind blowing her white hair up around her face. Azria kept herself steady as she rose, only stopping when she floated directly across from the older mage.

"So, you're the mage who is going to raise the island?" Iyzani said, her voice thick with age and scorn. Her dark eyes were narrowed, incredulous.

"I'm just glad to meet the greatest mage of Miz in person," Azria offered, wondering what her reaction would be. This close to her, in the flesh, Azria couldn't help but feel frightened. This was a woman who had sunk the Marauders' Island. Even if she hadn't killed her sister and brother-in-law, she still lowered the island into the sea, with all the people on it. Azria remembered the words of Red, the talk of ghosts who walked the waves.

"The greatest, eh?" Iyzani said. Her voice softened and she raised her white brows, obviously flattered by Azria's words. "Even after all I've done, all they've said I did, they still call me the greatest."

"You were The Innate," Azria said. Before her, Iyzani looked leaner than she had imagined her, how she had presented herself in Azria's dream. Age had softened her muscles slightly but Azria was under the impression this was a woman of some physical strength. Azria hoped the lessons Bolo had given her had hardened her some.

"What will they call you, girl?" Iyzani asked. The mage started to move and Azria instinctively moved with her, keeping the same distance.

"I doubt I'll get to choose," Azria said, holding back nervous laughter. Iyzani smirked back at her, the golden-orange glow of her magic swirling around her.

"But you can give them a bit of inspiration," Iyzani said, still slowly moving. As Azria moved in time, she realized they were circling each other. "I am The Innate. The Traitor. I didn't get those names for nothing."

"I'm too young to be one of the titled mages of Miz," Azria said. She said the words but Azria knew they weren't completely true. Back home, among the other Innates, she had been called many things. Once she raised the island, would those names melt into the sea, as the Marauders' Island once had? She felt the cloth of the spell engine around her wrist, the pull of the spell in her pocket.

"False modestly looks good on your face," Iyzani said, still moving, still coming towards her. "And how old are you, fourteen? Fifteen?"

"Sixteen," Azria said, trying not to sound upset.

"You're short," Iyzani said, evidently amused by the reaction on Azria's face. "Can't be too surprised, knowing who your father is."

"You know my father?" Azria asked. Her magic flared as her face grew hot.

"I do," Iyzani said, nodding. "Even though your mother isn't my child, we have the same heat in our blood. I followed it to the Golden Isles. I saw the boy become a man. Handsome. But short."

Azria closed her eyes, still moving in the slow circle, mirroring Iyzani in her movements. Iyzani knew more about her parents than she did. Someone else to add to the list. Azria tried to calm herself before she spoke again.

"I have many years of magic ahead of me, Innate," Azria said. "I'll do more than lift the island from the sea."

"About that," Iyzani said.

Iyzani blinked out of the circle and appeared before Azria. Azria could feel her breath on her face. "Why?" Iyzani said, Azria flailing back in defense, dropping through the cool air before she caught herself. Azria's face grew hot, trying to hide her embarrassment as Iyzani chuckled.

"You're going to a sunken island with more ghosts than coins, girl," Iyzani laughed. Azria hovered several feet below Iyzani, her mouth pulling into a grimace. "There are other treasures to be had on the Jeweled Seas."

"Are you nervous some little girl is going to undo your legacy?" Azria asked. "Not even full Mizian. All you'll have left are the lies people have told about you."

"Now your teeth come out," Iyzani said. It was almost a growl. "The rudeness of the young. The brazenness. The things they do, not understanding the consequences. Just like you, here before me. You left the safety of your boat, thinking what? That you could stop me from stopping you?"

"I know you don't care about the rest of the crew," Azria said. "But I didn't want you and my mother to face each other. I didn't want her to try to hurt you." Azria looked back over her shoulder, expecting to see the *Hen & Chick* on the horizon but just saw the empty blue ocean, surging beneath them. "You came to me in my dream, to tell me you didn't want to hurt me, to hurt anyone."

"I've hurt enough people," Iyzani said. "I have had my fill of blood, girl. All the salt water in the world can't wash it away. I have no appetite for it. Your mother has stirred my anger, trying to raise the island. For gold." Iyzani made a sound of disgust in her voice and spit to the side.

"Why did you sink the island, Iyzani?" Azria asked. Now seemed like the time Iyzani would answer her. Iyzani's brown eyes widened, as if surprised Azria asked so plainly. "I've seen the spell, I've felt its power. You knew you were going to do this thing. And you did it. With the help of others, but still." Azria watched Iyzani's expression change at the mention of other mages, her eyes softening. "It was a terrible thing you did, but you did not do it alone."

"Don't speak to me of terrible things!" Iyzani spat. "You have no idea." Iyzani narrowed her eyes at Azria, the clouds above her graying. "Do you know why the mages of my time were so great, how we were able to do such things? Because we had to be great!" Iyzani answered, not bothering to let Azria answer her question. "We needed more, so we desired more, so we did more. We sunk islands and raised them. We made Miz great. We made Miz whole. Now the mages allow their wills to be tempered by the chiefs, who speak of greater good but care only about their own households and holdings."

"Your sister and brother-in-law helped to make Miz whole, and look how they were repaid," Azria said, ready to dash out of the way if Iyzani's temper flared again.

"I didn't do that!" Iyzani said, her voice pitching higher with anger. "I didn't kill them!"

"I know you didn't!" Azria said. Azria remembered Zesh's words. "I know. But someone did."

"I might as well have killed them," Iyzani said. She let her head droop, her weariness evident in her shoulders and wrinkled face. "I couldn't stop those that did. Just like..." Iyzani's voice trailed off. "The Marauders who killed my parents. I wasn't there to stop their attack on my village."

Azria stared at Iyzani. That was why Iyzani had sunk the island. Not just for Miz. The spell in Azria's purse throbbed under her hand. "Iyzani..." Azria started, not sure what to say in response. She thought of the anger in the spell she had felt. "There are so many reasons why people can't be in places, why we're not at the right place at the right time." Azria frowned at her own words, knowing they must have sounded insignificant to the older mage. "Even as we make order out of chaos, the tangles of the past still affect the present." Azria thought about the history lessons she had received on the beach as a child, the stories Nana had told her, one event stated after the other. But when they happened, they were a mess of emotions, actions and thoughts.

"And here we are," Iyzani said.

"Raise the island with me," Azria yelped. She almost put her hands over her mouth after she said it but she balled her hands at her sides. Iyzani stared at her, as if Azria had just called her a cruel word.

"What, girl?" Iyzani said.

"Raise the island with me," Azria said again, more slowly, staring down at the ocean. "You regret sinking the island."

"Says who?" Iyzani said.

"Says me," Azria said. "You did it in your anger. An anger sparked when you were young. You felt helpless and you let it consume you and you fed it. Don't you want to be known for more than that?"

"It won't bring my sister back." The way Iyzani said it, Azria felt like Iyzani was trying to reassure herself.

"No," Azria said. "But it means someone other than Zesh may remember you for more than your past deeds."

"All you want is the treasure," Iyzani said. "Treasure gained through the bloodshed of people like my parents. Other Mizians. Our people."

"No, I want to raise the island because..." Azria felt the air under her, the wind whipping through the clouds. She could see the white crests on the waves below and the ombre hues of the sky fading from afternoon to early evening. "Because I want to see if I can do it. I want to be a mage of Miz. A great mage. And..." Azria looked up, looking Iyzani in the eye. "I want to make things right. What you did was wrong. You drowned the Marauders. You sunk the island. You undid what the Goddess did."

"The Goddess is asleep beneath the waves, girl," Iyzani said, her voice dry. "We are left to fend for ourselves. And I did what I had to do, to keep Miz safe."

"You did it out of revenge," Azria shouted, clenching her fists. "You sunk it to make yourself happy! To make up for the loss you felt. You and your friends, whoever they were. But you're not happy! And the friends who helped you sink it are gone too! All you have left is people's fear of you!"

"How dare you," Iyzani growled, still approaching her in a steady circle. The clouds swirled around them faster, their coloring darkening as they grew thicker around them. The clouds pressed in, and Azria pulled away, their chill seeping through her clothes. "I lost more than my parents the day the Marauders killed them. The pain in your heart, it's nothing compared to mine."

"I'm not saying your pain isn't heavy, Iyzani," Azria croaked, the winds drying out her mouth. "I'm not comparing our losses or our struggles or our abilities. I'm saying...the island was sunk. Let it be raised. Let life go on." Azria shook her head, running out of words to say to the other mage. "You can't reorder the past, not really. We can only put our hands to what we have."

Iyzani stared at Azria from across the sky. If she felt anything at that moment, Azria couldn't read it. "What I have put my hands to, you would undo! And you would show the blood on my hands! After all these years, it is still there, hot and red and full of salt. You would tell everyone I sunk the island, so you can say you raised it!" Iyzani's hands shook and now Azria could see the emotions on her face, the wind whipping up with her anger. "After I sunk the island, after we sunk it, I presented the seal to Kish and he...I could see it in his face. He was scared of us. Of the mages. I used my hands to protect our people and he wanted to tie them. He wanted to tie all of our hands."

Azria's lips parted, holding back her words. Iyzani sunk the island, and her brother-in-law, Kish...the destruction of the Marauders' Island had been the cause of Kish and Zaya trying to control the mages. Why they had moved to make laws against the mages. Why the mages had turned. "You," Azria managed. "You're the reason they left. Why they ran away."

"I had to tell my fellow Innates!" Iyzani shouted, her fists balled at her sides, the wind shrieking with her words. "I had to! We had worked together for so many bloody years. And they turned against the two people I cared for the most. I tried to stop them but even I, the greatest mage, could not stop them." She spat her words. "Enza, your grandmother, she cursed me that day, when I broke her knee. I was trying to find Kish and Zaya, to help them. And she thought I was there to hurt them, like the mages who came before me. My sister, who I loved more than my life, fled from me, Apzana within her." Iyzani still floated in the air, though her body seemed heavy, her dark eyes glistening with tears.

"Leave the island where it belongs," Iyzani said. "Below the waves. Leave its secrets to me. Go back to your mother's boat and sail somewhere else, girl. You are too young to be infamous."

"My mother means to get that treasure," Azria said, ignoring the trembling in her voice. "She wants it. She thinks I can raise the island."

"Your mother is greedy," Iyzani spat. "I left her alone

all these years because she is my niece, but she should not bring up this pain for gold. She is worse than the Marauders if she does this."

Azria stopped, ignoring Iyzani's words before she took a deep breath again. "I know I can raise the island. And I know you don't care what I say, but I am sorry about your family. All of it. I know it was a hard time, and everything after it...Nana told me about the years after the Triumvirate left, the lawlessness, the pain. But that's over! Miz is different now! And...maybe the people of Miz need to know this. To learn from these mistakes."Azria shrugged, noticing for the first time Iyzani had better control of her body as she hovered. Azria felt unsteady where she floated.

"You think you can raise the island?" Iyzani asked. Her voice was low but steady.

"I do. And, if I don't do it, someone else will, right?" Azria said, smiling as much as she dared. It felt good to smile, however small.

"Only Mizian magic can undo Mizian magic," Iyzani whispered, her words barely audible over the wind.

"Right," Azria said. Perhaps they had come to an agreement. Perhaps Iyzani would go in peace. Azria had never thought of herself as someone who was good at convincing people of things. Her smirk turned into a smile of relief as she watched Iyzani give her the slightest of smiles.

Iyzani lifted her hand. Azria felt the pouch on her belt open. Before she could stop it, the spell flew across the space between them, into Iyzani's open palm. Iyzani held it, the purple magic glowing so brightly in her grasp it made Azria wince.

"Hey!" Azria shouted, panic rising in her. "Give that back!"

"No," Iyzani said. "You've given me an idea. And you're going to help me with it."

"There's no way I am going to help you do anything!" Azria shouted, her face growing hot. She balled her fists at her sides, trying to stop herself from shaking.

"There is a way," Iyzani said.

In the blink of an eye, Iyzani was nose to nose with Azria. Azria screamed, flailing away from her. Iyzani reached out with her free hand, the spell glowing amethyst in her other. Azria felt the muscles in her face grow slack, her mouth falling open but no sound coming out. Her head fell back as the sensation rolled from her face to her neck, down her spine and spreading through her limbs. Numb.

The light of her magic faded as her eyes fluttered, too heavy to keep open. The ocean roared in her ears. Her panic did nothing to help her as the sea surged closer. Azria wanted to scream as she fell. But she couldn't. Before she fell into the hungry waves, darkness engulfed her, and the sound of the sea faded away to cold.

Azria sucked in her breath, spasms running along her ribs as she gulped at the air. She was dry but she was cold, so cold it made her muscles ache. Her hands were bound at the wrists. She moved her legs, finding her ankles bound as well. Her face still felt numb and her cheek was damp with drool. Azria wiped the side of her face with her shoulder.

Where was she? Forcing her eyes open she looked around. Oil lamps burned all over the strange room at different levels. Various colors sparsely illuminated the space. The walls were uneven and constructed at peculiar angles. As Azria's eyes focused, she saw the walls were natural, made of jagged rock. Lights and items were tucked into pockets and alcoves within the face. Had Iyzani taken her back to the shore? She couldn't hear the crash of waves or seabirds.

Azria rubbed her wrists together, trying to feel her bonds. "Don't bother," Iyzani's voice came, the mage walking into the room. She wore saffron-colored robes, her bare feet unhurt by the uneven ground. "The rope is enspelled. If you try to undo the bonds with magic, they'll grow tighter. Have you ever had a serious rope burn?" Iyzani cocked an eyebrow at Azria. "They're not pretty."

"Where are we?" Azria murmured, her mouth not cooperating like it should have. She couldn't help but look around the room. Various items hung from the ceiling on colorful cords, some glinting in the light, others strangely absent of color. The aroma of incense and wax and toasted black rice perfumed the air.

"If you can guess, I'll let you go," Iyzani said with a grin that made Azria lean back. "Where do you think we are?"

"You won't let me go if I guess right," Azria said. She was exhausted. She couldn't figure out if it was because of all the energy she spent flying or because of what Iyzani had done to her. What had she done?

"You are smart," Iyzani said. "I'll give you a hint. I'll be sad to see it go when we're done with it, but it's been a long time coming."

Azria leaned against the wall, the shapes of the stones digging into her back. She grimaced as she tried to sit up and support herself, too weary not to hunch over. "I don't want to play any games. I want to be done with you. Tell me or kill me." As the words left her parched lips, Azria wished she could pull them back. She didn't want to die. Not here. Not now. But she was frustrated and exhausted and with Iyzani standing before her, relief seemed so far off.

"I won't kill you," Iyzani said. "I am blood and magic only. I've had my fill of both. But this one last thing can be done. And," Iyzani added, going to one of the alcoves. She pulled the purple orb of Azria's spell out from within her robes and held it out, its light filling the room with its familiar glow. "You're going to help me with something. Try to remember what happened last time you refused."

Azria pressed her lips together, her mouth dry. "What?" Azria asked, her voice rasping in her throat. She coughed and blinked, her eyes burning, her throat raw. "What do you want from me?"

"I'm going to destroy the island," Iyzani said. The light of Azria's spell illuminated her face, giving it a ghastly look.

Azria blinked. "You already did that," she managed to say.

"I sunk the island," Iyzani said. "Now I'm going to destroy it. Every stone. Every grain of sand. Every coin, every bone on this cursed rock."

Azria's mouth fell open. Could she do that? Azria looked at the spell Iyzani held, Azria's spell, and thought. Azria had used her magic to augment Iyzani's spell. Could Iyzani transmute the spell again, using the energy to do what she said she would? "You can't," Azria whispered. It was all she could say.

"We can," Iyzani said. "You're going to help me do it."

Azria opened her mouth to protest but stopped herself. Her face tingled as the nerves woke up, one cheek feeling warmer than the other. A burn from the lightning Iyzani had chased her with. "I'm surprised you'd allow me such an honor," Azria coughed, unable to keep her anger from her words.

"Well, the *Hen & Chick* is still out there, somewhere. If you're not willing to help me with this, I'm sure I can find another way to fill my time," Iyzani said, putting the spell back on the shelf. Azria grimaced. There was a skull there, carved with symbols Azria didn't recognize, a bowl of water in its mouth.

"You said you didn't want to kill anymore," Azria said, sitting up straighter.

"Murder and misery are two very different things," Iyzani said with a shrug. "The young often don't know this. The choice is yours." Iyzani touched the spell again, making sure it was secure on the shelf before she started to walk away, out of Azria's field of vision.

"Wait!" Azria rasped, leaning forward. Her arms and legs still tingled, and she fell over onto the ground, catching herself on her forearms. The jagged floor cut into her skin, the pain slowly trickling through her limbs. "Where are we?"

"You wanted to get here so badly, I'm surprised you didn't guess," Iyzani said, turning to face her. Her dark eyes shone with excitement and Azria felt trapped under her gaze. The older mage pointed towards one of the walls. "Look there and you should be able to tell."

Azria winced as she pushed herself up, not sure if Iyzani's words made sense or if she was still dazed from what had happened. She turned her head to look at what she thought was a window. The sky was dark blue, well beyond dusk. How long had she been asleep? Azria narrowed her eyes. Something was strange about this window. As she peered closer, she jumped, started as something floated up close to the opening and then darted away.

It was a fish.

"We're underwater," Azria said. Azria's stomach turned, realizing where they were. "We're...in...we're here. We're in the Marauders' Island." She imagined the stretch of water above them, below the surface of the sea. Something was keeping the water at bay. Something magic. No one could find her here, no one from the *Hen & Chick*.

She was trapped.

"For now," Iyzani said. She turned to leave again, her bright robes fluttering behind her. "Rest up. We have much work to do."

If Iyzani's footsteps made sounds, Azria didn't hear them. Her body trembled as she stared at the opening, where she had seen the fish. "A trick of the light," she told herself. "Iyzani is lying to me," she said. But Azria knew the truth. Iyzani had taken her below the waves, to the Marauders' Island, to some cave kept dry by magic Azria didn't understand. This was Iyzani's stronghold. Azria slumped back down to the ground. The points of the rock floor pressed into her flesh, scraping her skin. Azria didn't know how long she lay there, thinking she was too exhausted to do anything but fall asleep. But the lump in her throat rose till her eyes filled with tears. Frustration and fear made the tears roll down her cheeks, hot and salty, as sobs made her chest and stomach ache. Azria wept on the floor of the strange cave, not sure what she wanted but knowing she was too exhausted to do anything else but cry.

Chapter 11
Escape

Azria's eyes snapped open. She sat up abruptly, her heart already racing in her chest. She must have fallen asleep. Her eyes burned from the tears she had shed, her face dry and crusty with salt. Her cheek still throbbed with heat. Azria looked down at her hands, still bound. Out of the corner of her eye she saw a cup.

Water. Azria swallowed, anticipating the feeling of cool water in her mouth. She reached out for it but stopped short. What if the water was drugged? Azria licked her cracked lips, wincing at yet another pain in her body. Would Iyzani drug her? It was a possibility. Perhaps the older mage would keep her drugged until she was ready to force her to destroy the island. But if she was drugged, she would be woozy and unable to cast a spell, not with the concentration this type of magic would require. Azria wrapped a hand around the metal cup, the cool feel of it a welcome relief. She placed the cup against her cheek, closing her eyes as the cold metal dampened the pain of her skin.

Azria brought the cup to her lips, praying she wouldn't drop it. She took one sip, tasting the water first. She recognized the flavor. Sea water which had had the salt removed. Azria had made gallons of this water for the *Hen & Chick*. It was one of the first spells she had learned, on the beach of Miz with the other Innates. Azria thought she had cried all her tears but she found her eyes watering as she took another gulp of the water, the memory of carefree days on the beach so far away. She managed to leave a mouthful of water in the bottom of the cup. Carefully, she aimed and splashed the water onto her face, rubbing her hands over her skin.

Nothing in the room stirred. The small window which wasn't a window was dark blue, the color of the sea at night. She must have slept for several hours. Where was Iyzani? Azria leaned forward slightly, realizing her body felt less numb, though her legs tingled. Her stockings were torn in places. Azria checked her wrist. The spell engine was still there, wrinkled, along with the bracelet her mother had let her take from the Vaults. Iyzani must have thought it was just a bracelet. Azria gave a sigh of relief. There was still a chance Azria could make all this right.

"Hello?" she whispered, eyes darting around the room. "Iyzani?" Azria closed her eyes and tried to feel any other presences in the room. Myriad energies swirled around, pulsed and throbbed as their magic ordained, embodied in the various objects left in the chamber. But none matched the energy of Iyzani herself. She wasn't silently lurking, invisible. Azria shuddered to think of Iyzani watching her.

"First things first," Azria said to herself. "Hands free. Then feet." Iyzani had said the ropes would tighten if she tried to undo them with magic. But sharp rocks weren't magic.

Azria tucked her legs under her and sat up, facing the wall of the cave. Several jagged points jutted from the wall. Picking the lowest spike, Azria rubbed the rope against the sharp edge, back and forth. As the fibers broke, hot blue sparks showered down. The spell woven into the ropes tore as Azria worked, the motes of magic rained down, singeing her skin and clothes. Azria grimaced, worrying the smell of burning rope and fibers would draw the older mage. Azria stopped, listening for some indication Iyzani approached. Nothing stirred within the small chamber, and Azria resumed, ignoring the sparks of magic raining down on her lap.

"There has to be a faster way," Azria huffed, looking around the room. All around her were various items, tucked away, chests and metal boxes. It reminded Azria of her mother's treasure trove. She was fairly certain everything in the room was magic, though she didn't recognize the workings or makes. "She dumped me in this room with her treasure. Like I'm some...thing."

The room was lit by candles and oil lamps. Azria turned and spotted a lamp not too far from her. Getting down on her elbows and knees, she scooted across the floor, not caring how ridiculous she looked. Her elbows and knees scraped against the rough ground, and Azria felt her skin tear. It didn't matter, not now. Cocking an ear towards the now visible exit to the room, she brought her wrists to the flame.

A stream of black smoke snaked through the air. Azria winced, feeling the heat of the flame on her wrists, already raw from the rough ropes. The flame crackled and sparked blue, Azria jerking her hands back instinctively. Her skin burned along with the enchanted ropes.

Azria grit her teeth and brought her wrists as close to the flame as she could stand, ignoring the pop and crackle of the spell destroyed by the pure fire, the searing pain on her wrists. Sparks landed on her arms, singeing her skin and hair, the smell of burning hair wafting through the air.

The ropes fell away. Azria wrapped her hand around her wrist, wincing as she cast a healing spell. She felt the heat of the inflamed skin dissipate and fade as the pain receded, still there but less sharp on her senses. After looking over her shoulder, she quickly turned her attention to the ropes tying her legs, fumbling to untie them.

Something moved.

Azria looked up. All she heard was her own heavy breathing. The movement had been on the other side of the window. As Azria stared, she saw it again. A soft, white glow swished in the dark depths beyond the window. "Probably a squid," Azria told herself. She tugged at the ropes, her tongue sticking out of the side of her mouth as she undid her bonds, throwing the rope to the side before she stood up.

Azria walked over to the far wall, where the spell rested in the alcove. She gave a quick glance over her shoulder before she snatched it from its resting spot, its warm, familiar glow brightening in her grasp. She had the spell. But now what? Azria looked at the spell engine on her wrist. The ink hadn't run. Somehow Iyzani had got them both down there completely dry. How was the water being held back? Perhaps there was a spell engine, or several spell engines at work. As she dropped the spell into her belt pouch, Azria looked about the room again, wondering if it was Mizian magic which held the water back, and how much energy it must take to do so.

Iyzani had a haven in the Marauders' Island. Something about this made Azria's stomach turn. She doubted the old mage lived there, and if she did, it was alone, not with her grandson. Would Zesh have vouched for his grandmother if he knew she kept a trove of magical items in the same place she had killed so many? She remembered the boy's face and how he spoke of Iyzani. He couldn't know. Iyzani must have kept this from him all these years.

Azria stepped as quietly as she could towards the window, hoping to gain some clue as to how the water was kept back. If she could learn how it was stopped, perhaps she could breach the barrier in some way, to escape. Azria reached out a hand to touch it, holding her breath as she flexed her fingers.

A glowing face appeared on the other side of the window.

Azria stumbled back, clapping her hands over her mouth to stifle her scream. The face. Azria shook as she stared back at the face in the window. The visage glowed white, its eyes pools of shimmering black that stared back at her.

"A ghost," Azria whispered. It must be. Azria remembered the stories of the sea above the Marauders' Island being haunted by their spirits. It was true. The ghosts were real. Azria gulped, not sure what she should do.

The ghost lifted a hand slowly, extending a finger towards the window. Azria took another step back in panic, hoping the spirit wouldn't pass through the window, into the room. Her fear melted away to curiosity as she watched it trace its finger along the outside of the window. It looked up at her before it did it again.

Azria's eyes followed the motions of the ghost's fingers, the lines and swirls familiar to her somehow. Her eyes widened as the realization hit her.

Writing. The spirit was trying to communicate with her. Azria rushed towards the window, trying to follow the path of the letters. It was probably writing backwards, Azria thought. But what script would a Marauder use? What language did they use? Azria pressed her finger against the window, where the Marauder's finger was. Slowly, she followed along as the Marauder wrote something again, trying to figure out what it was writing.

"This is Mizian script," Azria gasped. It wasn't exactly like Mizian, not the Mizian she was used to. This script had more hard lines than curves and the vowel marks were exaggerated, like they were in older texts. "But the words...that's not a word in Mizian." Azria thought for a moment. It was close to a word in Trade. Was it Tradespeak in Mizian script? If the Marauders had traveled all over the seas, their language would have been known to those who came across them. Tradespeak borrowed words from many languages, and used accents and pronunciations most pronounceable by all who used it. Who would have been better at crafting such a language than those who heard them all?

"Hidden?" she said out loud. Azria looked up, trying to look over the spirit without making eye contact. On first glance she had thought it to be a glowing, vaguely humanoid figure. This close, she spied the fine detail of the ghost's face and garments. Messy hair billowed around its thin face, its wide nose and full lips somber as it wrote the word again. Something about its features reminded her of Mizians but the hair and loose clothing made her think of Zesh. "What are you asking me?" Azria traced the word on the window, backwards, so it'd be easier for the ghost to read. "What?" she said as she wrote.

The ghost wrote again, emphasizing the word with accents. Azria thought back to older spells she had read in Mizian script, trying to remember conversations she had had in Trade over the last few months. "Trapped? Am I trapped?" Azria took a deep breath before she quickly scrawled the letters. "Yes!"

The ghost began writing again, Azria straining to make out the words. Iyzani could come back at any moment. Azria watched, thinking she knew what the words were. "I can help. Go up."

Go up? Azria gulped. "Where?" she wrote.

"Look." The ghost fixed its gaze on her, slick black eyes like two holes to the night staring back through the magical window. Azria pressed her lips together before she turned to better explore the room, ignoring the thrum of the magical items whispering to her in energies she couldn't quite decipher. The only exit to the room led to a dim hallway but there was a light ahead. Iyzani could be there. Hot tears welled up in her eyes as memories made just earlier that day flooded back. Something stirred. Azria froze in her tracks.

She looked over her shoulder, towards the small window out into the dark sea, the glowing visage of the ghost still looking back at her. It made a motion for her to continue on. Azria put her face in her hands, her chest tight. Should she trust this ghost? What if it was leading her into a trap? Still, if there was a way out of the cave, it wasn't in the treasure room. Azria hadn't freed herself to not try and escape. She had to get out, away from Iyzani. She put her hand on the pouch, feeling the spell hum under her touch as she stepped forward.

Azria walked as quietly as she could down the hall-way. A sound came from the room ahead and Azria leaned forward slightly, trying to figure out what the sound was. It was slow and steady, a growling sound that went in and out, in and out like the waves.

Azria jumped as a drop of water splashed onto her head. Pulling her attention away from the strange sound, she looked up. There was a hole in the ceiling. It led up through the rough stone, veins of other types of rock snaking through the walls. The slightest of breezes came from the opening, briny and cold. Could she get up there? Azria peered at the irregular wall, jamming the toe of her boot into one of the spaces. She had climbed trees as a child in Miz but that had been for fun. It would be a dangerous climb.

A snorting sound made Azria jump again. She leaped back from the wall, pressing herself against it as she tried to peek around the corner, into the dimly lit room. As her eyes adjusted to the light, she froze as she saw something on the ground. Another snort and it moved.

Iyzani was asleep on the floor. Snoring. Azria didn't know if she felt like laughing or screaming. For the briefest of moments, Azria remembered Nana's knife. She balled her hands at her sides. But the knife was on the *Hen & Chick*, so far away it made a lump form in Azria's throat. Azria wasn't sure if she could strike Iyzani. The words of the mages of Miz still sang in her mind, meant to be a comfort to all Mizians: mages of Miz were not to use their magic against other Mizians. It was meant to help their fellow islanders, to edify and build.

Iyzani was a part of Mizian history, The Innate. But she had used her magic, Mizian or not in origin, against Azria. To hurt her. To hurt others. Azria trembled as she watched the mage sleep on the floor, oblivious to Azria's presence, apart from the pain she had caused so many.

Azria had to get out. She watched Iyzani for what felt like too long, trying to gauge how deeply the mage slept. Reaching down, she picked up a small stone and threw it. The rock clattered quietly but Iyzani remained on her small mattress, asleep.

Azria had the spell and considered undoing the magic there, in the cave. She brought her hand to her pocket but then shook her head. She had to put distance between herself and Iyzani. If Iyzani interrupted Azria's casting, something worse than the destruction of the island could happen. But was there a way to trap her here?

Azria looked up at the opening in the rock again before she scampered back to the treasure. Maybe there was something here which could help her. She looked to the window and wondered if the ghost was still there, still willing to help her escape. A glowing figure passed by the window at a distance and Azria looked around.

She couldn't waste time inspecting every single object in the room. Several objects were obviously out of the question. A sword and spear hung on one wall, and Azria cringed, trying not to think on what type of weapon Iyzani might keep in her possession. In one alcove was a book, bound in leather. The cover simply read, *Book 1* in Mizian script, the way mages labeled their spell books and journals. Perhaps there was something about the objects in the room, some clue as to what

Azria could use to protect herself from the mage's grasp. She yanked the book down and opened the cover.

A list of names was written on the first page, all of them crossed out. Azria turned the page, noting a date at the top, several rough sketches of maps laid out in dark blue ink. Small burn holes riddled the page. At first, Azria thought the page must have been burned by accident but on second glance, all of the burn marks were located on the hand-drawn islands, all along the coast. Something about the black ringed holes made Azria grimace, and she could almost taste the burned paper in her mouth. Azria turned the page, eyes skimming the lines written in a meticulous but older Mizian script.

Azria almost dropped the book. "This is Iyzani's journal. About the Marauders' Island. And...." Azria read on, reading as quickly as she could.

I have found another settlement of these people, this blight upon the shore. While I can't deal with them as I have the others, they shall be paid back for what they have done.

Azria felt sick. Iyzani hadn't just sunk the island. She had hunted down other Marauders, those who had escaped. Those who didn't dwell on the island. If they were a seafaring people, it only made sense they would have other settlements on other shores. Azria's hands shook as she read on.

Page after page touched on rumors, travel and then the final blows. Iyzani hadn't always used brute force.

I have sown the rumor in the town. What they don't burn to the ground, I shall grind into the dust.

Small maps were drawn and labeled, tables of expenses drawn with a meticulous hand, the same as the entries. Azria tried to reconcile the account Iyzani herself had kept and the woman who had entered her dreams, the tears in her eyes. What was this? Azria wanted to believe Iyzani held regret in her heart, that the tears that gushed from her eyes were those of remorse. But this same woman had kidnapped Azria and was planning on forcing her to destroy the island. Who did Iyzani weep for?

The next entry lacked a date, titled instead. Azria read over the bold letters, To Trap a Soul, So It May Not Rest. More entries were written. Iyzani traveled the coasts first, seeking Marauders but then turned inland. Drawings and formulas covered the pages, her journeys interspersed with studies of the mundane and the magical. Foreign words and their etymologies filled pages, and spells hummed as Azria's hand drew close to the careful script to turn the page.

"I have to get out of here," Azria said, closing the book.

The ghost appeared in the window again, floating before the window. It traced out two words on the surface of the window, Azria squinting to make out the words.

"Go up, yes, I know," Azria said. She walked to the window and scrawled as neatly as she could, "Found the way up. Looking for help." If Azria could make it to the surface, what could she do? Fly back and hope the *Hen & Chick* was still on track to the island. The thought that Iyzani may have gone back to the *Hen & Chick* and dealt with it while Azria was asleep made her stomach turn. If the ship was wrecked, there could still be survivors. The fact that Zesh was nowhere to be found gave Azria hope. If nothing else, Iyzani would have saved Zesh before sinking the ship.

All the items hummed with their own energy, most of them giving off sensations Azria had never felt in all her years of casting. As she concentrated, peculiar combinations of color emanated from each object. If she had the time she would have consulted the book for reference, trying to match each item to an entry. As it was, Azria wasn't sure how long she had. If she did try to leave and Iyzani woke, she didn't want to leave the older mage with a full arsenal. Azria looked to the window, noticing the various glows which floated beyond the window. Other ghosts.

How did Iyzani keep the water out? Did the ghosts know? Azria approached the window and tapped on the window again. She held her breath, wondering if the ghost would hear. The ghost appeared before the window, large, dark eyes wide as it scrawled on the window.

"Hurry," it wrote.

"No," Azria wrote. "I need to prepare."

"For what?"

"To escape. And to raise the island."

The ghost stared at Azria. It brought its hand to the window and wrote one word.

"Mage?"

"Yes," Azria wrote. "I am a mage. I want to help."

The ghost faded away. Azria almost hit the window with her fists, resisting the urge to shout, to call the ghost back. Trying to think, she quickly pushed her will into the tip of her finger, tracing the words in light on the glass.

"Please, don't go. Help me. How can I..." Azria stopped mid-word. She was trying to think of the word that would make the most sense. "Slow her down, if she chases after me? Please, help."

Azria saw the glow of the ghosts pulse on and off as they moved in the dark ocean. Occasionally she would see the movement of a fish in front or behind them, a flash of black against their pale glow. Finally the spirit came back, putting its hand on the glass.

"Please, stop her," the ghost wrote. "Skulls. Box. Quickly."

Azria could only nod as the ghost backed away from the window, fading into the inky depths of the ocean. Skulls. "Alright," Azria said. "Skulls. That's not that hard." Azria thought. The spirit had also said 'box.' Was there a box of skulls somewhere?

Azria saw the skull in the alcove, the bowl of water in its mouth. Azria scowled at it before she looked about the room. Spinning magic with body parts was forbidden in Miz, an atrocity. The fact that Iyzani had not one skull but several confused Azria as she looked around the room. Growing up, she had been steeped in Mizian magic, learned about the inferiority of spells from other shores. Yet Iyzani, one of the greatest mages, had seen fit to keep these items, and learn the ways of their weaving.

Azria counted three boxes. Two were carved of dark wood and inlaid with a yellow metal. Their décor reminded Azria of several Kamerian items she had seen in the City of Peace. The third chest appeared to be made of a large bone, a single piece carved into a smooth holding case. Azria knelt before the white box first, bringing her hand up, closing her eyes as she tried to feel the energy within. A simple lock gave way to the slightest push from her will. Taking a deep breath, Azria lifted the lid.

She gasped. Even knowing she was looking for skulls, the contents still surprised her. Inside were three skulls, facing away from each other in a triangle. Symbols were carved into the stark white bones, stained deep blue and red with some type of paint.

Most unsettling, each skull had a nail driven through the top of the pate, into the cavity. Azria peered at the strange skulls and their peculiar accouterments, eyes widening as she inspected the nails further. They were made out of some kind of crystal.

She had seen this in the journal.

Azria popped up, looking towards the hall before she picked up the journal again, flipping through its pages. She looked back to the box as she reached the page with the entry.

To Trap Souls.

Iyzani had trapped the souls of someone in those skulls. Azria shivered. In Miz, the dead were buried for several months before the bones were exhumed and sent to the bottom of the sea to sleep forever. Azria looked over the rite. It wasn't a Mizian spell in origin, but there were aspects of Mizian belief in the instructions which filled Azria with apprehension. Mizians didn't believe in ghosts. But Azria had just communicated with one. Were the spirits of three people trapped in these skulls? And how would they help Azria?

Azria looked over the words in the book, reading the spell in her head and holding her hands in her lap so as not to activate the spell. The ritual was complicated enough but the crystal embedded in the bone was the likely catalyst for freeing them. Azria couldn't help but wonder who Iyzani would curse with this type of after-life. Someone who must have wronged her so much, she wouldn't even grant them death.

Azria took a deep breath, looking over the skulls. She could take them as insurance before she climbed up the tunnel, threatening to undo the magic if Iyzani cornered her. But Iyzani had attacked Azria so quickly last time, subdued her before Azria could react. And Azria wasn't so sure those Iyzani had trapped deserved their unrest. Azria looked around the room for something she could hold them in, opening one of the wooden boxes and finding a waxed leather bag inside. She put the book inside, feeling a bit smug as she tucked it away. Azria felt she deserved it and definitely didn't want Iyzani to keep it.

Carefully, she put the skulls in on top, taking a quick survey of the room. There was so much here, so much Azria didn't know what to do with it. She could learn about the magic of other places when she was back on the *Hen & Chick*, she told herself, the hopeful thought pushing her out of the treasure room and into the hallway.

Azria slipped her hand into the bag, resting her fingers on top of one of the skulls. The bones were colder than she thought they should be. She tried to ignore the feeling that seeped from the surface into her fingers. The longer she touched it, the more she knew something, someone was enclosed within the confines of the spell. Azria walked forward, wishing she wasn't alone. She wondered what the crew was doing, imagining them all racing to arrive at the Marauders' Island. Azria would try to have an island for them to find.

Azria stopped. Something was wrong. Azria tried to come up with what felt off about the cave, not sure what it was. Finally, she realized it. Iyzani was awake. The sound of snoring was absent from the cave. Azria stepped forward ever so slightly, craning her neck forward to look into the room without possibly giving away her presence.

The bed was empty. The blanket was still on the small pallet, crumpled from recent use. The lantern in the room was brighter. But the room was empty.

"Oh, I am out of here," Azria squeaked quietly, pressing her foot against the wall and grabbing the wall, hoisting herself up. She climbed the first few feet easily, hoping if Iyzani was close by, she couldn't hear her. Azria looked for another handhold, wishing the holes were deeper. Stone grated against her nails, her clothes catching on the rough surface as she dragged herself over it.

Azria exhaled as loudly as she dared once she cleared the hallway's ceiling, finding a small piece of rock jutting out she could sit on for a moment. If her legs were longer, it would have been an easier climb, she thought to herself. She was already sweating and Azria rubbed her hands on the surface of the rock, chalky powder soaking up some of the moisture on her palms. She listened to her breath and steadied it before she inhaled deeply, continuing her climb up the tunnel.

Something moved beneath her. Azria froze. Without thinking, she pulled out one of the skulls from her bag, gazing into its vacant eye sockets. Maybe she had just heard something.

"Girl?" Iyzani's voice came from everywhere, the cave shaking with the words tinged with anger. Azria gasped. "Where are you?" Azria put her hand on the crystal shard, hoping she would be able to pry it loose. She heard Iyzani curse under her breath. "So, you've stolen my things, now. Things you don't understand. Things you're too stupid to wield."

Azria wanted to shout back at her. She wanted to crush the island with Iyzani still within it. But she couldn't, not right now. Azria listened in fear as Iyzani moved below her, to the bottom of the tunnel. "Are you up there?"

Azria yanked the shard out of the skull. The eye

sockets lit up, the skull hot as fire in her hands. Yelping, Azria dropped it, the skull clattering down the passage as it bounced against the stone and to the floor below.

A flash of sickly green light illuminated the cave and Azria dug her fingertips into the wall as a hot, wet wind blew up around her. "Iyzani," a spectral voice rasped in Mizian, its tone emanating from every direction. "Now you are done."

"No!" Azria heard Iyzani shout. "You are in my stronghold! I have the power here."

"Your power is waning, witch," the voice said. Azria shivered to hear the spirit admonish Iyzani. "You are unraveling. You are spun from too many threads and now they are fraying. Your anger is the fire that will lick them all up. Nothing will save you from death."

"Shut up!" Iyzani screamed, her voice piercing Azria's ears. "Get out of my way. I need to find the mage who is going to help me."

"No one will help you," the voice said. The light was sucked out of the room and Azria edged away from the crawling darkness, not entirely sure what she had unleashed. "You are beyond help."

Azria cringed as a shriek filled the air. Flashes of light strobed through the tunnel as Azria clambered up, away. Golden light and red played against each other as the two continued to scream at each other. The stones scraped Azria's skin, dust soaking up the hot red blood as she continued to climb up. The bag on her back swung down, slipping down her arm. Azria turned to grab it, catching sight of the tunnel's floor.

Iyzani stood at the bottom of the tunnel. Azria screamed and pressed herself against the wall, trying to escape her gaze. "You!" Iyzani shouted. "Help me!"

A flash of red flame shot into the tunnel. Iyzani

threw up a hand, the red flames directed around her. Hot, dry wind rushed up the tunnel, blowing past Azria. Iyzani stared up at Azria, her eyes bloodshot, her teeth red. "Help me! Or he'll kill us both."

"Liar," came the voice of the ghost mage. Another volley of red fire rolled around Iyzani, the older mage screaming.

Azria reached into the bag and pulled out the second skull. She saw the fear and anger boiling behind Iyzani's eyes. "Don't you dare!" Iyzani screamed.

Azria braced herself against the stones before she yanked the crystal out, throwing the skull down as hard as she dared. Iyzani yelped, the skull bouncing off her head.

"I'll make you regret this till the day you die," Iyzani growled, ducking out of the alcove. Azria didn't bother waiting to see if she would come back. Closing the bag securely, she started her ascent up the tunnel, trying to ignore the terrible howls and flashes of raw energy that shook the entire island.

"Almost there," Azria reassured herself. The tunnel slanted slightly to one side and Azria would have to lean forward and scramble up. She was glad she still had the boots Eixon and Onacá had purchased for her back in the City of Peace. Pulling off the bag, she threw it ahead of her, hoping she didn't damage any of the items inside. Giving one more glance down, she leaned forward and swung her legs, scrambling up the bulge of rock that ended in a small, rough platform.

The ceiling was low, as was to be expected. Above her head was another window, like the one in the treasure room. Azria held her hand up and placed it against it, wondering how she would get out. She pushed against it with her hand, feeling the magical energy keeping the water at bay. The energy was somewhere else. Azria looked around, making sure to stay clear of any errant shots of angry magic. It had to be close by.

Something glinted within the recesses of the cave, catching her eye. Azria crawled on her hands and knees, trying to squeeze into the small cubby. Squinting against the dimness, she saw it. Another skull with a bowl of water in its mouth. "Someone really likes skulls a lot," Azria murmured, regarding the skull and water. It was like the one in the treasure room, and there had been a window there. Azria felt the energy it was giving off, the small size of the arrangement misleading in its power. The bowl of water was the key.

Azria closed her eyes and took several deep breaths before she inhaled, holding her breath. She grabbed the bag and fastened it closed, then she reached out and took the bowl of water out of the skull's mouth.

Cold, salty ocean water poured through the window, the spell broken. Azria resisted the urge to panic, to scream. She pushed herself towards the hole in the stone, hearing the screams of Iyzani below. If the water was pouring down, Azria could make her way through the hole and swim for the surface. How far below was the island? Azria hoped it wasn't far. Fish flopped on the ledge, their mouths gaping open and snapping shut as they gasped.

Azria took one more deep breath before she stood on the ledge. Cold sea water poured over her, soaking her to the skin. Azria tried to climb out, but the saltwater gushed, strong as a riptide. She pulled herself out of the stream, looking down. The floor was already starting to flood. She had to get out of the cave and to the surface.

A glowing hand reached out of the torrent of water.

Azria looked down before she reached out and grabbed it. A chill shot through her body, colder than the ocean water, creeping over her skin, through her muscles to her bones. Azria leaped off of the ledge, the spectral hand pulling her through the torrent and up through the hole.

Bubbles popped all around, the salt water stinging Azria's eyes as she tried to see where she was. Her eyes widened. All around her were the glowing forms of ghosts, drifting through the water like sea jellies. Their light shone off the irregular contours of the island, illuminating the fish and corals which had rooted there. In their sparse glow, Azria spied the surface. More than that, Azria saw the rise of the land. There was a part of the island which rose almost completely to the surface.

Kicking her legs, Azria swam through the water, trying not to lose the bag in the process. The pale-faced spirit who had helped her floated alongside her, somber as ever as she swam towards the surface. Her chest began to ache, her nose tingling as the need to breathe pushed her forward.

Azria gasped as she broke the surface. A cold sea wind blew over her, the world around her a dark blur. She turned in the water, noticing flashes of light pulsing below the waves, like lightning. The air tasted salty but sweet in her lungs as she inhaled, treading water as she tried to recall which direction to swim. In more strokes than she thought, she found her feet on solid ground. Azria stumbled and then walked, standing on the highest point of the Marauders' Island, the summit of the island only a few inches below the surface of the sea.

Her teeth chattered, the wind biting through her clothes. She still had the spell. It didn't pull anymore. It just glowed. Azria pressed her palms into her eyes, trying to wipe the water out of them. She panted as she turned around on her small foothold, exhaustion trying to settling in her limbs.

Azria squinted. A light?

Was it a planet coming over the horizon? Azria's mouth fell open. No, the light was too bright, and definitely on the waves. What was it?

It was a boat. It had to be. It was too small to be the *Hen & Chick*, and moving too quickly, more quickly than any boat Azria had seen. Still, it was someone. She rubbed her hands together before she popped off a small purple flare of light.

A sound floated in over the waves, so faint Azria thought she was hearing things. Another peal of light throbbed underwater. Azria craned her head forward, trying to hear it.

"Azria!"

Azria froze, her heart racing. Could it be? "Mama?" she whispered, disbelief quieting her words. Azria blinked and rubbed her eyes again, too scared to believe it was true. "Mama?" she shouted as loud as she could, hoping the waves weren't drowning out her voice.

"Azria, it's me! I'm coming for you!"

Azria pulled the spell engine off of her wrist. She pulled out the spell, glowing as brightly as the light which bobbed on the waves.

She didn't know how much time she had. Iyzani was occupied and her mother was coming.

Azria would give her mother a shore to stand on. She licked her lips and took a deep breath.

And then she began the spell.

Chapter 12
Blood and Magic

Azria held the spell in her hand. It glowed with anticipation, knowing what was to come. Azria unwrapped the spell engine from her wrist, the words she had written already shimmering. She gave one more glance towards the approaching light before she closed her eyes, her magic already churning in her stomach like the waves, ready to work.

Azria exhaled, feeling her breath move up her arms, to her hands. The orb levitated, floating in the air and the spell engine began to turn around it, orbiting the spell. It sparked gold and green at first but after a few steady breaths, the amethyst hue of Azria's magic glowed, comforting in its color and power. Azria smiled as she held out both hands, cradling the spell, the engine spinning faster as the glow grew.

"By my power and the power of Miz," she said, her voice trembling. Her heart raced with the excitement she felt, casting again. She felt most like herself when she felt the energy of the spell within her grasp, waiting for her will to direct it. "I will this land to rise." Azria pushed her will into the spell, the energy leaping from her fingers and into the engine, the orb glowing brighter. Its glow intensified with every breath, growing brighter and brighter, Azria too amazed to blink against its light.

The island beneath her trembled.

A crack formed on the surface of the spell. Azria tried to remember to breathe, to keep the energy flowing through the spell. The crack lengthened, audibly, as if something inside was hatching.

In a burst of energy, the shell of the spell fell apart, bursting away from the center. The shards orbited the spell as well as the energy poured into the water, into the ground beneath her feet. Water steamed and sprayed around her.

The earth moved. Azria continued her spell, speaking it over and over as the power continued to seep into the island, returning to the land. All she knew now was the spell, crafted by her hand and executed by her will.

The magic in the spell rippled through the weave of the world. It trickled through the watery abode of the Goddess, outlining the waves which rose and fell for miles around her. It harmonized with the wind that rippled, making way for the land which rose to meet it, steaming in the ocean air. The sea glowed with creatures, moving in their patterns of life and death, their cycles. The stars winked as they went along their tracks in the sky, soaring past the horizon before they all eventually plunged into the sea. And still, Azria wove her spell, the power returning into the land.

It rose. Azria watched her spell, her words constant

and flowing like water out of her. Her voice was louder than the waves, louder than the beating of her heart in her ears. Azria focused on the spell, keeping her gaze soft but as she spoke, she could see the land begin to stretch before her as more of it became exposed. The island trembled as it rose, as if unsteady on its feet. Still, the violet energy, mingled with gold and green, poured into the land, the island rising in time with the magic. The magic sang out across the sea and Azria could feel the protective energy of the spell around her.

The spell engine spun, so fast it was a blur around the orb but Azria could make out the words on the engine, written in her hand. She meant to pour out every mote of magic the spell contained. Steam rose around her, rolling off the energy of the magic. Azria felt light as the air as the magic coursed around her, through her body and into the ground.

Beyond the light of the spell she saw the light of the boat, so close. Encircled within the magic, she sensed the heat energy of it, the presence of four other people. Azria concentrated on the spell. She was almost done.

Azria gently coaxed the last of the energy out of the spell, the steady stream dwindling to a trickle and then a drop before it burst like a bubble. The scant remains of the spell shimmered on the air and floated away, dissipated among the salt and water. Azria watched it float on.

She had done it. She had raised the island. Azria bent down to pick up the spell engine and spent shards of the orb. Everything seemed so quiet, the colors of the world faded after the brilliance of the casting. Azria stared at the remnants of the spell, cracked and jagged. The faintest sheen of purple stained the inside, shimmering only under a certain light and perceivable only by those who knew to look for it. Azria smiled to herself as she looked over the island, the scent of hot salt and sea water strong in the air. Every stone was smooth and dark, still damp, and here and there, Azria could see the looming entrances to the many caves which made up the island. The skeletons of trees jutted from the stony soil, seaweed hanging from their branches. Everywhere underwater life lay exposed to the air, bubbling, gasping, colorful corals already losing their luster. A small fish flopped at Azria's feet, its mouth popping open and closed.

"Azria!"

Azria looked up. One of the life boats of the *Hen & Chick* sat on the beach. Azria looked around. The Marauders' Island stretched all around her, and she stood on the highest peak. "Mama!" Azria shouted, her throat raw. She tucked the spell engine and orb away before she began her descent down the hill.

The cold wind blew across the island. Azria remembered the ghost who had pulled her from the island, towards the surface. As she walked, lights began to glow here and there before they pulsed into being. Ghosts. Azria picked her way over the still-wet stones, trying to avoid swaths of sea urchins and corals and other sea creatures which had moved in. The ghosts looked after her as she passed by, and she avoided their gaze as she tried to get down.

"Mama!" she shouted.

"Azria!" Her mother sprinted across the beach and clambered up the side of the hill. Azria watched as she slipped up the wet stones and sand towards her. "Azria, are you hurt?"

"I'm...fine," she said, not sure if it was true. She could feel the exhaustion trying to set in but the excitement of getting off of the island pushed her forward. Azria looked at the small boat. A box was set in the back. It must have been the thing that propelled it. In the boat were Onacá, Red and...Zesh. Azria stopped. Zesh was tied up, his head bowed to his chest. Onacá sat beside him on the boat. She had a sword on her hip. Red held a crossbow.

Her mother had Nana's knife.

A rumble came from underground. This one wasn't from Azria's spell. Azria gave a single glance behind her before she hurried down the side of the hill, trying to dodge the ghosts. The air around them was colder and Azria didn't want to walk through one. Azria cleared the last stretch between herself and her mother and fell into her arms, her mother squeezing her so tight, Azria thought she would cry.

"Girl, my girl," her mother said. "Don't ever do that again," Apzana said, her cheek pressed against the top of Azria's head. "I thought I lost you for good."

"I'm...I knew what I was doing," Azria lied. For now. She'd tell her the rest later. The ground rumbled again and a flash of magic erupted from the top of the island, from where Azria had escaped. "Iyzani."

"She's here," Apzana said. Her mother pulled out the knife. "I'll kill her. This ends here. Go get on the boat. Sit with Zesh."

"Mama, why did you even bring him?" Azria asked. Azria noticed the ghosts all turned to look at the top of the mountain, moving in unison, soundlessly.

"In case I had to trade him for you," Apzana said. "I know you left of your own will but I didn't know if she would be keeping you prisoner or not. I had to, Azria."

"Zesh...he doesn't have anything to do with this, not this part."

"Get behind me, Azria," Apzana said. It was an order.

"No," Azria said.

"What?" Apzana said, eyes widening.

"I just raised this island. I'm not going to lose you." Azria stood next to her mother, setting her feet against the stony ground. "You need me. More than ever."

Apzana looked at Azria for a moment before a sad smile pulled at her mouth. She sighed as she took a step to the side, giving Azria more room. "You're right, you know."

"Of course I am," Azria said, hoping she was.

"Onacá, to me, Red, stay with that boy," Apzana shouted. Azria looked over her shoulder and watched Red hand the crossbow to Onacá, only to hoist up another. Onacá sheathed her sword and ran up the beach with the weapon.

"Glad you're okay," Onacá said breathlessly. Her knuckles gleamed white on the crossbow. "Maybe try to pick a place with fewer ghosts next time."

"Hey, she's the one who chose this island for a take," Azria said.

"Quiet, you two," Apzana snapped. "We can talk when Iyzani is dead."

Azria gulped. "I...I don't know what she's doing there. When I escaped, she was fighting someone else."

"Who?" Apzana asked.

"As far as I could tell...a ghost. With magic." Azria felt her face grow hot, her stomach squelch with fear. "I freed it. On purpose!" Azria wasn't sure why she added the last part. It didn't help the situation.

Onacá said something under her breath which could only be a curse. The lines on Apzana's face deepened as she frowned.

A blaze of flame exploded from the top of the island.

Azria lifted her hand up, throwing up a plane of protective magic. A rain of rocks and pebbles peppered the shield. A plume of smoke floated upward and Azria grit her teeth as she saw a figure blast out of the island, flying up into the sky. What if Iyzani just flew away? A part of Azria wanted her to. But they would spend the rest of their days wondering if she was right behind them, watching them. Azria dropped the shield and tried to stand firm on the land, hoping she looked as confident as she had when she had cast the spell.

"Come and get me, witch!" Apzana shouted, making Azria jump. She watched as Iyzani flew towards them, descending till she stood just a stone's throw from them.

Iyzani was covered in blood. Her clothes were torn, her gaunt body covered in shredded fabric. Blood steamed, red hot, on the side of her face, obscuring her eye and staining her teeth crimson. Her garments still glowed at the edge, still on fire.

Azria gasped as the gashes on Iyzani's arm began to close, the flesh audibly knitting together slowly. Onacá made a sound in her throat as if she would vomit. Apzana did nothing. "I am here," Iyzani growled, her voice making Azria tremble.

"You die today," Apzana said.

"I'll tear your flesh from your bones," Iyzani half screamed, half laughed. A bolt of gold energy crackled towards Apzana. Azria leaped in front of her mother, casting the protective spell again. The force hit it harder than the strongest wave, driving Azria back into her mother. Her mother tripped, Azria and Apzana toppling over to the ground.

Iyzani screamed. A bolt stuck out of her shoulder. Azria looked to Onacá. Her face was stricken with fear, the crossbow still in her hands. By some power, Onacá ran up and swung the crossbow at Iyzani's face, the sickening sound of hard wood against flesh and bone making Azria wince.

Onacá yelped. Iyzani's hand was around her throat in the blink of an eye. She lifted Onacá off the ground. The older mage's eyes glowed, her face covered in gore.

Azria took a deep breath. Iyzani wasn't a mage of Miz. It was clear to her now. Tears shone in Onacá's eyes as she fought back, kicking, trying to pry Iyzani's fingers from her throat. Iyzani grinned.

Azria lifted both her hands, bringing them together. She remembered the feeling back in the City of Peace, of the green magic and its vines that tried to wrap themselves around her. Motioning with her hands, two tendrils of magic exploded from her hands. They wrapped themselves around Iyzani's wrists. With a flick of her own wrist, she pulled Iyzani's arms, the mage dropping Onacá. Iyzani glared at Azria.

"Now you use your magic against me, another mage of Miz," Iyzani spat. Blood and spit were smeared across her face. "Now who is the traitor? Who betrays Miz, by raising the island, exposing what Mizian mages have done? What will they say about us?"

"You are no mage of Miz!" Azria shouted. Iyzani's face twisted, as if Azria's words were a knife. "You don't know who you are! You've spent so much time being angry, learning how to destroy, you're not even The Innate! You're blood spilled by hate, and magic gained by anger! That's it!"

A blast of light. Azria felt the wind knocked out of her. Something slammed into her back. A weight rested on her chest, crushing her into the ground. She couldn't breathe. The world before her dazzled her, millions of stars blinking in her eyes. Azria gasped, trying to force air into her lungs, trying to move her hands to brush the stars away. In her mind, she screamed.

Someone was talking. Azria moved her head, trying to make out who. After a moment, she heard Zesh's voice, pleading, so close he couldn't be in the boat.

"Grandmother, no!" he screamed, tears in his voice. "What are you doing? Please, just...stop! She already raised the island, there's nothing more to be done!"

"Of course you'd say that," Iyzani's voice came, so close to Azria it made her blood cold. "You failure! We tried your way and look at this! There can be no peace, boy, not ever."

"Please," he said. "Stop this! We can just leave! Let's just go!"

Something hit Iyzani from behind. Azria moaned as something hit her in the face, perhaps Iyzani's knee as she tumbled over her.

"She didn't kill your parents!" Zesh yelled.

Azria saw her mother walk by, the glow of the ghosts growing stronger, illuminating the air. A whistling sound in the air. Another growl from Iyzani. Azria sat up on the ground. Another bolt stuck out of Iyzani, jutting from her chest. Iyzani yanked it, blood spurting from the wound as she threw it to the ground.

"She kidnapped Azria," Apzana said, her eyes stuck fast on the witch. "I could have maybe put this all behind us, let her go. But she can't be allowed to live." Apzana pulled out the knife, her muscles taut as she gripped its handle. Apzana turned her head slightly towards the boy, the slightest hint of remorse on her features. "I'm sorry, boy. I believe you, that she didn't kill them. And I know this won't bring them back. But this may preserve us."

"Try and kill me," Iyzani laughed. Azria watched

Iyzani standing there, hands stretched to the side. Something about it reminded Azria of her dream. Of Iyzani, waiting for Azria to strike. Iyzani moved her fingers in a flourish and a rod of light formed in the palm of her hand, a long tail pouring from it. A whip.

Apzana lunged forward, blade in hand. Iyzani cracked the whip once before she aimed it at Apzana. Her mother caught the end of the whip around her arm. She winced. With a quick motion, the knife cut through the whip,

Iyzani lifted her free hand, sending a bolt of energy hissing towards Apzana. Apzana dove to the ground, grunting as she rolled out of the way. Iyzani lifted the whip.

Azria slammed her hand into the ground, sending a volley of stones towards Iyzani's head. The first two sent her head to the side with a jerk but Iyzani redirected the whip end and smashed the stones out of the air. Azria scrambled to her feet as Iyzani fixed her gaze on her, blood trickling down her face.

"Oh no," Azria said, rolling out of the way of a bolt of energy. Azria took a deep breath before she brought her hands together, exhaling sharply and sending a gale towards Iyzani. The old mage tried to hold her ground but fell, landing on her back. Her head smacked against the ground. Azria started to walk towards her, her hands balled into fists.

"Stop!" Zesh said, standing between them. He held his arms out to the side, surrendering for them both. "Please!"

Onacá ran past Zesh, holding a rock in her hands. Zesh turned to try to stop her. Apzana took the chance to run past the boy, the knife glinting in the glow of the ghosts.

Iyzani disappeared. Azria looked around.

"Damn you!" Apzana cursed. She shouted something else Azria didn't understand. Tears were in her eyes and she gripped the blade with both hands. "Show yourself, you coward!"

Azria looked around. Her mother and the rest couldn't see Iyzani. But Azria could. A cloud of golden motes floated, the sparks in the form of the mage. Azria could see the cracks in her form. Where she was injured. Bleeding. Iyzani walked behind Apzana. She looked over her shoulder at Azria, staring at her. Her eyes were two molten orbs of gold. Soulless.

"Mama, behind you!" Azria shouted. Apzana wheeled around. She brought the dagger down on the air.

Iyzani formed around the dagger. Her mouth fell open, her eyes so wide, Azria saw the whites around her pupils. Apzana drew the blade back with a grunt. Blood spurted from the wound, dropped off of the blade. Apzana took a step back as Iyzani looked down at the wound and then at the blade.

"It's not healing," Iyzani said. Her voice was quiet, and Azria heard the slightest hint of something else. Fear. The old mage brought her hands to the wound, pressing them against her chest. A glow of golden light formed around her but when she brought her hands away, she grimaced. Her hands were stained red. Her dark eyes shone. "What have you done to me?"

Apzana took another step back. Iyzani put her hands over the wound again, a growl of frustration curling her lips. She glared at the blade, screaming as she made to reach for it, a bolt of energy wrapping around it. In a moment, the blade was in Iyzani's hand and she stared at its hilt, her eyes watering.

"Enza," she whispered. "You crab. You've finally gotten me."

"Grandmother!" Zesh called. Azria held him back, suddenly aware the ghosts on the island were glowing more strongly now, gathered around them all. A ghost floated past Azria, giving her and Zesh a nod before it approached Iyzani. It was the one who had helped her, the one who had told her about the way out of the cave. A groan behind them made Azria look as Red sat up in the little boat, rubbing his head.

Iyzani looked the ghost in the eye, and Azria could see her through the ghost's spectral body, her blood even redder through the ether of unlife. A cold wind began to blow up and Azria looked up at the sky.

Freezing cold ran through her body as the ghosts all rushed Iyzani. Something grabbed her but Azria couldn't move, too stunned by the sensation and the spectacle. The only scream she could hear was the one in her head as the cold rushed through her. The crackle of ice rang in her ears and her head ached.

Azria shut her eyes, trying to drown out the cold and the sound, trying to breathe in steady breaths. Still, the ghosts rushed, blocking out everything with their forms. Finally, they stopped. A ball of light winked where Iyzani had been. Azria watched, bracing herself for whatever was next. She knew better than to think they were done.

Warmth filled the air as the light went from white to red, swirling with energy. Azria barely made out the form of Iyzani within the ghostly dome, kneeling, head bowed. A crackle ran through the air as the red light became opaque, a beam of light shooting into the sky. Azria watched it stream up into the heavens. Crimson light washed over the beach and the dome of light pulsed, like a heart.

The light dissipated, particles like ruby motes fluttering up into the atmosphere. Azria held her breath as she watched them go, flying higher and higher, painting the sky with their red glow. The Mage's Smile twinkled in the sky.

Iyzani was gone. All that remained of her on the beach was the dagger, its blade still red with her blood.

Something was still clinging to her. Azria looked down. It was Zesh, holding on to Azria for dear life. Without a word, he let go and ran over to the blade, dropping to his knees on the stony beach.

"Grandmother," he said, picking up the blade. He looked up into the sky, holding it to his chest. "Where did you go?"

"Be careful with that," Apzana said, walking over to him. "It's dangerous."

"I know," he spat, looking over his shoulder. It was the first unkind tone Azria had heard from him in the short time she had known him. "Not as dangerous as the hand who holds it."

"Zesh," Azria said. She walked slowly towards the boy, not sure what to say. "I...I know you loved your grandmother. She was a great woman, and she showed you a lot of kindness. But you have to know...I need you to know..." Azria's voice trailed off, trying to think of what to say. She didn't want to lie and too many unkind words could be said. "I'm sorry the good she brought to your life will be gone now."

Zesh looked back, still holding the knife. "I'm sorry she caused you all so much hurt. I'm sorry I couldn't help her more." Zesh looked down at the ground in front of him, lost in his thoughts.

"We should let him grieve," Apzana said. Something in her tone told Azria her mother didn't think there was much to feel sad about when it came to Iyzani. She took Azria by the shoulders and looked her up and down. "Are you alright, girl? After all of that."

"I'm fine, Mama," Azria said.

"I can have Onacá look over you, to be sure," Apzana said.

"No, she should look at Red," Azria said, looking over her shoulder. Onacá just nodded and walked up to the old man, who was still rubbing the side of his head. Zesh must have knocked him out to escape the boat.

"Are you really all right?" Apzana asked, uncertainty in her voice.

"I do need to sit down," Azria said, pulling away from her mother. She found a bare spot on the ground and sat, then decided she needed to lie back. The ground was wet under her, the cold sea water seeping into her clothes. Azria watched as seagulls circled in the air, ready to eat the dying sea life which covered the newly exposed land. Her mother sat down next to her, resting her arms on her knees.

"How...how do you feel?" Apzana asked quietly. "After all this?"

Azria looked up at the sky. She rested her hands on her belly, feeling her breath go in and out. She was aware of every small stone under her back. The warmth of the magic the ghosts had been able to unlock with Iyzani's death still warmed the air, wafting on the sea breeze. She had just seen one of the greatest mages of the earth killed by her mother. Azria had seen the island rise at her will. The tremors under the earth of battling mages, alive and undead.

"I feel..." Azria began. She stared up at the stars,

catching sight of the sparkling motes still. "I feel like...even though what we just did, you and I...even though it was such a big thing, I still feel...like the world is stretched out in front of me. Like time is stretched out in front of me. Everything is still moving. And there's still more. A lot more. But." Azria stopped, looking over at her mother. "But I'm here now. I feel part of everything but also just...here."

Azria stared back up at the sky, thinking about what she had just said. It was true. Azria had always felt her magic, felt it as a part of her, working within her. In Miz she had used her magic among the other mages, as was expected and as she saw fit, as part of her lesson or for personal interest. But the last few weeks had thrown her into the middle of a muddled and troubled history and she had taken part in it. She had raised the island. More would come of this. More would come of her magic. She hadn't felt it to be truer than right then, on the beach.

"You know, what's funny about that," Apzana murmured. "It's pretty much how I felt the day you were born. The day I first held you in my arms." Apzana smiled, a warm, almost timid smile at Azria, before she looked out onto the ocean. "I labored for a day, walking and moaning and crying and singing. I was a mess." She laughed, still looking towards the ocean, as if the memory was playing out on the waves.

"But after all the pain and screaming and crying, you were there and I held you." Apzana shook her head and pressed her lips together. "I heard you cry and I know the midwife and Nana were there but they weren't. It was just you and me. And all of life. The time I had with you, I felt it, even though I hadn't lived it yet. You looked up at me. And I swear, girl. I swear, time stopped."

"Maybe I did stop time, with my magic," Azria said, laughing at her own joke. "With my baby magic."

"Stop!" Apzana snorted, smacking her leg gently with her hand. "You ruined the story."

"I'm sorry, I just had to say it," Azria said. They both smiled, sitting together on the beach, the sound of the soothing waves lulling Azria to sleep. Her eyes fluttered closed.

"You are a great mage, though," Apzana said suddenly. Azria opened her eyes, looking at her mother. "I know that now," she said. "For certain. But Azria, I'm sorry to have put you in this much danger so soon. I didn't know Iyzani's state, what she would do. I just...wanted the treasure."

"In Miz they say, you cannot know what pieces you will draw, you can only order them in the best way," Azria offered. She thought about her mother's words. Her mother had called her a great mage. Something about it hadn't sunk in yet. The exhaustion of the spell she had spun weighed heavily in her body and she knew what she had done was great. But she was still Azria. Azria who ordered her life the way she did, whose magic glowed with the same hue as the inside of her favorite seashell.

"Well, these are the pieces we're dealing with," Apzana said, holding a hand out to Azria. Azria held her hands up and her mother dropped something into her hand. Azria sat up to look. Coins. Coins from every shore. Discs, cylinders and ingots, stamped and smooth. Currencies Azria didn't recognize. Coins she did.

"Where did you find these?" Azria asked.

"Just in this hole right here," Apzana said. A grin

brightened her face. "Can't tell how many the island is filled with."

Treasure. Azria rubbed the coins on her face. "Wait," Azria said with a frown. "You never told me, how did you all get here so quickly?"

"Right," Apzana said. She stood up, brushing her hands off before she offered a hand to Azria, pulling her up. "Well, the Hen needs its Chick. It's a skiff I had out-fitted with a special engine, made by a mage you might know, about this tall, can't take care of himself, smart but kind of annoying?" Apzana winked at Azria.

"An engine for motion?" Azria asked, following af-ter her mother.

"Don't ask me how it works," Apzana said. "All I know is, I have to put one end in the water and hold onto another and it'll go. It's for emergencies only, mind you. It's not big enough to push the big ship. Speaking of which, look who finally caught a good wind."

Azria looked up. There, on the horizon was the *Hen & Chick*, its black and white sails fluttering in the wind. Tears came to Azria's eyes as she watched it approach, bobbing on the waves.

"We'll load up as quick as we can and then set off," Apzana said. Her mother wrapped an arm around Azria's waist, the two of them standing and looking out over the sea. "Where do you want to go next? I could always...take you back to Miz if you want."

Azria pressed her lips together, shaking her head. After all that had happened, after all she had felt, she didn't want to go back to Miz. Not yet. Azria wanted some time to think about it all. In addition, there was money to spend.

"I want to see where this coin can take us," Azria said. "And maybe start a vault of my own."

"You're not a vault level yet," Apzana scoffed. "Maybe after a few more treasures." She winked at Azria and laughed. "I think I know where we should go. A nice coastal city northeast of here. Beautiful temples. A library. Great bathhouses."

"I could soak for a week straight," Azria muttered.

"I'd let you," Apzana said, squeezing her shoulder. Her mother sighed as she looked out at the boat. "Azria, I've seen a lot of beautiful places. But no place is as beautiful as the *Hen & Chick*."

"I've never been happier to see that ship," Azria said. It was the truth. After years of waiting for the ship to come and bring home her mother, now Azria was waiting for the ship to come for her. Something about it felt right.

Shoving the money into the bag, she broke away from her mother and ran into the surf, the cold water feeling clean and cool on her skin. Azria waved at the ship and the crew members, smiling from ear to ear. She thought she saw someone wave back at her, which made her wave again. "Welcome to the Marauders' Island!" she shouted into the sea wind, knowing they couldn't hear her but needing to shout it all the same.

About the Author

Tristan J. Tarwater is a writer of fantasy, comics and RPG bits. Her titles include The Valley of Ten Crescents series, Hen & Chick, Shamsee: A Fistful of Lunars, and Reality Makes the Best Fantasy. She has also worked for both Pelgrane Press and Onyx Path.

Born and raised in NYC, she now considers Portland, OR her home. When she's not making stuff up, she is usually reading a comic book, cooking delicious meals for her Spouse and Small Boss or petting one of her two cats. Her next RPG character will most definitely be an elf.

You can find her online at www.backthatelfup.com

Made in the USA
Lexington, KY
14 March 2017